ZOMBIE ZERO

SCOT
MCATEE

iUniverse, Inc.
Bloomington

Zombie Zero

iUniverse books may be ordered through booksellers or by contacting:

iUniverse
1663 Liberty Drive
Bloomington, IN 47403
www.iuniverse.com
1-800-Authors (1-800-288-4677)

Because of the dynamic nature of the Internet, any web addresses or links contained in this book may have changed since publication and may no longer be valid. The views expressed in this work are solely those of the author and do not necessarily reflect the views of the publisher, and the publisher hereby disclaims any responsibility for them.

Any people depicted in stock imagery provided by Thinkstock are models, and such images are being used for illustrative purposes only.

Certain stock imagery © Thinkstock.

ISBN: 978-1-4620-1001-1 (sc)
ISBN: 978-1-4620-1002-8 (ebk)

Printed in the United States of America

iUniverse rev. date: 3/30/2011

For Griffin, Gabrielle and Jen

Brains!

CHAPTER 1

The first thing Kyle Williams noticed when he awoke from a drunken stupor was a pair of legs sticking out from behind his couch. It was not abnormal for him to find strangers in his cramped two bedroom apartment after a hard night of drinking. Usually they slept *on* his ratty furniture, in front of it, or hanging off it. Sometimes they even ended up in his bed, but never before had someone ended up behind the couch.

As he slowly sat up, being careful not to jostle his brain against his skull, he became aware of other various aches and pains. The worst of them was his throat. It felt like a porcupine had crawled down it backwards and his face felt as if an extra layer of skin had grown over it while he slept. The urge to vomit was overwhelming.

Groggy, he wandered into his small galley kitchen, pushing the rising gorge down as best he could. Some people drank coffee in the morning to wake themselves up, Kyle drank a shot of whatever was on hand followed by beer.

"Great," he grumbled as he opened the cabinet where he stashed his booze. The only thing left was a cheap plastic bottle of some no-name Russian vodka. "The safety bottle."

No one who came to his home ever drank from the safety bottle because it tasted like the plastic that held it. Even Kyle hated the taste of the stuff but it was the only way he could be sure that there was always some alcohol on hand and for a man such as he, alcohol was paramount to his survival.

He sucked down a couple of mouthfuls of the swill and slid the bottle back into its spot on the shelf. Although it was the cheapest vodka available, to him it was still something to be worshipped. Plastic container or not, booze was to be treated with the utmost respect. More than one visitor had learned that the hard way.

Wonder if that's why the dude is behind the couch? Did I stuff him back there for drinking out of the safety bottle?

Once, a former girlfriend decided to clean out his refrigerator for him. In the process, she shifted his beer from one side of a shelf to the other. When Kyle later reached into the refrigerator and pulled out a bottle of mayonnaise, he lost his temper and threw her out on her ass, screaming at her that no woman would ever change his ways. Even though he still regretted how it ended—she had treated him better than anyone ever had— he had no remorse over the reason why it ended.

He took a few more belts of the plastic tasting booze and washed the ex-girlfriend out of his mind. "Gotta be a beer in there someone," he told himself. He rooted through the fridge for a few moments, sorting through fuzzy green chunks of astro-turf that had once been food, until he found a solitary beer lying on its side at the very back of the bottom shelf. He sighed with relief and headed for the living room. Plopping down onto his favorite chair, a crappy garage sale special recliner, he rocked gently back and forth as he waited for the pained edges of his skull to wear down.

"Oh man," he groaned quietly. "Must have really tied it on last night, huh?" He aimed the question at the feet.

He decided a little television might help. The remote was where it always was—stuffed between the seat cushion and the bottom of the armrest. He flipped on the TV and Woody Woodpecker appeared. He stared dumbly at the glowing phosphorus blobs on the glass as he waited for the alcohol to do its job.

Eventually, the gremlin inside his skull stopped wrestling with his brain and he started to feel human again. But he also became more and more aware of a thick stench that permeated the stale air of the tiny apartment. He sniffed at it like a dog. The closest aroma memory to which he could compare it was the smell of a dead cow rotting in late August. Why his home smelled like that he could only guess. What in the world had happened last night?

Did somebody freaking die? he mused. He got up to check the bathroom and noticed the feet again.

"Oh my God," he muttered unhappily. The odor was strongest nearest the feet. "Man, I'm not cleaning up whatever it is you did back there," he said. He contemplated his options though the gears of his brain were rusted solid and would not turn.

Not knowing what else to do, he kicked a foot. It barely moved. No response was bad news. The fellow didn't even twitch.

"Damn, dead out, huh?" Kyle observed. Something struck a chord as the words escaped his mouth.

"Oh shit!" he exclaimed as the dots suddenly connected and he was able to see the whole picture. The guy wasn't just dead out, he was literally dead out. Dead, as in completely dead and rotting dead! The mottled blue appearance of the skin was a dead giveaway.

Time paused as his heart went into overdrive. *What to do? What to do? Did I really just think the word dead that many times in one paragraph? Bad form.*

There were a number of options, but none of them were good. He could call the police and let them deal with it, but how would he explain a dead body stuffed behind his furniture? There's no way they would believe that he and some strange guy had gotten drunk together and then the dude just crawled back there and died. They would think it was some sort of weird sex thing because situations like that always turned out to be weird sex things. That would not do. At the very worst, he would be executed as a murder and at the very least, he would lose his cushy teaching job.

He could try to hide the body or wait until dark and then drag it down to the pond directly behind his apartment and chuck it in. Or he could roll it up in a carpet and throw it in the dumpster, although that was at the other end of the parking lot and meant someone might see him carrying the body to the trash. *No, those are stupid B movie ideas. Damn! I never thought I'd have to deal with this situation!*

It occurred to him that anyone who knew him would vouch for his character and surely the autopsy would prove he had nothing to do with the man's death. After all, he was not the type to murder anyone. His anger was introspective. The only person he ever punished was himself. But the authorities did not know him and would not be inclined to believe that he knew nothing about a corpse rotting in his own home. He suddenly had to urinate.

When he turned on the bathroom light, the visage in the mirror nearly scared him to death. A gory faced soul reminiscent of the Death Mask from The Exorcist stared back at him. It took a few seconds to realize that the monster caked in dried blood was him.

He opened his mouth and grimaced. There were bits of something stuck between some of his teeth.

"What the hell?" he gasped. "Man, I look like shit!" He started to clean himself up, wondering what he could have done that would have resulted in such a horrible appearance. There was no way that if he'd gotten into a simple fight he would have ended up so brutalized. Had one of those damn Mexicans in the next building over finally taken offense to his chides and tried to whip him? That would explain some of the blood, since he was big enough to kill those little pipsqueaks, but it didn't account for the desiccated look he was sporting. Too, he was no biter, so what were the cruddy things in his mouth? His own cheek meat? Maybe he had challenged all three of those guys at once and had taken a bit of a whipping.

Some of the clotted blood would not come away from his skin so he broke out a bottle of rubbing alcohol and dug into a jar of cotton balls, swabbing away at the dreadful clots. He scrubbed and scrubbed until finally, after he had built a tiny pink mountain of filth-covered cotton balls on the counter, his face was mostly clean. The dark circles around his eyes remained, though. *Man I look like Death Himself.*

Then he climbed in the shower and washed his entire body, discovering that he had purple bruises all over. Most weren't serious, just discolored and tender. But there was one spot that upon closer examination appeared to be a bite mark, not a bruise. It was as high up on his left thigh as it could be without being on his groin and it was sore to the touch. It was almost impossible to get a good look at it where it was, but he was young and limber and managed to contort himself around to get a decent view of it. There were two punctures, where the incisors of some beast had bitten him. They were angry looking holes, black and purple and red. He swiped at them quickly, ripping crusty scabs from both marks.

Freaking vampire? Holy shit, how is that possible?

Now scabless, the wounds began to bleed profusely. Kyle jammed his washcloth against them and clamped his legs together so tightly that he accidentally cut off the circulation in his legs. He grew dizzy and passed out.

When he came to his legs were still clamped but not as tightly. The wound had stopped bleeding and he was able to compose himself enough to finish his morning bathroom ritual. In his bedroom closet, he dug out a pair of old blue jeans and a shirt he'd used for painting houses back in high school. He was thicker than the last time he'd worn the clothes so it took a bit longer to stuff himself into them. He had to lie on the bed to button the top button of his pants.

"Feel like a chick..." he grunted, twisting and wriggling. "Got to lose some weight." He made a mental note to ratchet up his workout scheme first thing next week.

Back in the living room, he stood over the feet, waiting for an answer to come to him. His stomach rumbled loudly.

"Great big steak sure would be nice right about now," he muttered. He knew he had none in the house, and there were more pressing problems at the moment, but no answer was forthcoming and the longer he stood there, the hungrier he became. There was nothing he could do about the body until after dark, anyway.

"So hungry."

Finally he could take it no more. He gathered up his wallet and car keys and headed for the little bar down the street that served the biggest and best rib eyes in the county. What difference would it make if he ate some dinner before dealing with the body? It wasn't like the guy was going anywhere.

Though he normally preferred well done, he ordered his steak rare. When they brought out the monstrous slab of beef, still dripping blood and barely warm, he didn't think twice about his decision. It was the juiciest, tastiest piece of meat he'd ever had. He worked it over like it was the last steak on Earth. It was so good that when he was finished with it, he licked the last drops of blood from the plate like a starving stray dog.

The bartender was staring at him. "What?" he shouted.

The man glared at him with a strange, disgusted look on his face but said nothing.

Kyle was no animal, but when he got a whiff of the beautiful juice he had to finish it off. Who cared if others in the place were staring? Beef blood was every bit as good as steak. In fact, it was what really made the steak so good. It was too damn good to waste!

He ordered a Cherry Wheat Sam Adams and sucked it down. It was fantastic stuff, sweet but strong, and every summer since the stuff had been introduced he'd done his best to drink as much of it as possible. Today it tasted a bit off, though. It was tangy and tart somehow, like the cherries in that batch had gone bad. He shrugged it off and ordered another steak.

"Same as the last, only give me a bigger cut," he instructed the bartender.

"You sure?" came the response. "That was a sixteen ounce cut."

"I'm sure," Kyle replied. "Go bigger if you can."

They brought him a twenty-four ounce cut that was so thick the bartender had to warn him, "It won't be done in the middle. If you eat this and get sick, we won't be held responsible."

Drooling at the beautiful slab of cow, Kyle barely heard the bartender's words. He understood that a response was needed to dismiss the man so he could eat, so he obliged the man with a nod and then dug in.

On a normal day, it would have been impossible for Kyle to put away that much meat. But today, today was different. He was extremely hungry, and only meat would do. He scolded himself for partaking of meat he knew to be tainted by all sorts of chemicals and antibiotics, but so what?

"Starting to sound like Brad," he snickered. That's when it hit him who was behind the couch.

CHAPTER 2

Once he could force no more meat into his belly, he paid his bill and left. He usually never left a tip but seeing as how he'd eaten three times as much food as normal, he gave the waiter a fifteen percent gratuity, which he considered sizable. Then he climbed into his ancient Ford pickup and muscled the old beater toward home. Some of the events of the previous night started drifting back to him. At first, he recalled just a few seconds, but as he passed a billboard proclaiming the benefits of drinking a particular brand of Tequila, most of the night came rushing back.

Kyle hadn't always spent his summers in the tradition of his literary heroes, drinking like a fish and chasing skirts every chance he got. He had run track in college and had been so lean that he was almost skeletal. That was when he still treated his body like a temple. But since graduating with a degree in Business Education and carrying a minor in English Literature, he had let himself go. He devoted his entire life to literature and swore to follow in the footsteps of men like Kerouac and Orwell, men he worshipped. He dedicated himself to doing everything like they did, drinking himself into oblivion at least three or four times a week and conquering any woman who allowed him to dominate her. Secretly, he believed that if lived their lives, he would have the same successes that they did and he wanted to be a literary giant like they were.

He was still something of an Adonis, even though he had fleshed out a bit. He was the stereotype of the tall, dark, handsome mystery man. He had dark curly locks that dangled down to his shoulders and eyes as black as coal, which added a devilish hue to his gaze. Women pined for him, including his female students, and men wanted to be like him. Since they couldn't, they generally settled for just being in his company, hoping that some of the shine from his aura would rub off on them and make them more attractive to the opposite sex. He was the light to which human bugs were attracted.

He had been hired to teach Business classes at a high school in a resort town north of Lafayette. Truly, his bosses there were more interested in his ability and willingness to coach the Track Team, an assignment he despised since it severely cut into his writing time. Unfortunately, as a new teacher there was very little he could do about it. Older teachers grew families and became tenured, drawing back from their extracurricular requirements and focusing more on their own personal pleasures, leaving the younger ones to take over. Incoming teachers were forced to coach sports and sponsor clubs in addition to teaching their full slate of classes, which was counterproductive since the rookies needed the extra time to prepare. But what could he do? Say no and lose the job?

Kyle knew that after he signed his sixth consecutive teaching contract with them and had become a permanent teacher, he could then quit every extracurricular assignment he had. Last fall he signed that contract and immediately resigned from Track, citing financial problems as an excuse. "I can't make enough from my day job and coaching to buy a house here, so I need to get a second job that pays more." His boss was angry but he believed Kyle's story. Their school system paid the least of any corporation in the region. Kyle added, "Maybe I'll come back to coaching when everything settles down," but he knew he wouldn't. He was already living the life he wanted and there was no way he would consider altering it unless an Act of God forced him to.

Kyle recalled that one of his colleagues had shown up that afternoon for a visit— Brad— an English Teacher at the school. Married with two little kids at home, Brad shared Kyle's dream of becoming a published author someday and they had become fast friends. Although the two wrote about vastly differently subjects, they loved to talk about their work, the work of others, and ideas. Kyle wrote about the human condition and Brad wrote escapist trash. He knew that Brad's work was more commercial but he didn't consider it to be literary. Brad knew it too, but he didn't care. He had to write because it was in his blood.

They were both excellent teachers, but both did it more because it allowed them large amounts of time throughout the year to write and read and do whatever else they wanted to do.

Their conversations at work had evolved into beer drinking visits at each other's homes where they ranted and raved about anything and everything. They had become such good friends that Kyle sometimes found himself thinking that if Brad ever decided to move to another corporation, he would quit teaching all together and move on to the next big phase of his life. He wondered if Brad felt the same way.

That morning, awaiting a visit from his buddy, Kyle found himself lounging by the pool in his apartment complex, nursing a hangover with a bottle of whiskey and a case of Coors. He slammed a shot and guzzled an entire beer, belching loudly once the beer was gone.

"Mmm… Boilermakers rule!" he shouted. He found it extremely funny to yell that line since it was not only the appropriate comment for such a drink combination, but it was also the mascot of the local university, too. Every time he shouted the phrase, someone in the complex would lean out of a window or look up from their chaise lounges and holler out "Boilers Rule!" in agreement.

By early afternoon he was completely drunk. He still had a few beers left and a half bottle of whiskey but hunger pains began to nibble at him. He grabbed his bottle as he clambered to his feet and glared at the three Latino men reclining on the other side of the pool sipping tequila from snifters.

"Don't you damn Mexicans ever work?" he cursed across the pool. They stared at him angrily for a minute then laughed at him. "Hey culo," one replied, "You fucking teachers ever work?"

Kyle laughed. "Hey if you bastards will watch my beer for me while I go get some lunch, I'll share my whiskey with you when I come back. It's top shelf shit!" He held up the bottle so they could see it. They nodded and waved. One muttered something in Spanish to the others and they all laughed.

"Speak English, you spics!" he growled at them.

The smiles melted from their faces. The leader of their little pack threatened, "You want to watch what you say, bandejo! People get hurt saying things like that."

"Fuck you," Kyle replied. "Watch my beer for me or I'll call I.N.S. on your asses." He spun around, nearly lost his balance, and headed for his apartment. He chugged another beer on the way. They would protect his alcohol while he ate lunch and took a nap. They always did. It was the same thing every day. They would split the rest of his booze and laugh like brothers until dinner, when they left for work and he went home for another nap before going out to the bars.

The moment that Brad knocked on the door, Kyle realized that he had forgotten they had made an appointment to hang out. He invited his friend in and offered him a beer. Brad immediately sucked it down and handed back the empty bottle with a loud belch.

"Can I get another?"

Kyle replied, "What am I? A woman? Get it yourself!" Then he grinned and told Brad to bring him a bottle of wine while he was in the kitchen.

They drank for a while and complained about work, about people at work and about the world in general. After they both had a good buzz going, the conversation turned to literature and the arts. Kyle wasn't as well versed in the arts but he enjoyed talking about literature as much as Brad did and wasn't angered by Brad's obvious superiority in the area. It was surprising to Brad that a Business Teacher would have any knowledge of Shakespeare or Milton or any of the Romantics, but it was thrilling for him to have another friend who liked to discuss that type of stuff. Kyle could even quote various lines from a number of Shakespearean plays, which was impressive for someone who wasn't an English Major in college.

"But I was an English major before I decided I wanted to be a Business Teacher," Kyle explained. "I minored in Lit and loved it so much that I almost applied for that last position that came open in your department."

"Why didn't you then?" Brad asked.

"Too much grading," Kyle replied. Brad smiled and nodded.

"Dude," Brad grinned, "I have that down to a science. Ninety percent of it is filler. You only really have to grade ten percent of it, and I get that done at school. I haven't taken anything home in fifteen years."

Kyle then confided that the real reason he hadn't applied for the English job was because his job was so easy that he was able to work a great deal more on his own writings. "Sometimes, I can even work during my prep. I get about a thousand words a day if no one has any questions or problems and I can complete a novel in just over a semester if I plan it just right."

"How the hell do you do that?" Brad asked, amazed.

"It's easy," Kyle grinned. "I paid a hundred bucks for a piece of software that takes dictation and I trained it on my home computer. So at work I write the outlines for my upcoming chapters and then I go home and dictate the material to my computer. It's awesome, dude!"

Brad was really jealous then. It took him nearly a whole year to think out a story, plan it and then write a first draft. "So what was your first book?" he asked.

"It was about a guy who signs up to work eight years for the government but finds that he has been tricked into working over two hundred years before he is forced from his little cubicle home. He goes on this big adventure all around the world and discovers that the world is much better than it was when he started his contract. The only problem is that the head dudes in charge are pushing the human race toward an unnatural end with technology and so he stops it."

"Sci-fi, huh?" Brad sneered.

"Yeah, I love sci-fi. But it's more than that. It's an attack on the technological evolution of our race. Tech has become a virus that infects more and more of the systems on our planet and if it's not stopped or at least reigned in, we're going to burn up our planet and destroy all worthwhile life in the process."

Brad chortled. "You're a tree hugger!"

"No, I'm a realist. I love computers and technological stuff, but like the Great Book says, 'everything in moderation.' Tech is like a drug. Before you know it you're hooked and pretty soon it has destroyed your life and everything around you."

He offered his two pronged plan for achieving what he called the ultimate goal for tech.

"If you have one team of scientists researching the benefits of a particular technology and another team researching the effects of that technology, you can put out a better product, even though it will take a little longer to get done. That will decrease the impact we have on the planet and the human race will advance with a minimal amount of devastation. Remember, the entire planet is one big ecosystem and mankind has a particular place within it. If we step outside of our place, we will disrupt the whole process. I think that could lead to the ultimate apocalypse."

"Wow," Brad remarked. "You actually sound almost sober." He chuckled and then added, "You think way out there, don't you? Do you seriously sit at your desk every day and think about stuff like this?"

Kyle nodded. "Only since I lived in Asia for a couple of years and saw all the nasty pollution that was there. They used to have the longest life spans on the planet until the Age of Industrialization. Now their life spans are actually decreasing and in some places they've dropped twenty years. You can't tell me that it's not related to technology because I've seen it firsthand. So I started writing books about it. They all have some sort of underlying ecological commentary, even though they're wrapped up in a mainstream story that even a thirteen year old could understand and love. Shakespeare did that and now look at us—we still read his shit nearly 500 years later."

Brad shook his head. "You're one crazy bastard!" he said. "I can't believe the way that your mind works."

Kyle smirked. "Yeah, you should be inside my brain. I can't stop thinking. That's the problem. The more stuff I learn the more scared I become. I know the Pandora is already out of the box but I think it can be put back in. It just takes a few people to step up and say 'Stop!' for everyone else to realize that it can be done. And I know you're wondering how I can connect Shakespeare to a global ecological disaster, so let me just say this. Shakespeare performed his plays for everyone from the King and Queen to peasants. They were all in the same room together watching the same play and yet everybody was able to understand his point. It didn't matter what point he was making but everybody was able to understand it. You go back and read his 37 plays and think about the fact that everyone from the lowest scum in the Kingdom up to the King himself was watching the same story and you see what they got out of it. That's what I want to do with my books. They are good and simple stories that you'll like even if you've got the IQ of a gnat. You'll walk away having learned something, even if it's subconscious."

Brad shook his head again. "Crazy bastard, you're drunk." Secretly, he was jealous that his friend could carry such grand themes for an entire book and even across multiple books. He couldn't do that on his own. He simply told or retold stories that were moral plays or commentaries on how life was a waste of time.

Kyle guessed what his friend was thinking. "Dude, if you want to be a better writer, you have to develop your own rules for your stories and then follow them and no one else's. Will you follow a formula or will you do stream of consciousness? Will you stick to the conventions of writing or will you pull 'A Clockwork Orange' out of your ass? It's all up to you, but the crucial element is that you have a simple story under it all that people can latch onto and pull something from."

Kyle chuckled at his improper grammar and thought to say something but decided against it.

The beer flowed and they both got drunker. After a good long time, the alcohol caught up to them. Kyle yawned. Brad cursed him for it but followed suit. Brad rolled his head around, cracking his neck loudly. Then he passed out. Kyle was right behind him.

CHAPTER 3

It wasn't like a corpse was just going to get up and walk away on its own, unless the dead suddenly began to rise, but Kyle had been wishing that the body would just disappear on its own. Of course, that was ridiculous but he was still a bit disappointed to find the body still there upon his return. No, he was going to have to deal with his unwelcome guest.

A few Boilermakers later, he worked up the courage to pull the couch back and inspect the body.

"Oh my God!" he whispered. Although the face was chewed up, quite literally it seemed, Kyle was still able to determine that it was indeed his good friend Brad behind the couch.

He drank a couple more shots to calm his nerves, hoping to hit that sweet spot where he, like most alcoholics, functioned best. Until that happened he was fairly sure that he was going to be unable to decide upon the proper course of action.

"What would MacGyver do?" he wondered aloud as the edges of his consciousness smoothed out. It was one of his favorite sayings. It hearkened back to the television action hero from the 1980s who was able to solve any problem with a paper clip, duct tape, and a piece of chewing gum. MacGyver could stop a nuclear meltdown with those three ingredients and the only mullet that anyone ever thought was close to cool.

Although MacGyver had long since become a joke, it was still that can-do attitude that kept him in the back of Kyle's mind. He actually owned a VHS library of the entire series, though he hid it in the trunk in his bedroom closet. Every so often he would take out a few episodes and watch them with the same thrill as a thirteen year old boy discovering his father's secret Playboy stash. But never for a moment had he ever thought he would actually consider plot points from the show as real options for getting out of such a situation like the present one and yet, there it was.

He surveyed his living room for items that could be useful but nothing was immediately forthcoming. "Okay, I've got a dead body decomposing in my living room and I have to get rid of it so that no one knows I had anything to do with it. Go, go MacGyver brain! Go!"

He cleared his mind of all thought, a difficult task considering the circumstances. Within moments, a plan crystallized. It was counterintuitive, but it would work. He would remove the body during the middle of the day when everyone in his apartment complex would be at work. They all had real jobs, as they were fond of telling him when they ran into him at the pool. There were so many people in the complex and they were so mobile that if he waited till after dark, someone would see him.

"Okay, next. Where do I take it?" He couldn't put it in the dumpster because that was too close. Wherever he took it, it would have to be far enough away from his complex to point away from him should the body be discovered. Then again, Brad was married and had kids. It was better that the body should be recovered quickly so that the family could get closure and any insurance money Brad might have coming. Still, he didn't want it found right away because any DNA on the body would lead investigators right to his door. Wherever he took the body it needed to be near enough civilization but far enough off the beaten path that only someone like a hiker could stumble upon it while wandering through the woods.

There are woods near the Wabash, he mused. The image that came to mind was a small forested roadside park near the river on his way to work. The woods were dense enough to hide a body for a while but the only people who ever frequented that park were gay men looking for casual encounters, cheating husbands, and the occasional hard core hiker. Someone would eventually smell Brad's rotting carcass and notify authorities, but he doubted that it would happen very quickly.

"Good," Kyle commended himself. "Now all you got to do is get the body from here to there." Obviously, he couldn't drag it out to his truck and plop it down uncovered in the wide open bed. No, he needed something to wrap it in.

He surveyed the room once more. *Nothing usable.* He stared at the body and waited for the answer to come to him. A bit of slimy goo dribbled down the side of Brad's face and dripped onto the carpet.

Ugh, carpet's ruined, he noted. *How am I going to hide that?* Then he wondered, *Could I just use the carpet itself?*

No, a fat hole in the rug would cost him dearly when he moved out of the place and he was not going to pay for a new carpet in such a shithole.

He went out into the tiny garden behind his apartment and checked his neighbors' tiny fenced-in plots. There were beach towels draped over chairs drying in the sun, but none were big enough to use.

Hey, a little voice told him, *go to Target and get a blanket big enough to cover the whole body. No ties to you as long as you wear a disguise and pay cash.*

Off he went, settling for the thickest Egyptian cotton bed sheets he could find. He picked maroon colored ones so as to hide blood stains. Once home, he cut the tags off the sheets so that when the cops finally found Brad, they wouldn't know what lot the sheets were from, thus complicating any efforts to determine the time frame in which the sheets were sold.

Then he quickly and firmly wrapped the body in the sheets. He made sure that no bit of his friend was protruding from the tight roll. *Looks like a giant joint,* he snickered to himself, *or a fat burrito.*

When the body was wrapped as tightly as he could get it, there was nothing to do but load it into the back of his truck and go. He propped open his apartment door with a pair of rolled up socks and tiptoed out into the long hallway to the front of the building, checking for neighbors. The building was empty and quiet, as was the parking lot. He backed his truck up to the front door and left it running. Then he hustled back into the apartment and yanked the body up over his shoulder. He kicked the socks from under the door and the door swung shut behind him, locking. It was the only time in his life he was thankful for that particular feature. Too many times before, he had managed to lock himself out of the apartment.

Stepping quickly into the open, he swept across his entire field of vision, searching for anyone who might witness his morbid deed.

He hoisted the body up over the tailgate and let it drop. It hit the bed of the truck hard enough that Brad's skull bounced twice. Had he been alive, it probably would have caused brain damage. Thankfully, and Kyle couldn't believe that he was actually using the word thankfully, Brad was not alive to feel the pain. He wondered for a second if the skull had accidentally cracked open. *Oh well, no time for such worries.* If he got to the burial place and found a bloody puddle of brain on the truck bed, he would worry about it then.

Relatively certain that no one had seen him, but not bothering to check for fear of drawing attention to himself, he strode purposely to the cab of the truck, climbed in, and drove off. He was careful not to go too fast but it was hard not to stomp the accelerator. Once he was on the frontage road that paralleled the Interstate and bordered the complex, he drove nervously toward the intersection that would bring him to the freeway entrance. The cops were thick in there because there was a Waffle House there they frequented.

It probably wasn't the wisest of choices to take such a heavily traveled road as I-65 as there were all kinds of semis that traversed the road. All of them were taller than his truck. Any truck driver could look down and see a body shaped blanket sausage lying there for anyone to see. It wouldn't take too many working brain cells for them to figure out what was actually inside that cotton burrito. Unfortunately for Kyle, he was such a creature of habit that he didn't even think twice about trying to find a more secluded back way. It was the way to work and he was so preoccupied with scanning for police that he was on autopilot. Before he realized it, he was merging onto the double-lane blacktop and then it was too late to turn back. As the first semi passed him and honked loudly at him for cutting him off, Kyle tried to convince himself it wouldn't have made a difference anyway. By the time the cops could have shown up, he would be off the highway and out of sight.

Fortunately, no one else passed him during the short run up the road. With only one mile left to go before he was off it, he even began to feel comfortable with the situation. That's when he noticed something flapping behind the truck, in his rearview mirror. As he fixated on the object, watching it grow taller in the whipping wind, finally reaching into the air above the cab like a sail, he realized that it was Brad's wrapper.

He let off the gas a little bit and the sheet smacked the back of his cab like a wet towel. He couldn't risk pulling over and drawing attention to himself on the highway, though. Indiana State Police officers tended to pull over and help stranded motorists and that was the last thing he needed.

His heart fluttered as he watched the blanket holding Brad's corpse grow from a wispy rag politely waving hello at him into a wildly waving flag. He slowed down as much as he dared, causing the sheet to shrink back into the truck bed a bit, but it didn't stop it completely.

He twisted around enough to peer down into the bed of the truck. Brad's mangled head was hanging out, chewed up cheeks and all. His eyes were open again. Kyle had used a pen from work to force them shut back in his apartment because it was too creepy a scene to deal with otherwise. But they were open again and Kyle's heart skipped a few beats. Was it possible that Brad was not dead after all?

He stared at Brad's face for such a long time that he nearly missed his turn. He had to swerve and cut across the white striped median, narrowly avoiding the crash barrier at the end of the concrete. There was a thunderous roll from the bed of the truck as the truck bounced up the incline and onto the ramp. When Kyle glanced back he saw that Brad had rolled over a few times and was now laying face against the tailgate. The sheet was nearly completely off.

At the top of the ramp, he slammed his truck into park and leapt crazily out of the cab. Time lurched to a stop as he worked feverishly to rewrap the body.

Just as he was finishing, a car flew up the ramp. *Of course-- a cop!* Frozen, Kyle could only stare as the patrol car pulled up next to him and stopped. The passenger's side window rolled down and the officer asked if he needed any help.

"No," said Kyle dumbly. The officer stared at him for a second too long and Kyle started to panic.

"I'm good. Just securing my load, Officer," he added respectfully. Hopefully, the cop didn't sense his panic. Kyle thanked his lucky stars that the police cruiser was built so low to the ground that the cop couldn't see what was in the bed unless he got out.

The officer stared at him a bit longer, then picked up his CB and mumbled something into it. He waited a moment for a response, and then flipped on his lights. Kyle's heart nearly leapt out of his chest. Mentally, he surveyed his cab, searching for weapons he could use to fend off the cop. But before he could move, the cop gunned his engine and roared off.

"Holy shit!" Kyle sighed as the cop sped out of view. When the car was finally gone, he climbed back into the cab and held up a violently shaking hand to check his nerves. Dropping the shifter into gear, he drove slowly away in the opposite direction as the cop had gone.

Ten minutes later he arrived at his destination. He nudged the truck down an overgrown track into the midst of a tiny forest on the edge of a farm and parked. There was a small clearing at the back of the woods that would be perfect. They were close enough to the road that when vehicles zoomed by he could hear the thump of their stereos, but far enough that it was difficult to catch anything but a flash of colored metal as they passed. There were a couple of houses a quarter mile away but no closer. If he was lucky it would take at least a few days for someone to stumble on the body. If not, the chances of tying the corpse to him were that much better for the authorities. Still, this July was one of the hottest on record. Hopefully Brad would rot fast.

He dragged Brad's body over to the edge of the clearing and piled some tree branches on it to hide it while he escaped, then surveyed his work before deciding there was no evidence. The ground had been baked hard by the hot sun so there were no footprints.

There wasn't enough room in the little clearing for him to turn the truck around, so he had to back out. That meant his license plate was visible for anyone to see and every moment he stayed there was another moment in which he could have been caught. His heart pounded as a Cadillac cruised slowly by. The driver stared him in the face as he passed. *Oh great, he got a good look at me. Well, maybe he's gay and looking for love.* Kyle flipped him a middle finger. That did the trick. The Cadillac instantly sped away.

When he finally backed onto the road, he watched in his rear view as other cars passed the overgrown path. He fully expected someone to pull in and find the body, so when he saw brake lights appear momentarily in his rearview mirror, his heart leapt into his throat. But the lights went off and the car resumed its journey.

"Thank God!" he cried, breathing a deep sigh of relief. This is what Norman Bates felt like when the car wouldn't go down into the swamp.

Slowly, carefully, he drove home.

CHAPTER 4

Pulling into the same parking spot from which he'd left only an hour before, Kyle was surprised to see his three Mexican pool buddies standing in front of his building. They saw him approach and pointed at him, laughing in Spanish.

"What the hell are you losers looking at?" he barked at them as he climbed out of his truck, worried that perhaps they had seen him leaving.

One of them pointed at the back of his truck and said something in Spanish. Another one pointed at Kyle's shirt and raised his eyebrows. "Man, what the hell happened to you? You got blood all over you."

Kyle glanced downward slowly in order to give himself time to think up some story.

"Oh, that," he replied nonchalantly. "I hit a cat on the way home."

The Mexican who had been pointing at the bed of his truck piped up and asked him, "That must have been a big cat, huh? You got blood all over the back of your truck."

Kyle smiled weakly. "Well, I guess he wasn't quite dead when I threw him in there."

All three men roared with laughter. Kyle smiled nervously.

"Hey, I'm going to go get washed up and then I'll be out there. Are you boys going to have a swim?" He knew very well that they were headed to the pool, but not to swim. It was the time of day when all the college girls would be out sunning and they would not have missed it for the world. Still, they nodded and patted their coolers.

SCOT MCATEE

"Got our suntan lotion right here," one of them joked.

"Yeah," said one of the others, "and all the bottled water we can handle." He held up two bottles of Vodka.

Kyle smacked that one on the shoulder playfully and headed for his apartment. The other men headed for the pool.

Once inside, he surveyed the damage to his apartment. He hadn't noticed before but there was blood on the wall behind the couch and some soaked into the carpet. A foul stench permeated the living room. He knew it would be impossible to completely rehabilitate the room but with enough elbow grease, most of the stains and the smells would likely fade away. Still, he would have to live with the mess until then.

He spent some time surfing the Internet looking for ways to clean rotten meat out of a carpet. He found a few companies that did biological cleanups of crime sites and one of them detailed how they got the gore out of murder homes. He followed the links and within minutes he was ordering various types of cleaners guaranteed to get the job done. Satisfied with his solution, he went into the kitchen and made himself some lunch.

After a nice hot shower he put on his swimming trunks, dug out a bottle of lotion, and headed for the pool. He begged some alcohol from the Mexicans as he claimed to be completely out. They were happy to oblige because he had always shared his booze with them.

Half a bottle of vodka and a fistful of beers later, he staggered home and passed out on the couch next to the nasty pool of rot percolating on his floor.

When he came to, it was still light out. Was it possible he had slept through the night and it was really tomorrow? He wasn't sure but it didn't really matter anyway. Work was still a month away.

Slowly, he raised himself up into a sitting position, brain fluids sloshing around wildly in his skull. For a moment, it seemed like everything had been a dream but as he looked around, he knew that it had all really happened. The dank odor of the nasty puddle on the carpet confirmed it.

"What to do now?" he asked himself. He had plenty of writing he could do but that would have to wait until the fog cleared from his head and since it would be days before the cleaners arrived, there was nothing to do but to move on.

He poured himself a glass of water and headed back to the pool. But as he pulled back the gate in the tall wooden privacy fence surrounding it, a horrific scene revealed itself to him. There were red spatters all over the far wall of the sundeck and misty red clouds floating lazily in the chlorinated water. In one of the clouds Kyle could see the top of one of someone's head.

"Holy crap!" he exclaimed. "What in God's name is this?"

He stepped forward and the wooden gate slammed shut behind him, boxing him in.

The floater was not the only corpse in the pool area. In one corner of the sun deck was a pile of girls in bikinis all curled up against the fence like they had climbed over each other to get away from their assailant.

Whomever or whatever had gotten them was brutal. Not a single one of them had been left wholly intact. Nasty slashes across their faces and bodies suggested an animal. One girl's jaw hung loosely by a thin thread of muscle. The body of the girl closest to him had been disemboweled. Her guts drooped out of her abdomen and lay sprawled on the deck in front of her. Her dead eyes stared unseeing into space.

But as gory and shocking as the scene was, he did not feel nearly as repulsed as he had at finding Brad's body. He had no idea why. Maybe he was still in shock after finding his friend dead. Maybe he was getting used to dead bodies. Maybe it was because deep down he hated those girls. Regardless, it was terrifying but not paralyzing.

He counted four bodies at the bottom of the pool. In addition to the three girls in the corner of the sundeck and another four or so scattered randomly around the pool area, the total number of people who had been dispatched in the time he had been passed out was at least eleven.

It was hard to believe that such an incident could have occurred without waking him up. Then again, he had been known to sleep through tornados.

In a daze, he wandered back to his apartment and plopped down onto his favorite chair. He didn't know what to make of it all. Life was becoming more surreal with each passing hour.

Someone had to have seen or heard the event. The commotion had to have been terrible. So why weren't the police all over it?

He felt relatively safe locked away in his little apartment—safe from whomever or whatever murdered those people. He did not fear death. But, he was afraid. He was afraid that the authorities would come and question everyone in the entire complex and that they might poke a little closer than he would like. They might even discover his secret.

What would they do when they saw the nasty stain on his carpet? Would they blame him for the pool? It really would not matter then that it was Brad's leftovers on the carpet and not the co-eds.

"What a freaking mess." The thought of spending the rest of his life caged in a tiny prison cell like a dog in a kennel was scarier to him than dying in a shootout with police. He hoped it never came to that, but he decided then and there that if it did, he would go out in a blaze of glory. But it wouldn't come to that, would it?

So there he sat in his chair waiting and listening for the telltale sirens to herald the approach of the police. He waited until well after dark before he moved from his chair and even then it was only to go to the kitchen. There was nothing edible left in the refrigerator and his freezer was nearly empty too. There were frozen peas and tater tots but not even enough for a full portion. A snack would only make him hungrier. He would have to go out.

The thought of running into a killer in the dark was less than appealing to him. Thankfully, he did have a nine millimeter handgun and he was a pretty good shot, so he fished his weapon out of his bedroom closet and loaded it.

There was a large department store near his complex that was open 24 hours a day. Normally, even on the best of days, it was not very crowded as there was a Wal-Mart only a mile down the road. Kyle had never been one for crowds and Wal-Mart was the worst of the bunch when it came to gobs of people. He liked to call it Hillbilly Heaven, as the never-ending parade of trailer park trash streamed in and out. Of course, many of those so called "poor souls" made more money doing slave work than he made sitting behind his desk, but class was more of a state of mind than of the pocketbook.

As usual, his preferred store was deserted. There were only about five people working in the store and not a single customer anywhere in sight. Normally he enjoyed having the store to himself, but in the context of the bloody mess at his apartment complex, it felt eerie to be alone. It felt like someone was secretly watching.

He stocked up on canned goods and alcohol and a few frozen items. When he had gathered a week's worth of items, he headed for the checkout line. The cute young cashier smiled at him as she scanned his items.

"Not very busy today is it?" Kyle asked.

"No," she replied politely. "I really hate it when it's so slow. It just makes the hours drag by. Not like I have anything to do after work tonight anyway..." She turned her eyes coyly away from him.

He picked up on the cue. He scented prey and went into hunter mode. "Yeah, me neither. I'm just basically hanging out at my apartment and writing stories."

Although he was not in the habit of picking up girls who were not old enough to ring up his alcohol without calling the manager over, she was shapely and cute and had a nice voice and it had been a long time since he'd had a girl. She might be just the distraction he needed. The problem of the carpet stain and the stink of his apartment disappeared, momentarily, while he stalked her.

She rang up his items extra slowly, he thought. He played along, flirting and making small talk until another customer came roaring up and nosed his cart into her aisle. Flustered, she quickly jotted her phone number down on his receipt before dismissing him with the obligatory, "Thanks for shopping with us. Come back soon."

His father had trained him to believe that men should be the aggressive ones in a relationship and that women should be the passive ones. In college however, he had discovered that women were just as aggressive as men and sometimes more so. Back then, he had thoroughly enjoyed the aggressive ones. They were so much easier to read and much more willing to experiment. These days it was about an equal mix for him. Sometimes he needed to hunt and sometimes he wanted to be hunted.

According to the unwritten local rules of dating, he should have waited a couple of days to call her, but he disagreed with that one. He preferred to call them right away so that they reacted to him instinctively. That helped him to catch them off guard, when they were more likely to accidentally tell him exactly what was on their minds. Women always thought they were in control, but with him they weren't—they just believed they were.

Keeping one eye on the front door as he loaded his food into the back of his truck, he was careful to avoid the shiny black spot on the floor so as not to get Brad's putrefaction on his food.

Once the pushy guy behind him came out of the store, Kyle took out his receipt and quickly dialed the phone number the girl had given him. He watched her through the giant plate glass window as she fished her cell phone out of her pocket. She picked up after only one ring and sounded surprised. "Hello? Who is this? I don't know anyone at this number."

"It's me, Kyle, the guy you just gave your phone number to a few minutes ago."

She spun around and looked out the window, but didn't immediately see him. There was an awkward pause. He hadn't expected her to search the lot for him, but it made sense. She started shifting her weight and playing with her hair, then rocked from side to side. He started to think that maybe he had played it wrong but she cleared her throat and said, "Wow, I really didn't expect to hear from you so soon." There was uncertainty in her voice, almost a scared quality to it, but her body language betrayed her voice. She was interested.

"Well, just to put your mind at ease, I'm not a stalker. I just figured there wasn't any point in waiting two days to find out if you gave me a fake number."

"Oh," she replied. Her voice was suddenly alive. "Well that's okay, then. I really didn't expect that you would call at all anyway. Most guys just want your number but then don't call."

"What? Why?" he queried.

"It's just some sort of dumb game they play with their buddies to see how many phone numbers they can get. They ask for numbers even when they're not interested. Some sort of stupid macho thing, I guess."

Kyle was aware of the routine and she was right that it was all about status. "Well, that's a frat boy thing to do and I'm no frat boy."

"Good to know," she said.

"Well, now that we have each other's real phone numbers, maybe you would be interested in going out with me. How does dinner sound?"

"Sounds good," she replied. "When and where?"

"Well I don't see any point in beating around the bush," he said, "What time do you get off work tonight?"

Almost instantly, she replied, "Eight. How about Olive Garden?"

"Fine," he responded. "You want to meet me there or do you want me to pick you up?"

"No, I'll meet you there. It's on my way home and I won't want to come back here to get my car when we're done."

"Fine. Eight-thirty at Olive Garden, then," he told her.

"Good. I'll see you there."

Kyle knew everything he needed to know. She was adventurous and open to new things or she would not have agreed to go out with a total stranger that very night. But she was smart because she was meeting him in a public place and driving her own car. That left her an escape route if things went horribly wrong. So she wasn't a nut job or some chick with a death wish. Neither was she looking for a long-term relationship. It seemed that the stars were beginning to align for him and his pretty little checkout girl.

CHAPTER 5

Excited more than he had been in a long time, he raced home and cleaned his apartment enough so that a woman would not be thoroughly disgusted when she walked through the front door. Unfortunately, the blood stain in the carpet was still there and the stench seemed to have grown stronger. It was a puddle of revulsion that seemed to keep on growing. He weighed his options. In the end, he knew there was nothing else to do except to cut out the portion of the carpet that was completely ruined and remove it from the apartment. He could air out the apartment all he wanted, but until that spot of decay was gone, the stink would only grow worse.

He kept a carpet knife under the bench of his truck, as a defensive weapon, which was the perfect tool for the job. He tried to keep the hole as small as he could but eventually he ended up cutting a roughly two foot square out of the carpet. Then, he dragged the couch over to the missing section and placed it over the bare area and hoped for the best. The couch was not centered on the wall so it looked oddly placed, but luckily Brad's corpse had been resting up against the wall and not in the middle of the room. Had it been in the center of the room, things would have been different. Kyle took it as another sign that his lucky stars were in force for this evening's festivities. He was going to get laid tonight.

After another shower and a load of laundry, which smelled particularly foul, he wandered across the hall and asked his neighbor if he could borrow something to mask the smell of rotten meat. She loaned him a can of Febreeze, apologizing that she didn't have anything more powerful.

"That's all right, I'm sure this will do the trick." He used nearly half the can before the stink diminished enough, but then the flowery chemical smell of Febreeze became so overpowering that he had to open all the windows just so he could breathe again.

At eight o'clock he headed for Olive Garden. He was not normally in the habit of arriving early, but he didn't know the girl at all, so showing up before her would be seen as respectful, if nothing else. Plus, he would be able to see if she was early or late. Early was good, it meant she was interested. Late was bad— it meant she would have to be convinced she was interested.

At 8:20, she appeared in the doorway. Immediately, she caught sight of him and bounced up to him, merrily planting a kiss on his cheek.

"You're early," she grinned.

Caught off guard by the smooch, he tried to appear contained and cool. "So are you."

"I wanted to see how long it would take you to show up. You can tell a lot about a man by how early or late he shows up to a date."

"Really?" Kyle smiled, secretly impressed that they were already on the same wavelength. "Do tell."

"Over appetizers, hmm? I'm starving." She took his hand and led him over to the hostess stand.

"Two for non-smoking and tucked into a quiet little corner," she said in a low tone.

Kyle was instantly aroused. He liked a woman who was willing to take control without being forced. They were all sorts of fun in the bedroom.

Once they were seated, she ordered a glass of wine and a beer chaser. The waiter asked for her ID and when he nodded and handed it back, Kyle breathed a sigh of relief. It would have been inconvenient if she wasn't twenty-one yet, because it would have meant night clubs and bars were out and that was usually a relationship death knell for him.

The drinks came quickly and she alternated sips between the beer and the wine, cementing the idea in Kyle's head that she was a bit of a wild child. She saw him watching her imbibe and said, "Don't worry, I find I get a much quicker and smoother buzz if I drink like this. It also lasts longer and I don't have to drink as much. And since I have to drive home…"

He got the message. She was not going to go back to his apartment. Normally, that would have made him lose interest right away, but she was different and he wanted to find out what made her tick. She was… challenging.

"So tell me what I need to know about you," she said.

Surprised at her forwardness, Kyle replied, "Wow. You like to get right down to business, don't you?"

"I just don't believe in wasting time if I don't have to," she answered.

"Well what exactly do you want to know?" he returned playfully.

"Why do you exist?" she fired back.

He stared wistfully into her face, trying to wring some sort of hint from her face that would tell him how to answer her question. But all he could discern was that she had something particular in mind. Normally, he would have thrown a bunch of bullshit at her, the typical date drivel, in hopes of scoring with her quickly. But from the expectant smirk on her face, he guessed that she was already testing him, trying to separate him from the rest of the pack. He was different alright, but how could he prove it to her?

"I exist to write," he answered honestly. Her eyebrows flicked upward.

"Oh. You're a writer," she responded condescendingly. "That means I can't trust anything that comes out of your mouth."

He smiled feebly, unsure how to answer. *Dammit! Wrong answer!* He sized her up again and decided the best approach, honesty, was still the simplest.

"You can believe what you want to believe. I write fiction, I just don't speak it."

"Well," she responded smiling, "You can't believe anything that comes out of any man's mouth until after you've had sex with him. The only time they tell the truth is after they've gotten what they wanted. Pillow talk is the only time when men don't lie and it's because they don't have to anymore. So why don't we just get right to the point. Do you want to have sex with me or not?"

Had she checked under the table at that moment, she would have had her answer. But Kyle answered anyway. "Of course. Why wouldn't I? I am a man, after all, and you're a hot bitch!"

If she wanted to play games, she might not like how it ended, but he sincerely hoped she would. "As long as we're being truthful, let me ask you the same question: Do you want to have sex with me?"

Her smile widened a bit and she replied slyly, "Of course I do. I wouldn't have agreed to come out on a date with a total stranger if I didn't. The thing is that I'm sure the sex between us would be raunchy and hot, but I'm just trying to figure out if you're worth wasting any more than just one night on."

There was an awkward pause, both of their minds racing for something to say that wasn't related to sex. She was the first to come up with something. "So, what are you writing about right now?"

"I'm writing about a character who goes through life observing all the injustices of the world and who wants to change the way things are done, but he can't figure how to achieve his goal."

She smiled condescendingly again and remarked, "You're doing a victim piece? Victim pieces aren't real literature."

"No," he huffed indignantly. "I don't write victim pieces. He's not a victim. He's a dictator in training. And what are you, a Psych or English major?"

Without missing a beat she answered, "Both. So a Napoleon complex, then?"

Again he huffed. "No. He's not a Napoleon either. It's more about a man realizing his place in the universe and stepping up to take his proper place."

"A coming-of-age piece?"

Kyle sighed. "I guess you'd just have to read it to understand."

"You know, a good writer could explain what he's trying to say without using that tired answer," she said. The corners of her mouth flicked upwards in what he took to be an evil smile. She was trying to get a rise out of him.

"I don't really like to be talked down to, thank you very much," he groused. "I'm in the middle of writing it. I don't know where the story is going to go. I don't write that way. I start out with a character in mind and an event. The character steps into the event and the plot evolves from there. It writes itself."

She smirked again. "Good authors map out their plot first, then fill in the story as they go."

His blood was beginning to boil. "Well, this sure isn't the way to get into my pants, denigrating my work without ever having read any of it."

"Who said I was trying to get into your pants?"

"Actually, you did. But if you're going to be a bitch about my work, then you can go find someone else." He made like he was going to leave, pushing his chair back to stand up.

"Okay, I'm sorry," she hurriedly apologized as she reached out to touch his wrist. "Please sit back down. I just wanted to see if you were actually passionate about your work. Obviously you are, so I know you're not full of shit. That's all I was trying to see. Please stay," she cooed softly.

She seemed sincere so he sat back down. Turning the tables hadn't worked very well. It was time for a different tack.

"Let's try this again," she smiled politely. "Why do you exist?"

With that same little smirk on her face she answered, "I exist because I'm a survivor. That's all I do. I survive."

"And what are you surviving right now?" Kyle returned snottily.

She looked away, knowing that he was exacting revenge for her earlier attack. She fidgeted uncomfortably in her chair. "Oh I don't think you want to hear my sad little story," she said. "It's pretty much the same story as every other girl."

"No, I really do want to hear your story. Go." He crossed his arms and cocked his head. She could tell he was losing interest already. She had made it too much work for him.

She took a deep breath and spit it out. "I survived an abusive father, a mother who played ignorant to the whole thing, a brother who tried to take over from his father, and a few suicide attempts."

Kyle had expected some middle class sob story, not an abusive one. Once again, she had surprised him, but now he was no longer aroused. He didn't know what he was, but it wasn't anything that could even remotely be labeled aroused.

"Yeah," she said, staring at the salad plate in front of her. "But I survived it and I'm surviving. I'm not crazy, I'm not suicidal anymore, and I am a survivor. I can survive anything. And I do."

Kyle uncrossed his arms and said, "Well this conversation suddenly just became very painful. Do you suppose we could change the subject once more?"

"Of course," she agreed. "Maybe you'd like to know my name. Or maybe you'd just like to ditch me now. Either way it's up to you. Which is it?"

He sighed again. "Wow, you're something else. A real roller coaster. No, I wouldn't like to leave yet. And yes, I would like to know your name. I assume from the fact that you asked that question that it's not Wendy, like your name tag says?"

She tapped the name tag on her chest and snickered. "Oh, you know that trick, do you? Well no, it's not really Wendy. It's April, after the month I was conceived in. My father thought that was so cute and my mother was too much of a milquetoast to stand up for what she really wanted to call me."

"And what was that?"

"She wanted to name me Desiree after her mother who died while giving birth to her."

"And your father wouldn't let her?"

April looked down at the table and with a bit of blood in her voice said quietly, "I told you, my father was abusive. Not just to me, but to the whole family. You know that song 'A Boy Named Sue?'"

Kyle gasped in disbelief. "Oh, no. You've got to be kidding. He named your brother Sue?"

"Mary," she answered quickly. "Or to be perfectly accurate: Marion. The doctors wouldn't put Mary on the birth certificate for a little boy. Said it was cruel. But Marion was okay. John Wayne or somebody like that had the real name Marion, I guess, so they let him put that down."

Kyle had to shake his head. If that was her lot in life, then he completely understood why she was a Psych major. She needed to understand her father better, to blame his behavior on something he couldn't have controlled. Even though she probably hated him for all the terrible things he did to her, she was still his little girl and most likely she wanted desperately to find a way to love him.

April started to tell him about various beatings and the mental abuse. "It was never sexual," she explained. "It was all about power with him."

He could only imagine what he would have done if he were in her place. Even as a child, he asserted his authority. If someone tried to control him or to take advantage of him, he lashed out at them. Sometimes that meant verbal spats, other times it was fists. He had no fear of attacking kids or adults whenever he felt the slightest bit wronged. It wasn't until somewhere about age twelve, when most kids were losing control of themselves, that he learned to control himself.

"So where is your father now?" he asked.

"Oh he's dead," she replied with an ironic grin. "He was such a cheap bastard that he wouldn't replace the tires on his car until they were almost bald. One night one of them blew out and he crashed headfirst into a tree. He was too stubborn to wear a seat belt too—he got multiple tickets for not wearing too, which he called Freedom Taxes—and he flew through the windshield and smashed his head open on a tree. I put a big cross up by that tree, and every time I pass it I sing a happy song in my head. Occasionally, I go out to his gravesite and piss all over it. There's no headstone to mark the grave, because we didn't have any money for that. So the county put one of those little brass markers on it just so they would know where the casket was. One of these days I'm going to scratch the letters off so he will be gone and forgotten forever. Now, let's have a few beers and a nice meal and go back to your place and fuck."

She noticed a 'funky' smell when she entered his apartment, but she quickly forgot all about it when he swooped her up into his arms and kissed her roughly. He carried her into his bedroom and dropped her onto the bed, pawing at her shirt.

"Tear it off and take what you want," she commanded. Completely and utterly aroused by her assertion, he did as he was bade. They kept at it until the sun came up, at which point April slid exhausted from his bed. Stiff and sore but completely satisfied, she began to put her clothes back on. Kyle lay limply on the bed, watching her dress.

"Oh man," he chuckled. "I think you're going to have a couple bruises on your ass."

"You mean bite marks, don't you?" she sneered. "I thought you were trying to eat me there for a while. My left nipple is still bleeding a bit."

"Sorry, don't know what came over me," he apologized softly.

"Me either, but I liked it. It was so primal." She checked out her posterior in his full length closet door mirror, surveying the bite marks and tracing them with her fingers. "Guess it's a good thing I don't sit down at work. That one's already swelling."

"Maybe we need a code word next time so we know when a little is too much?" Kyle suggested.

"Next time?" she gasped with faux surprise. "You really think there's going to be a next time? What would be the point? You think we can top this?"

He couldn't tell if she was serious or not. "Well, yeah, I think so. I mean, I want there to be a next time." He started to babble but she cut him off.

"Stop, stop. You're jabbering like a virgin after his first time. I like strong men who take what they want. Don't ruin this."

He obliged her, then stood up. He pulled her to him, spun her around so her back was to the bed and pushed her down onto the still warm sheets. He slid her panties down around her knees and hoisted up her bra just enough to get at her and took her again.

When he'd had his fill of her again, she groaned, "Do I get breakfast now?"

"Sure, anything you want as long as it's not more than ten bucks."

"Ten bucks?" she howled indignantly. "That's all I'm worth?"

"No, that's all I have left until the next pay day," he said.

"Fine," she answered with a tone that told him he would pay for his cheapness later.

He asked if she wanted to join him for a quick shower, but she declined his offer, stating that she would do it at home. "That's where my makeup is," she added.

But as she began dressing again, she felt a stirring desire to watch him in the shower. She stood in the doorway, watching his fuzzy shape through the semi-transparent shower curtain. She could sort of make out the water running down his sore muscles and her brain clarified the image for her. That was enough. She flung open the door and the next thing Kyle knew he was getting the most intimate scrubbing of his life.

She wanted to do breakfast at the local IHOP, a place he drove past almost every day but never had the courage to visit. The smoky windows betrayed the air quality of the atmosphere within and he knew that it was some place that he would never enjoy. He tried to talk her out of going there, citing his hatred for cigarette smoke.

"Yeah, well, don't forget they outlawed smoking inside restaurants in the entire county months ago. It's okay in there now," she informed him.

Even though it was against his better judgment he acquiesced, even though he suspected that he'd be home taking another shower shortly after the meal.

Finally, all cleaned up and ready to go, they strolled out of the apartment and headed for the parking lot. Kyle pushed the outer door open and stopped dead in his tracks, as did April, for at the end of the walkway stood Kyle's three Mexican pool pals, covered from head to toe in what appeared to be blood and gore.

CHAPTER 6

"Hey you bastards, get a job before I call I.N.S. on you!" Kyle shouted at them somewhat tentatively. April jabbed him in the ribs with an elbow.

"You can't say that!" she whispered. "That's racist!"

"Trust me, I know what I'm doing," he whispered back, his eyes glued on the Mexicans. They didn't move. They didn't even blink. Their mouths hung open. Red-tinted saliva drooled lazily from the corners of their mouths.

Kyle and April stood stock still, waiting for them to do something, anything, but they didn't. They were statues. One's arm was nearly chewed off, another's cheek was missing a chunk of flesh and the third, the one that he thought of as the leader of their pack, had a good sized portion of his neck ripped away, which revealed the underlying muscles and ligaments that kept his head attached to his shoulders.

"Uh... I think we ought to beat a retreat to my apartment," he told April quietly. She agreed nervously.

"They don't look right, do they?" she suggested as she grasped his hand tightly and backed slowly toward Kyle's door.

"Ha, understatement," he agreed.

Until that moment, Kyle had assumed that the deadbolt on the hallway door was there only for when the building was completely unrented, but now he was thankful that it was there. He slid the bolt home, locking the Mexicans out.

He pointed to the long panes of decorative glass that ran up and down either side of the door and told April, "It's not going to keep them out for long, but maybe it will buy us some time."

April looked at him, puzzled. "What are you saying?"

"I'm pretty sure they're coming in," he said hurriedly. "Come on!" He pulled her into the apartment and locked the door, then quickly pushed his couch in front of the door. He piled other pieces of furniture up against it to bolster the strength of his blockade and then started throwing smaller items atop the heap to give it heft.

April watched tensely as Kyle stacked all his belongings on the mound and wondered what in the world was going on. She pestered him for an explanation, which he tried to provide between trips from the bedroom.

"I have no idea what's going on," he grunted as he lugged a heavy nightstand to the edge of the couch. "But I'd say those guys are out for blood. Literally."

"What do you mean?" she moaned. She was on the verge of hysteria.

"Well, I know how ridiculous this is going to sound, but did you get a good look at them? Did you see those bite marks all over them? To me that pretty much means something is fucked up about them. Did they seem really alive to you? Me neither. If this were a movie, I would guess they're zombies. And if you know anything about zombies, you know they like to eat human flesh. But even if they're not really zombies, they look like they want to make hamburger out of us, so I'd say we got to get this door covered up in a hurry. Why don't you help me now and worry later, huh?"

April shivered and clasped her arms around her midsection. It was unbelievable to think that there was anything valid in his statement. Zombies weren't real—they were the stuff of fiction and horror movies. But she had seen the men. She had seen the bite marks and saw the way they glared at her and Kyle.

"But zombies aren't real..." she muttered.

"I wouldn't have thought so either," Kyle replied, now rushing frantically around the apartment in an attempt to fortify their position. "But I can't think of any other explanation, can you? You ever see anyone that chewed up who was still alive and walking?"

She had not. "Maybe they're on drugs?" she offered. Before she could say anything else, there came the sound of breaking glass in the hallway outside. They were coming in.

April could barely see the door for all of the furniture in front of it. She prayed that it would keep them out. But as she looked around, she noted the sliding glass doors that opened onto a tiny concrete patio. What was to stop their attackers from just walking around the building and coming in that way?

She cried out, "Hey," and pointed at the patio doors. He turned to see what the problem was and immediately understood.

"I just hope they're stupid zombies," he said.

"But zombies aren't real!" she repeated. "Maybe they're just high on some weird designer shit."

It was obvious that she was about to lose her composure. "Don't freak out on me," he commanded her. "You're a smart girl. Do the math. All myths come from a grain of truth. You know there are real zombies in Haiti, don't you?"

She nodded. "Yeah, but those are drug-induced and they don't eat human flesh."

"Sure," Kyle agreed, "But there are cannibals out there in the world too, right? So is it much of a stretch to say that maybe a virus makes them into zombie-like creatures and then makes them hungry for human flesh?" He had no idea what he was talking about, but he didn't know what else to say. April had not seen the pool massacre. She only saw three near dead guys standing on his front lawn with bits of flesh ripped out of their bodies.

"I wouldn't believe this if it was a movie or a book or anything else," April cried, "And I can't believe it now." Tears of panic started to flow down her cheeks. He pulled her tightly to him and held her for a moment, but then thrust her away. There wasn't anymore noise from the hallway. It was silent.

"I don't hear anything," he whispered. He rushed to the sliding glass doors and peeped out between the blinds that covered them. He glanced from side to side to see if the Mexicans had made their way back there. "I don't see them," he said.

He ran into his bedroom, which faced the front of the building, and plopped down in front of the window. He pulled back the blinds and poked his head up just enough to see over the edge of the window sill.

"They're just standing there," he whispered back to April, who was standing in the doorway.

"What else are they doing?" she whispered back.

Kyle suddenly let go of the blind. "Oh crap, I think they saw me." He jumped up and ran out of the room, pulling the door shut behind him. He brushed past April and ran into the other bedroom looking out the window to see what they were up to.

"They're heading for the front door again," he narrated. A few seconds later he said, "They're trying to figure out how to get in."

There was splintering wood and more glass breaking, followed by a crash and a huge thump. They were through the door.

"They're in!" Kyle hissed. "Quick! Now we get the Hell out of here!"

Together they raced through the living room to the sliding glass doors. At the same moment that he got the one door open, the door to his apartment began to quake with the weight of three murderous men pushing up against it.

Kyle leapt through the doorway and pulled April behind him. He slid the door shut as quickly as he could, which would only stop them for an extra second or two at the most, but every second might mean the difference between life and death.

"Let's go," April enjoined him.

"Wait," Kyle replied, "I just want to make sure they're committed to the assault before we split. I want to trap them inside the apartment, not the hall."

The furniture tipped and rocked as the door began to give way. His nightstand fell off the top of the pile and the entire mound of furniture began to crumble. The pounding grew more intense and finally the top of the door snapped off. One of the Mexicans began to climb through the opening.

"Now! Run!" Kyle shouted. He grabbed April by the hand and dragged her around the corner of the building. In seconds they were at the truck and he was fishing his keys out.

"Damn thieves," he mumbled, cursing his neighbors. If it wasn't for the dirtball kleptomaniacs in the next building over, he wouldn't be standing there fumbling with keys while maneating zombies were hot on his tail. "Ah, finally." He got the passenger door unlocked, shutting it as quietly as possible after April was in. She reached across the cab and unlocked his door while he ran around.

He jammed the key in the ignition as fast as he could and mouthed a quick silent prayer. Murphy's Law dictated that anything that could go wrong would go wrong but for Kyle it was more like anything that could go wrong at the exact moment he needed it to go right would go wrong but only at that moment.

He turned the key over and floored the gas. The truck lurched forward and died. "Oh Lord! Please don't be flooded!"

Again he tried the ignition. The starter turned but the motor wouldn't kick on. He tried again but had the same luck.

"They're coming!" April hissed. "Go!" Kyle kept at it, but the motor wouldn't catch.

He kept working at it, staring wide-eyed in the rearview the whole time, watching the men emerge from around the corner of the building. They weren't slow like zombies in the movies but they weren't running either. It was somewhere between a Night of the Living Dead shuffle and a 28 Days Later sprint. They meant business.

One of them reached the back of the truck and began to climb into the bed. The other two crept up the passenger's side of the truck.

The one in the truck bed managed to reach the cab before the motor finally roared into life, causing the truck to lurch forward again. Kyle gunned it and the truck roared away. Their passenger was summarily ejected.

April looked out her window and screamed. One of the Mexicans was still holding onto the door handle and staring at her intently. He latched the other hand onto the side of the truck. She screeched continuously as the thing inched closer to her until it was touching the glass.

Kyle reached the end of the parking lot and jerked the wheel hard to the left. The back end of the truck fishtailed and the Mexican disappeared from view for a moment, but he popped right back up. He had just slipped down the side of the truck and out of view but once the truck was going straight again, he was able to climb back up the door.

They roared down the road, back toward the superstore where April worked. There were commercial buildings all along this stretch of road and Kyle got an idea. Turning the wheel toward the closest building, a public storage barn, he looked over his shoulder to see the Mexican now straddling the side of the truck like a jockey on a horse. They only had a few more seconds before the guy would get both feet in the bed of the truck and then their window of opportunity was lost.

"Strap in, this may hurt a bit," he commanded April. She obliged, pulling her shoulder belt across her chest and snapping it tight. Kyle strapped in, too, without ever taking his eyes off the approaching structure.

The Mexican was on his feet, leaning around April's side of the cab, when Kyle veered to the left a hair and scraped the passenger's side of the truck along the side of the barn. Metal scraped against wood and was immediately followed by a meaty 'thwack' as the Mexican's head hit the wall of the building.

Kyle jerked the wheel to the left and the grinding noises halted as the truck pried itself away from the building. He did a full circle and came back around to face the Mexican. When the nose of the truck was pointing at the crumpled up body lying at the corner of the building, he idled the engine.

He and April stared for a long time at the limp body. The head was nearly pulverized on the right side, but the left side was just about normal. There didn't appear to be any other real damage to the body but from the force of the collision with the building, Kyle knew their attacker was nothing more than a bag of mush.

Or was he? The Mexican began to twitch and shake. Slowly, he climbed to his knees, and finally to his feet.

"I think I'm going to be sick," April gagged. The sight of the man wobbling to his feet with a smashed head made her ill. He lurched around and locked onto them with his one good eye and started for the truck. He was not as much of a threat, at least in Kyle's estimation, but that would not stop him from doing what needed to be done.

"You may want to close your eyes for this part," Kyle told April as he mashed the accelerator down. The truck rushed toward the gory caricature. April put her hands up over her eyes and then decided it would be better if she just lay down on the seat.

Kyle smashed into the Mexican, crushing his ribcage against the sturdy old Ford's radiator. When he slammed on the brakes a few seconds later, the monster flew backwards into the next building, hitting one of the rollup garage doors so hard that the door collapsed in on itself like aluminum foil. Something flew up out of the mess and even though Kyle only caught a glimpse of it, he later realized that it was the man's brain breaking free of its compromised container. He saw it splatter on the roof overhang and then fall back to the ground like a lump of jelly. There was no way he could tell April, who was still lying on the seat with eyes closed, what he had just witnessed.

He idled there a moment longer to make sure that the guy wasn't going to get back up before leaving the grisly scene.

"Some first date, huh?" he said drolly as they turned onto the frontage road.

April threw up on the floor of the cab. "Take me home," she groaned.

 CHAPTER 7

State Road 26 was packed with minivans and pickups, just like every summer evening. As Kyle and April rolled through the intersection, Kyle wondered if those people had any idea that two angry zombies were on the prowl less than a mile away. It was unreal to think that they had just survived a zombie attack. It was even more frightening to think that no one else seemed to be the slightest bit aware that the undead were roaming the streets of Lafayette and about to unleash Holy Hell upon the entire town.

"Do you think these people know?" he said to April, not really expecting a response.

She shrugged. "I don't know. How could they? I don't care. I just want to go home." She surveyed the traffic, the vast majority of which was headed out of town, and wondered aloud, "Was there a game today or something? Traffic is only this bad out here when there's any kind of home game at Purdue."

"No," Kyle replied. "It's July. There are no major sporting events in Lafayette in July." *That must mean they know something*, he added mentally.

Upon reaching April's apartment, a third story walkup tucked into a quiet corner of a rundown building occupied mostly by students and blue collar families, they barricaded themselves inside. She had a walkout balcony complete with sliding glass doors and after a quick inspection of the area below the balcony, Kyle decided that only the tallest of zombies would be able to scale the railing and get in that way.

Still, he pulled the blinds closed for good measure. Then he turned on the television, keeping the volume down to a bare whisper.

There was a small television station in town. It had its own news crew and a fleet of trucks. Their coverage area was the doughnut counties surroundings Lafayette, since their sister station in Indianapolis covered everything else in Central Indiana. It was excellent in its coverage of its hometown, but there was nothing about the zombies, no "Breaking News" segments or anything. It was all talk shows. Kyle took that to mean that the situation was not well known yet.

By the time the noon news came on there had still been no stories about zombies or Mexican corpses. They were now on the far side of town, far enough away from the event for Kyle to relax enough to address his growing hunger pangs, even though both of them were still scared shitless.

"What've you go to eat in here?" he asked politely. "I'm not feeling brave enough to go out again."

"Me either," she agreed. She went to the kitchenette and rooted through her fridge. "Tuna work for you?"

"Fine with me," he replied.

They dined on tuna sandwiches made from lightly moldy bread and a can of soup. April wasn't much of an eater so she didn't have much of a menu selection. She explained that she only shopped for a couple of days at a time. "I hate to waste food or money," she said.

"But you work at a grocery store," Kyle laughed.

"Exactly," she replied. "I get a discount, too, but I don't like waste."

After lunch, April showered again and coaxed Kyle into taking one, too. Playfully, he tugged her towel off her while she was doing her hair and happened to note that the two bite marks on her butt had turned red and puffy. It occurred to him that most zombie viruses in the movies were transferred by human bite. He knelt down to inspect the marks closer.

April thought he was messing around and smacked him with a hair brush. "What are you doing, you perv? Stay away from there."

He put his face close up to the bites and ran his fingers over them.

"I'm looking to see if you have any broken skin here," he told her as he fended off another hairbrush attack. He explained his idea about virus transference to her but that only served to upset her.

"Oh my God!" she cried. "You mean you might have turned me into a zombie? You bastard!" She started clubbing him with the hairbrush.

He whined for her to stop but she didn't. Finally he cried out, "If you were going to get it from me, then I would have to be a zombie, right? Well I'm not, am I?"

"No, I guess you aren't. But who's to say if it didn't pass to me through the air. Son of a bitch! I'll kill you if I turn into one of those sick bastards!"

He tried to soothe her. "Your ass would have had to been out in the open air around them when they were close enough to spread it, and I don't remember that happening. If it had, I might have bitten your little round peach butt myself!"

"Again you mean?" she replied, her voice a little softer now. "From now on, no more rough stuff till this whole nasty episode is over."

He nodded in agreement. They got dressed, she in nice fresh clothes, he in a spare pair of extra large gym shorts and a very tight wifebeater T-shirt. Then they curled up together in front of the television and waited for the news that they both knew must eventually come. At some point, they dozed off.

It was dark when Kyle awoke to a buzzing tone that sounded much like the tornado sirens mounted on telephone poles around the county. The tone was coming from the T.V. and there was an emergency symbol on the screen. A ticker ran across the bottom of the screen informing users to tune to the station's radio channel for more information.

"You have a radio?" Kyle nudged April.

"Yeah, in the bedroom. It's my alarm clock," she mumbled sleepily, trying to avoid waking up.

He retrieved the clock and tuned the radio to the sister channel, but there was only static. "Should have known," he grumbled.

"Known what?" asked April, sitting up and rubbing the sleep from her eyes.

"Well, I think the shit has hit the fan. Channel 18 is out, so is their sister radio station."

"What about the Indy channels?" she wondered, reaching for the remote. She flipped through the half dozen or so stations, but they were all fine. "Hmm, weird. No news on any of them…"

"Wonder what's going on out there," she said. She went to the balcony and peeked out between the curtain and the glass. "I don't see anything."

"Um, I might not do that for very long if I were you," Kyle suggested. "Longer you look, the more chance someone or something will see you."

She shivered, recalling the events from earlier in the day and quickly pushed the blinds shut again.

"Don't want a repeat of that, do we?" she shuddered.

"So what do we do now?" she asked, plopping down on the couch. Of course, looking at her lying there, clean and cute in her skimpy little shorts and tank top, he smiled and crawled across the floor toward her.

"Uh, no, not that," she said, quickly crushing his libido. "I'm not going to be in the mood for quite awhile after this morning."

He grunted, paused long enough to decide she was serious, and gave up the attempt.

"Then I don't know," he said. "What've you got on the DVR?"

"Oh, network stuff mostly. It was set to tape CSI tonight because I missed that episode back in the spring."

He suddenly had a thought. "On what channel? Indy or local?" he asked hurriedly.

She picked up on his thought and grabbed the remote. Kyle could tell from the look on her face which channel.

They played back the tape from earlier and were amazed to find that the DVR had in fact taped something.

There was a breaking news report during the soap operas in which on-the-spot reporters showed footage of a number of zombies scrambling from building to building in Kyle's apartment complex. There were screams and people jumping out windows or being mobbed in the parking lot by discolored creatures who proceeded to tear them apart and munch on their flesh. If Kyle hadn't just lived through it that very morning, he would have never believed it. He would have dismissed it as a publicity stunt. Unfortunately, he knew it was no stunt.

A few minutes later, as the reporter stood there jabbering on about "no police patrols in sight," a corpse in the background of the shot stood up, stumbled over to the reporter, and bit him on the neck. The reporter screamed and crumpled to the ground. The zombie turned on the cameraman, who had the good sense to drop the camera and run. After that, there was nothing but static.

The news anchors came back on the screen. They showed supplemental footage from another crew. Apparently the zombies had spread through the entire commercial district near his home. The Feeding Trough, a family buffet, had become a horrible scene of carnage. They showed a zombie running through the parking lot toward the front doors and a brave worker trying to block the doors but the zombie smashed right through the glass and ripped his arm off.

There were a few moments of silence followed by screams. Minutes later, a mob of undead streamed from the building, all headed right toward the cameraman. The camera shut off and the beautiful young anchorwoman came back on the screen.

"Ladies and gentlemen," she said as she tried to maintain a comforting but fake smile, "that is the last feed we have. But we have in-studio an eyewitness."

"Oh no," Kyle said, a thought occurring to him. "This is not going to end well."

"What do you mean?" April asked.

"Well, we know that the entire station went dead a little bit ago, right? I think that means that the station must have been attacked. And who is our most likely candidate to do the attacking?"

April shrugged and then looked back at the screen. Then it dawned on her. "Oh... him." She pointed at the eyewitness. Kyle nodded silently.

They watched the rest of the broadcast like it was a slow moving train wreck in the making. They could not look away as they waited for the ending that they knew was coming.

When the moment came and the eyewitness turned blue and keeled over dead on the spot, then arose a few moments later and viciously attacked the petrified anchorwoman, Kyle's sense of anticipation turned to horror and disgust. Still, he could not look away. The anchorwoman turned almost instantly. She immediately attacked her coworkers like a rabid monkey and ripped them to shreds. The cameraman cursed and ran from the studio, leaving the camera taping. Kyle would never forget the image of the petite beauty leaping on the back of the weatherman and nearly ripping his head off with her teeth. The resulting blood spray was something out of a Monty Python skit. If they hadn't been witnessing it on live (taped) television, Kyle might have thought he was watching a comedy show.

For a second, he even thought about rewinding the tape to watch her other on-air kills. Before the weatherman hit the floor she was on a couple of stagehands. She dispatched them with a ferocity that Kyle had only seen in animal attacks. One of them lost a limb and bled out quickly while the other was summarily disemboweled.

The last thing that the footage showed was the news reporter stomping out of the studio like Godzilla. Thanks to the wireless microphone pinned to her chest, the entire world could hear the screams and wet gargles of her coworkers as she caught them off guard and killed them. Eventually, she went outside the maximum range for her microphone and the sound went dead. After that, there was about an hour of dead air before the signal finally snapped out.

Almost absentmindedly Kyle suggested, "So real life zombies aren't as stupid as they appear in the movies."

"Well that would just rewrite the zombie books, now wouldn't it?" April replied sarcastically. "We can't have that. How in the world will we kill them?"

To Kyle, her comment was a relief. It suggested that she was strong and resilient, a survivor liked she claimed.

He reminded her about the zombie who had been hanging onto the back of his truck. "But apparently if we separate the brain from the body, just like in the movies, we win."

"Or so you hope," she answered.

"Yeah, I do. Let's just hope it doesn't get any harder than that. It's one thing to shoot a zombie through the head from a long distance, it's another entirely to have to get close enough to them to cut their heads off their bodies. I really don't relish the thought of either."

She agreed. "I don't think I can sleep tonight," she said, shivering.

"Maybe you should call your parents and see how they're doing?" he offered. "Once this hits Indianapolis news, it's going to go nationwide and the phone lines will all jam up."

She harrumphed. "Well I guess you just found the silver lining for me."

"How so?" he asked.

"Well, I told you my Dad was dead. What I didn't tell you was that my Mom was killed in a car accident about two years ago. All my Grandparents are dead, too. I don't have any family anywhere. So no one to worry about me."

He scooped her up in his arms and whispered in her ear, "Well, you've got me."

She hugged him hard and long, maneuvering around to where she could wrap her legs around him. "Bedroom. Now."

CHAPTER 8

April awoke at the sound of her toilet flushing. She stretched out for a few minutes and shook the sleep out of her body. Joining Kyle on the couch, she scratched her ass and asked him what was new.

"All the Indy stations are gone," he told her.

"Christ!" she exclaimed.

"That was my exact response," he mused.

"Great minds think alike, huh?"

He went to the balcony and pulled back the blinds a couple of inches and looked out.

"What are you doing?" she demanded. "I thought we wanted to stay hidden."

He opened the sliding door and stepped out onto the balcony. Leaning on the rail, he surveyed their surroundings. "We can't stay here forever," he mumbled. "You don't have enough food for starters. Also, eventually, the power is going to go out and then it won't be long until society breaks down completely. We need to find some place that's more secure than this."

Though she was not sure what could be more secure than a top floor apartment with easy roof access, the thought of an inadvertent fire or attack by an undead neighbor crossed her mind. She hadn't seen or heard a single person moving around the apartment building since they got home yesterday. Where had everybody gone?

Was it possible that the zombie attack had started well before they were aware of it? Could they both have been so oblivious that they had gone on living their mundane lives in the middle of the Apocalypse? There had been no signs to imply that's what had happened, but maybe there had and she had just missed them.

"Oh, wait," she sighed, suddenly realizing there had been at least one sign. There had been a long line of people trying to get onto the Interstate. Now that she thought about it, business at the store had been really off the last two or three days. Maybe everyone but she and Kyle knew about the outbreak. He had mentioned something about not being much of a TV guy.

The fact that most of the people in her life were college kids who also lived within a bubble did not help. They were the kinds of people who stood on their balconies when a tornado was coming and videotaped it instead of finding a basement to hide in. They were the ones who never drank a drop of alcohol during high school but got to college and went so crazy with the stuff that some of them ended up in the hospital or dead. Taking away parents was like letting loose dogs that had never been out of their pens before. And so, which of them really cared enough about the outside world to follow the news?

"Don't zombies head for the place that meant the most to them in life?" she asked.

"So George Romero would have us believe," he answered. "Why?"

"Oh, no real reason." Mentally, she ran through a checklist of her neighbors. Which of them was most likely to remember she was here? Those were the ones she was most concerned about.

Kyle broke her out of her daze. "Oh shit!"

"What?"

Kyle pointed at the north end of the parking lot. "We've got company and he's headed this way." She stuck her head out the door far enough to see where he was pointing. He was a squat little zombie all covered in blood.

"Oh my God, that's my next door neighbor!"

She ducked back into the apartment and ran to the door, turning to yell at Kyle. "Hurry up! Get back in here!"

Kyle waited a few more seconds until he was sure that the zombie was, in fact, headed for them before going back in. He closed the door and the blinds behind him. Tapping his teeth with his finger, he mulled over their options.

So that part of the myth is true.

Hopefully he wouldn't sniff them out, but what if he did? There was a fire axe in the hallway. He had noticed it when they came in because it was so Day-Glo orange that no one could miss it. He hurried out and grabbed it. Then he told April to shut and lock the door until he told her to open it again.

Of course she argued with him, pleading for him to come back in the apartment with her, but he could not be convinced. It was almost comical how much like the horror movies their argument was, but when they heard the shuffling steps of the zombie on the stairs below, April hissed, "Fine. Nice knowing you!" and slammed the door. He heard the dead bolt slide home and then the pitter patter of her feet as she ran into her bedroom and slammed that door too.

"Mental note, her walls are even thinner than mine."

It didn't take long for the zombie to get up the stairs. Although it moved like it was in a daze, it was a great deal faster than Kyle would have expected. He stood next to the stairwell, hoping that the zombie would not realize that if it looked straight up, it would see him peering over the rail at it. Zombies weren't known for being extremely aware of their surroundings. They were more often focused on such things as, "BRAINS!"

When the monster finally reached April's floor, it turned toward her front door instead of its own. That's when Kyle stepped up to him like a batter to home plate and swung the axe as hard as he could.

It made a flat smacking noise as it glanced off the dead man's shoulder blade and deflected up into his neck, where it lodged in the bone at the top of his spinal cord. The zombie registered the attack and started to turn. Quickly, Kyle yanked the axe back and took another swing. This time, he sliced through the neck with ease, though he did not get all the tissue. The zombie's head leaned forward until it toppled over onto its chest, attached only by a single muscle and a bit of skin. The body took two more steps before it flopped over, landing across April's doorstep.

It was a horrible image and Kyle could do nothing but stare as the rush of endorphins subsided. Eventually he was able to move and speak again.

"Okay," he called out. "You can unlock the door!" With the axe blade, he sawed at the bit of flesh holding the head on, severing it completely. Then he kicked it down the stairs just for good measure.

He had expected blood to spray from the body, but it had not. It just oozed out and puddled on the concrete. It was nearly black in color. Did that mean the blood was clotting or was it just rotten? Maybe if the blood clotted and turned solid, the body would be unable to move. Either way, he hoped to never have to find out.

He laid the axe down and dragged the body over to the rail. Quickly, he poked his head out over the rail. No more zombies. He tried to lift the thing, but it was too heavy so he got the axe and blasted an opening in the railing. Then he used his feet to shove the headless corpse over the edge.

The wet smack hitting the asphalt was enough for him. He didn't need to see it. He was no killer. He could do what had to be done, but he didn't take any pleasure in it. But much like every hero of every zombie movie he had ever seen, he figured that eventually he would become numb to the entire situation and maybe even become flippant, but at the moment, he was still human and life was a horrible nightmare.

He went back to April's door and banged on it again. "Okay baby, you can let me in now. I've taken care of that nasty old zombie."

April opened the door a crack. "Where'd he go?" she asked, looking all around. With one hand he pointed at the head, while with the other hand he pointed at the hole in the railing. April pieced it together from the trail of blood that led to the opening. "You threw him off the balcony?"

"Part of him," he grinned, wagging his head in the direction of the landing below. April saw the head and retched.

"Oh my God," she cried as she choked back her vomit.

"Hey, don't get all grossed out," Kyle said. "He was already dead. I just made sure he wouldn't come back and try again."

She examined the axe. It was coated with coagulated blood. "Ugh," she retched. "Leave that out here."

Kyle shook his head. "No, we need to have it inside in case somebody gets through the door. But I tell you what, I'll put it out on the balcony."

"Fine, just don't let any of that nastiness get on the floor."

Later, when they were scanning for working channels on TV, Kyle latched onto another idea.

"I don't suppose you have any neighbors that have satellite television, do you?"

She shrugged. "How would I know? I don't really have time to visit with my neighbors. I spend all my time working or studying."

"Oh, new detail. I sort of suspected that. You seem too intelligent to choose cashier for a career."

Sarcastically she returned, "Well, thank you so much for your vote of confidence. And yes, I just work there to pay the bills. Plus, it's nice to get an employee discount on anything I purchase there. That makes it just as cheap as Wal-Mart and the quality is better."

"You sound like a commercial". They both snickered. "No, seriously—do you have any neighbors who have satellite dishes mounted on their balconies?"

"I have no idea. I never looked. And even if they did, what makes you think they're going to let us in to watch their TV? I wouldn't let a stranger in to watch mine, especially considering all the crap that's going on right now."

"Yeah, but I don't suppose you've seen the people who live in your building any time in the recent past, excluding zombie dude of course, have you?"

She shrugged. "That's what I thought," he nodded.

A quick trip around the building netted a few possibilities. There was a dish one floor below them and a few on balconies on the other side of the building. He settled for the one below them.

"Do you know if they're students, too?"

She shrugged. "I don't know, but pretty much everybody in this building is a student. Why?"

"Well," he sighed. "Here's the plan. I'm going to go down there and knock on their door and see if they're home. I would assume that most of the students have already bugged out and headed for home, like everyone else in town. That's what I would do if I were them—I would get the heck out of Dodge. So, if they don't answer, I'm going to kick in their door and steal their satellite. Then we're going to find out if this has spread any farther."

"That's breaking and entering," she warned him. "I don't think that's a good idea."

He chuckled. "Yeah, like B&E is way worse than everything else that's going on." He waited for her to agree with him, which she finally did. Then he went on. "I'm not going to steal anything else, at least not right now. I just want to see what's happening out in the real world. And if life returns to normal sometime soon, we'll take it back."

She could tell that he wasn't going to change his mind, so she dismissed him with a grimace. "If you get arrested, I'm not going to bail you out. I don't have the cash for that."

"No problem," he said. "Haven't seen any cops around lately anyway." He fetched his axe from the balcony and headed downstairs. She heard him rap lightly on the door a few times, then silence. Another knock, a moment of silence and then a loud, "Whack!"

Two minutes later, she heard someone shuffling heavily up the stairs. Another moment of silence. She knew whoever it was standing just outside her door. Then, heavy thumping on the door.

"It's me," Kyle whispered. She opened the door and there he was with a bed sheet tossed over his shoulder like Santa preparing to slide down a chimney. She let him back in and he spilled the contents of his pack onto her floor.

"This ought to get us started," he said as they peered at the crazy pile of cables and electronic equipment.

"You know how to hook it up?" she asked.

"Not really, but I'll figure it out. What else have I got to do?"

She huffed. "That's sort of funny."

While he worked at setting the system up, she lay on the couch watching him. He was handsome and strong and she was glad she'd taken a chance on him, especially considering the circumstances. She wouldn't have wanted to face those Mexicans or the dead neighbor by herself. He was proving to be everything a girl could want—protector, lover, provider.

Though she felt she could stare at him forever, after a while of watching him toil with machinery, she became bored. One could only watch another work for so long without getting naked. Her mind wandered and eventually she began to think about her friends and neighbors. Suddenly she was curious to know if he had seen any sign that the neighbors were still around.

"Well, kind of," he said not bothering to look up.

"What do you mean?"

"To put it politely… I don't think your neighbors are going to mind too much if we borrow any of their stuff," he said. "That is, if your neighbors were a young guy and girl."

"You mean…" she started, not wanting to finish that thought.

Kyle cocked his head to one side and explained the scene in that apartment. "From the looks of it, the zombies had a pretty good feast. Maybe they didn't want them coming back from the dead. They seemed like a cute couple, based on some of the pictures on their walls, so maybe some jealous zombie didn't want the competition and ripped them apart."

"Stop!" she groaned, thrusting out a hand. She didn't need to hear anymore.

"Sorry," he apologized. "I don't know how else to deal with things, so I joke about them. Bad habit of mine."

He gazed over his work and exclaimed, "I think I'm done. I'll just need you to watch these bars on the screen and tell me when I get the dish pointed at the right spot."

"Okay," she said in a mousy voice. She was busy trying not to picture the handsome couple torn apart.

It only took about two minutes for Kyle to get the dish lined up. Once that was done, they had a sharp, clear image of CNN, which was still live, and stared with rapt attention at reports coming in from around the entire country about wild and crazy zombie attacks.

"Damn, it's just like Night of the Living Dead," he mumbled.

"I never saw that movie," April said. "And after today, I never want to."

They watched as on-the-spot reporters filmed corpses wandering down the streets of one large city after another, chasing after anyone who was stupid enough to be out in the streets. One clip showed half a dozen zombies turn a man coming out of a hotel into spaghetti.

Neither Kyle nor April could look away even though it made them physically ill to watch the goriest of scenes. Eventually though, April could take no more. "Turn it. I think we know everything we need to," she said. "The whole country's caught up in it now. Is this Armageddon?"

Kyle didn't move quickly enough so she grabbed the remote from his hand and changed it herself. The next channel was also stuck on the zombie situation. She kept flipping until finally she found Nickelodeon Channel. SpongeBob and Patrick were in the midst of some misadventure in Bikini Bottoms.

"Don't change the channel again while I'm in the room," she ordered him. "I don't want anything more violent than SpongeBob on that TV. Do you understand?" Kyle nodded. She was upset and he had seen enough to know what was going on out there, so he complied. Besides, he had nowhere else to go. By now, his entire apartment complex was probably one giant bloody mess, a real massacre. He did intend to go back as soon as he could, though. He wanted his books, his small but highly prized personal library of first edition classics. Still, he wasn't about to go back until he was positive that he wouldn't be eaten in the process.

So he left the TV on SpongeBob, even though neither one of them really watched it. They were both lost in their thoughts, wondering how the world could have turned upside down so fast.

Besides thinking about his own situation, Kyle wondered how Brad's family was faring, especially since they would never know what happened to him. They would say that he was attacked and killed by a zombie and that would be that, but he knew the truth. He was the only one who ever would. After a while, his thoughts went to his own family, especially his younger sister. He knew his parents would be fine, but Elaine was a teenager and still emotionally fragile, even though she was somewhat of a tomboy.

April's thoughts were more self-centered. She thought only about her own preservation and what she would do if she had to trust her life to this semi-stranger. Was he one hundred percent trustworthy? Only time would tell.

Of course they wondered about other things, such as how they were going to feed or protect themselves if and when the undead swarm came for them. For now, they could only sit and plan. Maybe if they were lucky they would ride out this thing together in April's little apartment and come out unscathed.

"Fat chance," Kyle muttered.

"Hmm?"

"Nothing. I'm hungry. Want something?"

She shrugged. He headed for her kitchenette.

According to CNN, the outbreak had spread around the globe. They were saying that authorities had only been aware of the problem for two days and that there were no reports of problems before that.

"Two days ago, huh?" Kyle mused. That was the same day he had found Brad's body behind his couch. Since Brad had been there overnight, that suggested that the Lafayette outbreak had to be at the bleeding edge of the outbreak. Could little old Lafayette, Indiana be Ground Zero?

There was a large foreign population in town, thanks to the University. It didn't take a rocket scientist to figure out how quickly zombism could have come to town.

April hadn't touched any of her food yet.

"What's the matter?" he asked her. "Are you feeling okay?"

She shook her head. "Stupid question. Of course I'm not."

"That's understandable, but you have to eat something. You don't want to get sick when you're stressed out. When my sister was a baby and would get sick, she wouldn't eat and her blood sugar would drop real low and she would have seizures. It was really scary and nerve-racking, even after we found out what was causing it. That's why, no matter what happens I make sure I eat three square meals a day, even if I'm not hungry."

She bobbed her head up and down in agreement, but his comment was not going to change anything. "I just don't feel any hunger right now. I can't eat when I'm not hungry. I'm sure this will pass. I never heard of anyone starving to death that had a refrigerator full of food before."

"Me neither," he grinned.

"Maybe you should go lay down for a little while," he suggested. "Sometimes a good nap is the best cure for anything that ails you."

She slid her dinner over to him. "I think I will go lie down. You can have mine if you want."

"Thanks, but I'm full."

"Okay then," she said absently as she stood up. "Nighty night." She went to the bedroom, making sure to close the door most of the way, but leaving enough of a crack to let in light from the living room.

Kyle heard the springs of her bed creak as she lay down and after a few minutes her breathing became calm and regular.

He polished off her dinner and then went back to the TV. Though he flipped between news channels it was all the same. No one knew exactly how or when the epidemic began, but they could all agree that it was spreading like wildfire. When the international authorities recognized that intercontinental airplanes were carrying the disease to far-flung corners of the globe, all air travel was shut down. Next, they quarantined any boats still in the ports and those at sea were forced to stop where they were. There were reports of cruise liners becoming nightmarish massacres.

Road and rail travel were also shut down. No one was allowed to travel anywhere without prior authorization from the authorities. Every person on the road was another potential zombie waiting to happen.

"Damn, like Nazi Germany," he commented.

Experts, if they could be called that, were likening this situation to the Ebola outbreaks of the late Twentieth Century. One egghead put it this way: "The biggest difference between this outbreak and those was that the Ebola outbreaks never got the chance to spread too far because the diseased burned out its hosts too fast, whereas the Zombie Plague shows no signs of burning itself out. If anything it appears to be growing at an exponential rate, and our best guess is that by the end of the week it will have affected nearly every place on the planet. Even those tiny little backward places you would go to escape it appear to be headed for a holocaust of sorts."

The media always made things seem more dangerous and scary than they really were, but something told Kyle that, if anything, this time they were underestimating the danger. If something didn't happen soon to stop the plague in its tracks, the entire race of man might be extinct as soon as next month.

Maybe the whole thing is natural. Nature had a way of bringing things back into balance when they got out of whack. When one species became too populous, she wiped them out with disease or famine or a corresponding rise in predators. Man was not immune. With so many people running around all over the place consuming everything and burning through all of the planet's resources, an extinction level event was bound to occur. In fact, he knew that every generation of mankind faced at least one extinction level event. Usually it was from a virus such as Bubonic Plague or Ebola. But this time, it appeared that mankind would literally eat itself. The irony of such a notion struck him as morbidly funny and he burst into laughter.

It was nearly dark before Kyle could pry his eyes away from the television. He thought he heard noises from outside, so he went to the balcony doors and peeked through the blinds. He couldn't see anything, so he shut off the living room light and gently slid the door back just far enough to squeeze out.

He tiptoed to the rail and peeked over. In the parking lot below were a half-dozen zombies loitering around a car. Kyle couldn't tell if anyone was in the car, but since they were pawing at the windows he felt safe in assuming that someone was in there.

There was a middle-aged man and a middle-aged woman. Two of the zombies were small children, a boy and a girl. The other two zombies appeared to be in their early twenties, as best he could tell. The longer he stared at them the clearer it became that they were a family, except for the twenty-something female zombie. He surmised that she must be the girlfriend of the young adult male.

It was a comical scene, an entire zombie family beating on a family sedan. It was like "Simpsons" meets "Dawn of the Dead" or "The Cemetery Man." But as funny as he found the sight of them thumping away on the car, it was still tragic. He suppressed the urge to laugh even as a smile crept across his face and a chuckle built up in his throat until he had to sneak back into the apartment to let it out.

"Oh shit!" he cried out. The front door was wide open!

He raced over to it and slammed it shut, producing much more noise than he knew he should have. He locked the knob and slammed the deadbolt home and then spun around and surveyed the apartment.

No zombies in here. But what about April's room?

In five giant steps he was in her bedroom. There was no zombie and there was no April. There were no signs of a struggle and no blood anywhere that he could see either. Where was she?

He checked the bathroom. Nope.

Was it possible that she had gone outside to get some fresh air? Not likely, but if she had then he had just doomed her. By slamming the door he had caused enough noise to attract the attention of the zombie family below.

"Jesus save me," he whispered, screwing up the courage to open the door. Leaping through the door in one quick cat-like move, he landed in the center of the hall and spun around. No zombies, no April.

He peered down into the stairwell, just in time to catch a glimpse of her ankle disappearing from view. He raced over to the rail where he'd tossed the neighbor and peered out. The zombie family was still there surrounding the car but they had stopped beating on it. They were staring at the hallway where April was.

As if she did not see them, she strode stiffly into the parking lot and walked toward the street. The dead family peered at her but did not approach. They simply stared at her. Frozen like a deer in headlights, Kyle waited for the scene to unfold.

April strode into the parking lot without a care in the world. She didn't even notice the zombies huddled around the car though they were less than twenty feet from her. She kept walking till she reached the street. Kyle and the zombies watched as she disappeared behind a nearby building. Unfazed, the zombies went back to pounding on the car, all except for the youngest one, who turned to follow her.

He wanted to scream, tried to scream, but no sound came out. He felt lightheaded. As the little dead girl followed April out of view, Kyle finally regained his breath and screamed at the top of his lungs. "No! You evil little bitch! You stay the hell away from her!"

Of course, the scream drew the attention of the entire family. In unison, they shuffled toward the building. When they reached the stairs, Kyle grunted in anger. He had effectively cut himself off from April.

The axe was back inside the apartment! "Shit!" he spat, realizing that by the time he got to it, they would be no more than a floor away. If he didn't hurry, they'd be upon him in no time. He scanned the surroundings, searching for a glimpse of April, but she was gone. The beasts were only a flight below him now.

By the time he grabbed his axe, the remaining child zombie was crossing the threshold. He opened his mouth and reached out for Kyle, groaning hungrily at him.

He pulled the axe back like a baseball bat and swung it around, catching his shoulder blade at an angle and nearly slicing his head clean off. The putrid little zombie stumbled and nearly toppled over but somehow stayed on his feet.

"Nuts." He yanked the weapon back and leaned into it this time, cleanly cleaving the head from body. The corpse dropped straight down as the head arced backwards through the doorway and bounced into the hallway.

Next up was the pair of young adults. The male crossed the door frame and was just about to step over his dead brother's body when his head too flew off. Kyle swung so hard he buried the blade in the wood of the doorframe. He had to dig it out quickly as the young woman was only steps away. He backed up a few steps to get a good swing at her but the rest of the family went over like dominoes.

As he climbed over the putrefying corpses, he took care to plant his feet against something firm before he lost his footing. Wouldn't want to put in all that work just to get their undead cooties all over him.

Knowing that neither he nor April would ever return to her cubbyhole, he didn't bother to attempt to clean any of the mess. And as he bounded down the stairs and raced into the parking lot, he wondered how April had been able to get past them with no problems. Wouldn't they have smelled her as she walked past them? Or did they think she was dead? The thought crossed his mind that perhaps April herself had somehow become a zombie.

"No, not possible," he growled through clenched teeth. He refused to believe that she could be a zombie.

By the time he reached the main road, he was too late. It was too dark and she had too much of a lead on him. He had no idea where she was going since it obviously wasn't to her home. He ran around the neighborhood like a crazy man until he attracted too much attention from a few wandering zombies and had to retreat.

The rest of the night he spent driving around town looking for her, but he never did find her. She had totally disappeared.

CHAPTER 9

After a fruitless night of searching, there was nothing to do but head for home. He would get some sleep if possible and then figure out the rest later.

But about halfway home the truck's engine overheated and he had to stop. Since there was no traffic, he simply stopped in the middle of the highway. Even before he climbed out of the vehicle and propped up the hood, he knew what had happened. A small branch had punctured the radiator hose a while back. He had never gotten around to removing the stick due to sheer laziness. In time, he had forgotten it was there, but now it had finally worked itself loose, probably from the rough ride at the storage facility, and had been draining the engine coolant slowly but steadily ever since.

"Crap." He was right. The stick was gone and so was the radiator fluid.

Luckily for him, he had broken down in front of a large department store where a number of cars were still parked, apparently abandoned. He could risk entering the store, but images from any number of horror movies whizzed through his mind and that made the decision for him. He didn't know how to hotwire a car but he also knew that he wouldn't have to. There was an old Indiana trick some people knew, like him, that woulc come in handy right then.

He went to the oldest car in the lot and tugged at the door handle. It was open, just as expected, but no keys were in it. So he went to the next oldest car and so on until he found one with keys still in the ignition.

Once, he had a roommate with a clunker who told him that he always left the keys in his ignition and the door unlocked. "Who's going to steal that piece of shit?" the guy used to laugh.

Funny how the Universe provides, he thought. Never before that moment had he thought his old roomie's piece of wisdom would come in handy, but it had. The logic was simple: if your possession is so nasty that no one would even want to steal it then you don't have to protect it.

From where he was, it was three miles along the busiest stretch of road in town to his apartment. That meant he would probably have to pass through Zombie Central to get there. He could walk, but the odds of surviving the walk were not in his favor. One man, one axe and a whole city of zombies. He might be able to take out a few, but not a mob.

"The Gods are smiling," he quipped as he fired up the faded yellow 1969 Oldsmobile Delta 98 and turned the monstrous boat towards home.

At the intersection to the Interstate there was a police checkpoint. Two officers sat on the hood of their car with matching shotguns on their hips.

As Kyle rolled towards them, they motioned for him to stop and asked for his driver's license. Kyle had no tolerance for bureaucracy but had to bite his tongue at the request since they had guns and he only had an axe.

One cop told him that he should just turn around and go back where he came from. "Trust me," he said, "There ain't nothing east of the highway that you want to be messing with. They think that's where this whole mess started, by the way, and they ain't even found all the bodies yet."

Kyle sighed. He wouldn't admit it to anyone, but he hated stupid people. *No, not really stupid people but people who were so lazy that they made themselves stupid.* There was a huge difference between the two. Deep down he knew that's one of the reasons he became a teacher—to eradicate laziness from the general masses.

The other officer heard him sigh. "We ain't out here to keep anybody from their homes," he explained. "We just don't want to see you back here in twenty minutes after you get chewed on by one of them undead suckers. If we can save one life... you know what I mean?"

Kyle nodded, "Yeah I think I see your point, but this is a pretty solid car and I've got an axe. If I get attacked I'm going to take some of them with me before they get me. And then you can go right ahead and shoot me because I really don't give a fuck about anything anyway. You know what I mean?"

The cop grunted. Kyle knew the guy was calling him an asshole in his mind. But he shrugged and waved him past anyway. As Kyle drove away he checked his rearview mirror, just in time to see a zombie rush the officers. As he watched, one officer raised his shotgun and blew the zombie's head clean off its shoulders. Both officers shared a good laugh and went back to lounging around while they waited for the inevitable mob to appear.

"Pieces of shit," Kyle remarked.

His apartment complex looked more like an uprooted graveyard. Bodies hung out of windows, broken glass was everywhere. Doors had been ripped off their hinges and cars were mashed together in the center of the parking lot as if someone had tried to build a fortress out of them. Black puddles of filth stained everything.

Kyle got out of the car, careful to spin it around so that it was facing the exit of the lot. He left the driver side door open in case he needed a quick escape and of course, he left the keys in the ignition. After all, who was going to steal that big old piece of shit?

For some reason he had expected to find nothing but a crater in his apartment. He was shocked to discover that it was just as he had left it, except for the fact that the front door and the sliding glass door had been smashed beyond repair. It appeared that no one else had been in the apartment since he and April had to escape. Then again, it had only been a couple of days. Why had he thought it would be any different than he had left it?

Without doors it was not a very safe place to be, but he had to have his books and he wanted them bad enough to risk his life for them.

He kept an eye on the windows and an ear tuned for any noises while he loaded boxes of his precious first editions into the 98. A few books he tossed into a separate pile. Those were the ones he could live without, ones with zero value to him. It was a small pile.

He was able to load the entire car full of books before he heard any noises. A crashing tinkle of glass stopped him dead in his tracks as he was going back to check for any books he might have missed. He was halfway between his building and the car, as vulnerable as could be. There were no other noises, no shuffling feet, no groans, and no more breaking glass. So he did one last check and headed back to the car.

Probably better hit the store one last time for a food run and maybe some other supplies before setting off to wherever I'm headed.

There were no cars in the department store's lot and the doors were wide open. He drove up to the front doors and then decided after surveying the width of them that the behemoth might fit. Of course, he would have to knock out one doorframe in the exterior and interior sets of doors, but he was sure the metal monster was sturdy enough for the job.

Looping around the lot, he gunned the engine and shot right through the double doors, knocking the first doorframe out like a toothpick. The interior set was not quite all the way open and he clipped the right door with the front fender, smashing it inwards. That barely even slowed down the old car.

Flipping on the headlights, or rather, flipping on the one working headlight, he zipped down the main aisle, past the frozen section and stopped at the end of the canned good aisle. He grabbed his axe and sprinted into the darkness.

Something stinks, he noted. *Probably the frozen foods section. No electricity, no refrigeration.*

He made sure to get cans of tuna and other various types of potted meats as well as fruits and vegetables. He rushed back to the car and tossed the cans in the back seat, pausing to check for noises or shapes in the dark. He made four or five more trips, even ventured bravely into the next aisle before he decided he had enough food.

It wasn't until he climbed back in the car and began to back down the aisle that he realized he did not have a can opener. He gunned the engine and coasted toward the aisle marked "Kitchen Tools" where, as luck would have it, was an endcap full of can openers. He grabbed an entire box of them from the bottom shelf, then noticed eating utensils hanging from pegs. He shoveled them into the car. *Can never have enough of these things.*

Just then he heard a low moan. It was very close. He climbed back into the car just in time to see a dead man, dressed in the company's uniform, step into the orange glow of the car's parking lights.

"Not sweet," Kyle said, dropping the car into reverse and backing away.

The tires slipped on the highly polished tile floor as he gunned the engine. When he had backed as far as the delicatessen, he hit the brakes. Then he mashed the accelerator down and shot forward. The engine roared as if it was its last hurrah. The zombie lumbered towards him, not realizing its second life was about to come to an abrupt end.

For just a second, Kyle thought that he could see sudden despair on the dead man's face. The next second, the man's face smacked into the steel hood, bounced into the windshield, and then slid up over the car.

"Done?" Kyle called out the window. He kept his eyes glued to the rearview. Sure enough, the dead man got up. His face was contorted into a caricature, like a Spy versus Spy comic. Kyle dropped the car into reverse once more and plowed over the man on his meteoric surge toward the front doors. The thump and crunch from the man bouncing along the undercarriage was strangely satisfying.

The car shot out of the entryway like a horse on fire. Kyle hit the brakes, whipped the wheel around, dropped the car into Drive, and hit the gas in imitation of his favorite James Bond maneuver. Surprisingly, considering the weight of the Oldsmobile, it worked.

That particular store branch had a company branded gas station at the far front of the parking lot and since the gas gauge read nearly empty he zoomed over there to get some gas.

"Damn it, should have known there would be no electricity." The pumps wouldn't work without it and there was no one in the kiosk to turn them on.

"Never a solution does a problem solver pass up," he mumbled to himself as he picked up a metal trash bin and chucked it through the plate glass window. He climbed through the hole and flipped on the switch for the pumps. He credited all of the pumps for $100. "That ought to be enough."

As he was pumping, he surveyed his surroundings. The noise he'd created would surely bring the dead running. It had. A dead worker had emerged from the store and was sprinting across the lot. It was only about 300 yards from store to station so it wouldn't take long for the monster to reach him.

He looked back at the pump, watching the readout climb higher and higher. It seemed to slow before his eyes.

"Come on," he cajoled the machinery. In the corner of vision there was movement. There were more zombies appearing all around. Most were in the subdivision across the road and far enough away that they were of no consequence, but three zombies had emerged from a parked car about fifty yards away. They had spotted him.

Then he noticed a dozen or so faces in the window of the store. They were banging on the glass, trying to get at him. It wouldn't take long for them to find the way out.

The pump chugged slower and slower as his pulse went faster and faster. He remembered why he didn't like to fill up at this station. Even when there was only one person using a pump, it took forever to fill your tank. He had always guessed it was some marketing scam— take forever to fill so you would buy a soft drink or candy or some other convenient item you wouldn't have bought in the store. Capitalism at its finest. He didn't fault them for it but the one zombie was already halfway across the parking lot and the three from the car were lumbering towards him too. The tank wasn't going to fill before they reached him.

"Geez, how big a tank you got, bitch?" he griped. It was up to fifteen gallons and showed no signs of stopping. Granted, it was a Sixties gas guzzler.

"No wonder we're dependent on foreign oil," he moaned. "It takes a 55 gallon drum to fill you, you thirsty bastard."

The running zombie was close enough that he could hear its feet slapping the pavement as it scrambled toward him.

"Fuck it," he cursed, dropping the nozzle to the ground and hustling into the car. The beast fired right up. He dropped it into gear and floored it, looping around in a lazy circle towards the single exit. Kyle could see the sunken eyes in the hungry man's sockets. "Whites of the eyes!" Kyle screamed at it.

He mashed the accelerator and launched the car at the dead man in a twisted game of Chicken. The zombie came at him with outstretched arms, sensing a meal but not understanding that his afterlife was about to become a post-afterlife.

Kyle plowed through him, the zombie exploding like a piñata. "No worker's comp for you," Kyle quipped. He turned the car toward the other group and ran them down too. They clunked as they hit the hood and bounced off, body parts coming unglued and flying across the asphalt.

"Blood on the asphalt," he grinned. It was a reference to the driver's education video they forced teenagers to watch.

This is almost fun, Kyle thought to himself. Scary how fast the human psyche can adjust to horrible situations.

There was a crash of glass from the direction of the store and he turned just in time to see a mass of rotted corpses spill out of the burst window.

"Uh oh, time to go," Kyle sang out. The car shot out of the lot. Once he was on the main road, he noticed a slapping sound from the engine compartment. *Crap, is that the fan?*

The more gas he gave it, the louder and faster the slapping became. It was obvious that the car was no longer road worthy, especially not for any sort of long distance trip.

Now what? Before he realized it, he was home again. He wasn't sure where he would go, but he didn't want to risk his life on a car that was older than he was and that sounded like something out of a Three Stooges clip.

His parking lot was full of vehicles. A truck would actually serve his purposes better than a car. There were no shortage of them here either. But he wasn't as lucky this time as he'd been when he stumbled upon the car. No one left their truck unlocked in this part of the country because trucks were much more valuable than cars in Indiana and there were plenty of scum who would steal them in a heartbeat.

Should just bash in a window. But what good was a truck with a broken window in the midst of a zombie attack? They could just reach in and pull him out or eat him where he sat. No, he was going to have to take a vehicle intact and that meant finding the keys.

So it was down to breaking and entering. He would have to search apartments until he found keys. That was time and labor intensive, which meant hours of vulnerability. What other choice did he have?

Two buildings over from his there was a nice big box truck parked serenely in a slot, ready to roll. Most likely, the truck was parked as close to home as possible, so he started with the nearest entrance.

He crashed through the two bottom floor apartments before he found any keys. Unfortunately, they weren't the right ones, so he had to continue the search.

The third apartment had a bedroom full of weapons and ammo. "Dang," Kyle gasped at the armory. "Looks like I found me a new home base, if nothing else." The fourth apartment had piles of porn stacked around the place, which he might return to later for entertainment purposes if he was still around, but still no truck keys.

So the search expanded, eventually reaching into the opposing building. Just as the light was fading, he found an unlocked and untouched apartment that apparently belonged to one of the pool girls he had frequently lusted after. He knew he wouldn't find the right keys there, but he spent a half hour rooting through her drawers, checking out her lingerie and underwear, before he realized how gross lusting after a dead girl was, and left the place.

He spent the entire next day searching but to no avail, so he gave up and hit the internet. Surprisingly, it was still working through his cell phone. That was handy. It took less than five minutes to find directions for hotwiring a truck. In an hour, with a screwdriver and a pair of pliers, he had the sturdy Ford running.

"Life is good sometimes," he congratulated himself.

He was going to need to test drive the vehicle before he entrusted his life to it, so he gently depressed the accelerator and dropped the truck into reverse, letting out the clutch slowly. The truck immediately lurched backward twice and died. He tried again and had the same result. The next time, he floored the gas and popped the clutch. This time the truck surged backward with unbelievable power. He had to slam on the brakes to avoid smashing into the cars behind him, but he managed to keep the motor from dying and even managed to get it into first gear without killing it.

It took a little while to get used to the shifter, but once he was, he was off and running.

There were a few zombies wandering down the road as he rolled by. They were coming from the subdivision to the north of his complex. Nice homes, nice families. Kyle used to jog through there. Some of them used to wave at him as he jogged past. A few even stopped him for a conversation. A couple of housewives had been extra friendly. He liked those people as much as he liked anyone.

But now, as he watched them shuffling along in search of God-only-knew, any fond memories he had of them melted away the second he saw their discolored faces and sardonic mouths widened by encroaching rigor mortis.

In life, those people were the ones who followed the rules and lived healthy quiet lives. Now, even in death, they were good little zombies, sticking politely to the side of the road so as not to get run over. Kyle reckoned that some people were just too brainwashed to change, even in death.

One of them, however, heard the truck coming and turned around to take a look. Unfortunately for her, she stepped too far into the road, right in the path of the truck.

Kyle was only going about forty when the cab of the Ford E350 Super Duty pulverized her. Reddish black slime exploded over the windshield and pieces of decayed flesh crawled across the glass. He retched but choked back his puke. He ran the wipers but that only spread the mess out further.

Now he could only see through a tiny bit of the windshield but he wasn't about to stop. There was a carwash half a mile away. He made a beeline for it in hopes of reaching it before the hot July sun could cook the gore onto the truck. He hit two more zombies on the way, both unintentionally, but neither of them exploded like the woman. They crunched under the wheels. In his rearview he could see them tumble along the asphalt the same as small animals did when you hit them.

At the carwash, the truck was too tall to fit in the automatic carwash, but it didn't matter anyway because he had no idea how to turn on the system, so he drove around to one of the do-it-yourself bays and blasted the truck with pressurized water, reveling the whole time that the electricity in this part of town, which seemed to be hit hardest by the outbreak, had remained mostly on.

As the guts and slime ran down the truck, he replayed the movie of the woman exploding in his head. He tried to find the humorous side of it so that he could let it go. It was the only way to keep from losing his marbles. "Damn she was like a ripe melon."

As the last bits of her dripped from the bumper, he wondered why she was the only one who had swelled up like a balloon and popped. *Ours is not to wonder why…*

Once the truck was clean, he drove around a little more to get a feel for it and then he headed back to his not-so-favorite gas station to fill it up. He was more careful about running down zombies this time, only hitting thin ones who tended to slip under the wheels. He didn't want to have to repeat the carwash experience.

"Okay, gassed up, ready for a real ride." No zombies had managed to reach him in the long minutes it took to fill the ravenous tank. He ran the truck around the parking lot once more, smashing a few more undead for good measure. *This baby can really nail 'em*, he noted. It was all good clean fun until he ran over a woman who was nothing more than a stick with crazy hair. He knew as soon as the abomination fell from view that something was wrong. The truck lurched and dropped to the right, like he'd hit a pothole. There was a loud hiss—escaping air!

"Sonuvabitch!" he cursed. Flat tire. Behind the driver's seat he found a jack and tire iron.

"Sure enough," he said when he saw a chunk of skull protruding from the passenger's side tire. He set about jacking up the wheel and removing it only to find that the spare tire was frozen in its cradle under the truck bed. He worked the tire iron as quickly as he could, stopping every so often to check for zombies. None were close enough to cause him any stress. But the process of freeing the tire took longer than it should and by the time he had the tire free, two zombies were close enough to be worrisome.

He worked furiously to get the tire mounted and let the jack down. But after all that, the spare was flat. "Fuck," he cried. One of the zombies was only about thirty feet away. It was a slow mover. He ran at it and smashed it in the forehead with the tire iron. It fell over like a bag of bones and did not get back up.

Kyle climbed back into the cab and sparked the ignition. He waited for the remaining zombie to get within five feet of the front of the truck, then gunned it, slamming the corpse to the ground. The truck pulled heavily to the right and was impossible to steer but it did move.

Back to the gas station. There were three cans of tire sealant left in the kiosk and he took them all, managing to inflate the tire and then to get the truck rolling again.

It still pulled to the right a little but he went very slowly and was able to reach home with no further trouble.

He spent a while transferring his precious books from the 98 to the truck, then went scavenging for food and water. Along the way, he picked up a few other items of interest, such as weapons from the one apartment and some porn from the other. Then, taking no more than a moment to take a last look at his home for the last few years, he loaded himself up and headed for the Interstate.

At the bottom of the ramp he paused, trying to decide which direction to go. His parents and sister were south. Work and Brad's family were north.

He had good reasons to go in either direction. He felt responsible for Brad's death, even though he wasn't sure why or how, and that meant he felt responsible for his family, too. His parents both had their own guns: high powered rifles and shotguns. He was sure they could handle themselves. But his sister was at IU in Bloomington and although she was capable of taking care of herself, she had no guns with her. She was a smart girl and chances were good that at the first sign of trouble, she would have headed for their parents' home, but he couldn't be sure until he had some sort of contact with her.

It was an easy choice when viewed from that standpoint. Brad's wife would simply assume that her husband had been mauled in some zombie attack and that he was either wandering around dead trying to eat people or that he himself had been consumed. She never had to know the truth.

He gunned the engine and headed for his parents' home.

CHAPTER 10

His parents lived in a two-story farmhouse on a gravel road outside Huntington, Indiana. Huntington was a small town that had shrunk with the passage of time. Each new generation of children would grow up, graduate from school, and disappear to the big cities to make their mark on the world. Huntington had become an old town with old people, a city of grandparents. It was a nice place to live, and the countryside outside the town itself was also beautiful, but for Kyle and his sister and anyone else who was young and full of life, it was a graveyard—and that was before the zombies.

After fighting in the Vietnam War, his father wanted nothing but quiet. He was too afraid of city life after having fought three urban battles in the war. Although he would never admit to it, he suffered from Posttraumatic Stress Disorder. He couldn't go into a town or city without becoming agitated because at the crack of any loud noise, he would fly into a panic. Most days, if anyone needed to go to town, he would send his wife. If he absolutely had to do it himself, then he would do it "Terrorist style" as he called it—in and out before anyone could notice he was there. Frequently, after even just a simple trip to the bank or restaurant, his father would have to spend three or four hours out in his barn workshop, making small wooden toys for local charities. That was how he relaxed.

Kyle stopped once for gas in the middle of nowhere. It wasn't that he was out, he just wanted to top off the tank before he reached a populated area. There was nothing around that station so he figured it was relatively safe.

Finally, after three and a half hours, he reached the gravel road that led to his parents' fifty acre farm. By modern standards it would have been considered a hobby farm, but back in the Seventies and Eighties it was large enough to support the entire family with all the eggs, milk, meat and vegetables that they could desire and still pay the bills.

There were two little hills before his parents' driveway. As he rolled over the first one, the creek where he spent his boyhood summers catching crawdads came into view. He checked the water level as the truck crawled over the corrugated steel tube that had been plopped down in the creek bed and then backfilled to create an earthen bridge. His father called it a 'country bridge.' Once when a tornado had suddenly appeared in the field west of their home, it became a life-saving tunnel that kept him from being swept away. If it weren't for that country bridge, he knew, he would have missed out on a lot.

The nearly empty truck rumbled up the other side of the slight incline and over the second hill. The family spread appeared, calm as always. It was about a quarter mile up the road. Nervous energy washed through him. It had been a long time since he had been home but even if it was under threat of attack from an impossible source, it was still a safe place that made all his fears melt away. Nothing could touch him at his parents' place.

Everything was the same, he noted as he edged up to the property, except for one thing. There was a deep trench along the road where there had only been a small ditch. To be more accurate, there was a moat ten feet wide and probably ten feet deep around the entire farm. Since his father's loader was parked in the driveway by the house, it meant that it was freshly dug. His father was anal about taking care of his equipment. He didn't leave the loader out unless he was using it. That meant the moat had been finished today and that at least his father was still alive.

He turned off the motor, climbed out of the truck and walked around to the side facing the forest green, two story house. There on the front porch were his mother and father sitting in matching rocking chairs, rifles across their laps.

"Who the hell is that?" his father hollered out like some old mountain man.

"It's me Dad, Kyle."

They both stood bolt upright and charged out to the trench to meet him. His mother babbled incessantly with joy. His father cursed up a blue storm. To anyone outside the family he would have appeared extremely angry.

His mother laid her rifle on the ground and started jumping and clapping. "Kyle, oh Kyle, I can't believe you're still alive."

To be honest, that was the most animated he had ever seen his mother. She was normally a very stoic person. Father's enthusiasm was also out of character for him. "Jesus Christ boy. Get your ass over here and give your old man a hug."

Kyle rolled his eyes at his father. "How the hell am I supposed to do that, old man? Looks like you dug halfway to China."

They froze like statues. Both of them examined the trench as if they were seeing it for the first time.

"Well hell, I guess I didn't think anybody live would be coming out here anymore," his father remarked. "Well, I tell you what. You just jump down in that hole and come on over to this side and I'll pull you up."

"Or you could just go back and get a ladder out of the garage," Kyle suggested.

The old man clapped his hands once and raced off to the garage.

They dined on chickens from the deep freezer. That meant it could have been up to two years old. Father was too afraid to kill any animals for fear they might come back to life. "Nothing scarier than a goddamn zombie chicken!" he said in all seriousness. Mother nodded sullenly in agreement. Kyle burst into laughter.

"Zombie chickens!" he roared, imitating one with a weird groaning squawk and wide eyes.

"Ain't funny," Father scolded him even as the corners of his mouth turned upward.

Kyle jumped up and did a cross of a human zombie squawking and strutting like a chicken. He cackled like a crazy rooster and soon Father was doubled over with laughter. "Okay, fine, goddamn it. It's funny, now STOP!"

Mother, who had been chuckling silently to herself, let out a big guffaw and roared with laughter. "Zombie chickens! HAW!"

Eventually, when they were able to stop laughing, the tone turned serious once again.

"Have you heard from Elaine?" Kyle asked.

Mother nodded. "She called right after the first news of the outbreak. She wanted to come home but we told her to stay there. We figured she was more protected in that dorm she's living in than in driving across the entire state."

"That makes sense to me," Kyle agreed. "I had a few problems driving here myself."

His mother and father looked at the truck. The hood was again coated in blood.

"What the heck?" his father teased, "Did you swerve to hit them?"

"Yeah," Kyle answered back. They couldn't tell if he was joking or not.

After lunch, they sat on the porch, catching up on Kyle's life. He didn't hide anything from them, which they both appreciated and disliked because at times he was more honest than they would have liked. He went into graphic detail about his and April's short time together and his mother had to clap her hands over her ears. "No mother wants to hear that stuff. Just stop talking, please."

Kyle didn't understand what the big deal was. He never had the 'stopper' that precluded him from talking about such things. If someone asked him a question, he answered honestly. That's what he wanted from his friends and lovers and that's what he gave them. And if he hadn't gotten that from his parents, then where had he gotten it?

He told them about the three Mexican zombies in the bloody apartment complex and the family he dispatched when April disappeared. To his surprise, none of his tales made them even bat an eye. To them it was the same as if you would have explained how to hack the head off a chicken. He found it comforting, though a bit strange, that his parents could take such an unbelievable story in stride.

"I thought you guys would be freaked out when I told you all that stuff," he said when he was finished.

His father stared off into the forest across the road in with a faraway look in his eyes said, "I've seen a lot of death, son. I've seen enough of it to know that it's just part of how life is. This isn't any worse than Vietnam. The only difference here is that you can tell who the enemy is. Back there, your enemies and your friends looked the same."

Kyle was not especially fond of discussing Vietnam with his father. The old man had not gone willingly and he never agreed with the war, but when called upon to do his duty to his country, he did it without question. Hoping to keep his father from starting into a tirade about the government and the way the world was, he switched topics. "So, have you guys seen any zombies out here?"

Both parents shook her head. His father answered, "No, not yet. But everybody out here goes to town and the towns are spreading the disease. It won't be long before one of the neighbors turn. And it won't be long after that that I have to blast one of them into Kingdom Come. I'm just hoping that it's not anybody on our road. We have pretty good neighbors out here."

Mother piped up. "Who are you kidding? We all know you wouldn't have a problem sending any of them to Jesus. Remember when you shot the Jones' dog in the ass with rock salt for shitting in the yard and then threatened to shoot Mr. Jones in the same place just to prove it wouldn't hurt him any more than it did the dog?"

Even though he should have been used to it, Kyle was constantly amazed by his mother's knack at inserting slicing, yet witty, comments at just the right moment. She had a way of knocking you down two pegs while forcing you to laugh at yourself. If his students and coworkers ever met his mother, they would know from where his sense of humor came.

Right after she said it, Mother got up and went into the kitchen and made them a nice fried chicken and mashed potato dinner with homemade cottage cheese and a garden salad. Kyle ate it like it was the last meal on Earth. Then again, it was entirely possible that it might be.

After dinner they went back to the porch, Mother and Father armed with rifles and Kyle armed with a shotgun. They reminisced quietly about days gone by until the sun began to set, then grew quiet.

"Got to be able to hear the damn things sneaking up on you," Father explained, though he had not been asked. Mother scanned the dark, listening for telltale dragging or groaning.

For three solid hours they sat in near silence, listening to the sounds of the night and peering into the darkness. But no zombies came. Finally, Mother yawned and got up to go to bed. Father stayed right where he was. "Don't turn on the lights until you're sure you have the blackout curtains sealed."

She nodded. "I know, I know," she grumbled like a persecuted teenager.

"And don't let the door slam shut," he added. She slapped the back of his head in response. He didn't flinch.

Once she was in the house though, he cursed her quietly. "Damn woman." Then he turned to his son and said, "First night of the outbreak, she had all the windows open and lights on. Didn't stop to think that it would attract those dead bastards like moths to a flame. We'd be undead right now, I'll bet, if I hadn't turned off the power." He shook his head and carried on the commentary in his head.

After a while, Kyle asked quietly, "Why did you dig the moat so deep?"

"You ever met a ten foot tall person?" Father replied.

"No," Kyle answered.

"Me neither. Take a bunch of zombies to fill it before they can start climbing back out."

"Hmmm." The old man was pretty smart sometimes.

"Only one problem…" Father added. "I should have parked the truck on the other side. Now if we have to evacuate, we'll have to use your box van over there." He bobbed his head at the van.

"Hey, that's fine," Kyle chuckled. "It's not mine anyway."

"Oh," came the response. In another world, Father would have ripped him a new asshole for thieving the truck, but not in this one. Instead, he dismissed the comment with a yawn. "Time for bed, I think."

Kyle was surprised by that. "You're not going to do an all-nighter?"

"No need," replied Father. "They can't get out of the moat, remember?"

"Why'd we stay up so late then?" Kyle mumbled.

His father pulled back his sleeve and revealed his Timex to Kyle. "It's only eleven," he said, pointing to the watch.

"Oh, feels a lot later."

"Always does when you're on patrol, son."

CHAPTER 11

It was well after ten the next morning when he finally made his way down to the kitchen. His parents were nowhere to be found but there was a plate of eggs, bacon, and toast wrapped in cellophane on the stove.

"Aw, thanks Mom," he said as he stuck the plate in the microwave. He guessed they were either on the porch, waiting for target practice, or tending to chores. So after his breakfast, he checked the porch just to be sure, but finding no one there, headed to the barn.

His mother was collecting eggs and feeding the chickens. Father was busy shoeing one of his two horses. "Can I help, Dad?" he asked.

"Of course you can, Son," Father grunted from under the horse's backside. Let me finish with this. I've got some other stuff we can do."

Father hammered home the last couple of nails and let the horse put his leg back down. Red-faced, he straightened himself up, grunting as he did.

"I'm not as young as I used to be," he said with hands cupping his lower back.

"But not as old as you're going to be," Kyle grinned.

Sarcastically, Father replied, "It's just like you never left."

Kyle made a silly face. Father added, "You still don't get up till noon, eat whatever's laying around, and only come out to help when the work is almost done."

The smile melted from Kyle's face. His father let him believe that he was serious for a moment longer and then clapped him on the back. Together they walked out to the box van.

"Every moat has got to have a drawbridge," said Father. "I've got some angle iron and some boards in the garage. I'd like to weld me up a nice bridge so we can just drive out of here when we need to. I was thinking we put it right across the driveway, since the gravel will make a nice bed for it. But I'm not so sure that putting a bridge right out where they can see it is such a smart idea. What do you think?"

Kyle shrugged.

They walked around the entire edge of the property, examining the moat for a better spot. The east had the road, the south was down in a swale, and the north end of the property bordered the stream and was too soft. The west side held the most promise. They could hook up a pulley system to the garage so that in case of a full frontal assault on the homestead, they could easily winch the bridge over the moat. The only problem there was that they would be driving into a cornfield and that would be slow going as the ruts ran parallel to the moat. But unlike the north and the south ends, they would not have to fjord any stream. As long as they drove straight west, they would come out at the next county road and be free. They agreed it was a good plan and set to work.

It took the entire afternoon to weld the frame together. Kyle worked on the wood decking while his father strengthened the underside. Before the sun had set, they had a fully finished drawbridge system.

"Time to test it." They stared hopefully at each other.

They tied a rope to the trailer hitch of Father's Toyota pickup and looped it through a massive pulley that had been cannibalized from the barn, then tied the other end to a steel eye welded on one end of the bridge. On his father's order, Kyle let out the clutch and nudged the truck away from the bridge. The pulley system did its job and the bridge gracefully slid across the moat, coming to rest gently on the other side.

"Okay, time to try out the welds," his father said. "You want to do the honors?"

Kyle sighed. "If that thing falls down into the moat, I'll never be able to get out."

"It will hold," Father responded. "I'm a great welder."

Ever so slowly, he eased the truck across the bridge. Though the wood protested from the weight, the little bridge was sturdy. Kyle reached the other side with no problem. He drove into the field, gunning it as he spun the vehicle around. Then he ran it over the bridge again, a little faster this time.

"Satisfied?"

Father nodded. "Yes, that will be just fine. Just wish you hadn't done a doughnut in Old Man Headdy's corn. I'll never hear the end of that come harvest time. Assuming he stays alive that long. Now, let's get this thing retracted and then we'll hook everything back up so we're ready for the worst."

That night, as they sat on the porch watching for intruders, Kyle made the comment that he wished they had satellite television. "At least we would know what was going on in the world outside."

There was a long pause and it was Mother who answered. "You already know what's going on out there. What do you want to see it again for?"

She had a point. But even in the face of Armageddon, he felt the need to know what was happening. Was it getting worse or better out there?

"Well, do you at least have a radio that works?"

"Of course, and we still have the same stations here, too. Remember? You hated all three of them. One was country, one was oldies and classical, and the other was..."

Kyle smiled. "News! 24 hour news channel! Where is it, Mom?"

"Where it's always been," she said nonchalantly, jerking a thumb at the house. "Been there the whole time."

There it was, in the cupboard above the stove, like it always was—an old Bakelite radio that had been passed down from his grandparents. It only picked up AM stations, which is why they only got three stations on it. Sometimes you could get Toledo, Chicago or even St. Louis on that thing, if you held it a certain way when the weather was just right.

He plugged it in and turned it on. The power light came on, but no sound came out. It always took a while for the tubes inside to warm up. Even so, it seemed like forever as he waited for the sound of static

84

to rattle the speaker, which was the sign that it was nearly ready to go. Quiet at first, the telltale static strengthened in volume until it was so loud that he had to turn down the volume. The last time he used it, he must have left the volume knob all the way up, or maybe Elaine had done it as a prank.

It should have been tuned to one of the three locals but it wasn't. Or maybe it was. He began to get a sinking feeling. Back when he and his sister had lived at home, Mother always had that radio tuned to the country station. Kyle hated country, but as long as Mother was around, they had to leave it on that station. So it should have come up right away.

Suddenly troubled by the implication, he cranked the dial all the way to the right, then started back slowly to the left. Eventually, he did actually manage to pick up the faintest sound of people speaking. The Bakelite had two knobs, one for rough tuning and the other for fine tuning and he had to use both to bring in the channel as best he could. Then remembering that the antenna was built into the frame, he turned the whole assembly around until finally a voice popped out of the plastic box loud and clear.

"It's the top of the hour, eight o'clock, and this is the news at the moment." What luck, he'd found the news channel right off the bat. "The living dead population continues to explode across the country, both literally and figuratively. Sorry for the pun, but if I can't laugh about something, I'll probably shoot myself. And as they say, the show must go on. So, the undead population continues to grow at a phenomenal rate. The government is urging everyone to hole up in their homes as if this were a hurricane or tornado. Most rural areas still have power, but authorities are urging people to fill up their bathtubs with water in the eventuality that the power goes out. People should move freezers and refrigerators to the coolest part of the house, preferably the basement, and you should freeze everything perishable so that it will last longer when the power does go out."

Thought the news people were supposed to have no personality, Kyle noted. *Guess in the end, even newscasters are human.*

"The President today declared the entire country a disaster area and said he would release funds to help local government address their issues. The Army and the National Guard continue to do cleanup duty, going from house to house, eliminating threats as they emerge. The cities are clogged with the smoke of rapidly multiplying bonfires that have sprung up in every neighborhood. The smell of burning, spoilt meat hangs heavy in the air and only those with the most resolute constitution can handle being outside more than a few minutes without vomiting.

Scientists from the CDC repeated what they said just a few days ago. They believe that the virus that causes people to reanimate is passed by bodily fluid. They advise that if you see a zombie coming, you should not attempt to deal with it yourself. They urge that you call the authorities and leave the area immediately. Those people who have attempted to kill the undead have sometimes found themselves in serious jeopardy as blood spatters from the killing gets on them. It appears that the zombie blood can soak into a living person's skin and transmit the disease as quickly as it does through bites or open wounds.

Reports of suicides continue to stream in. An entire family of 16 was found in Utah with gunshots to the head. A note alongside the father's corpse read simply, 'God forgive me.'

America is not the only country suffering. The outbreak has spread via the airline industry to every continent. Rio, Paris, Kampala, Tokyo—all have become massive graveyards. All commercial air travel has been halted and only critical sea travel has been allowed to continue. The President had this to say about the travel situation…"

Kyle turned up the radio a bit more as the President's voice came on. "The experts tell us that in order to minimize the impact of this horrible situation, we need to keep the power going. I have issued a temporary order nationalizing all the power companies. The Army will keep the lights on. You can help us by turning off anything electrical that you don't need. It's July. It's hot. We need the power. Thank you."

The announcer came back on and talked about other things but the only item of any real interest to Kyle was related to baseball. All Major League Games had continued at first but when zombies began wandering into the ballparks, it became a real problem.

"Over 10,000 people at Wrigley Field in Chicago were attacked during a game last night with the Houston Astros. Mobs of zombies clogged the exits, biting everyone who tried to leave, which in turned created more zombies. Spectators leapt onto the field to escape but the zombies followed. A handful of people were seen swinging bats at the undead, but eventually they succumbed to overwhelming numbers. The MLB quickly moved to postpone the season until the situation has resolved itself. It's possible that if the season is cancelled the Cubs, who have the best record in all of baseball but haven't won a World Series since before World War I, will be declared Champions. So I guess this really is the end of the world."

Kyle turned off the radio while thinking to himself how unbelievable it was that it would take a zombie attack to get the Cubs crowned World Champions.

He rejoined his parents on the porch. "You hear anything good?" Father smiled sardonically.

"Cubs are in first and if they cancel the season, they'll be Champs!" Father always knew how to take the wind out of his sails, so Kyle knew it was coming.

"Doesn't count if there's no World Series," the old man replied.

"A win is a win," Kyle shot back.

"If you don't play, it's not a win. If there is no Series, there is no World Series Champ. Remember the strike year? There was a theoretical champion, but no one recognized them as the actual champions and no one remembers who it was. Seems to me that was the year the Cubs did really well, too. Those losers just can't catch a break, can they?"

Father was egging him on, looking to start something. Who could blame him? Sitting out here in the boonies with no TV and no radio, with only your wife to talk to while waiting for a bunch of demons to come down the road and try to eat you? It could drive anyone mad.

Normally, he would have succumbed to the temptation and argued with his dad, but it wasn't worth the trouble.

Thankfully, his mother ended the conversation for him. "Don't you two start. I've got a gun and I know how to use it." She had a totally serious look on her face and even though both men knew she was kidding, they understood that she was not in the mood for one of their playful discussions. Plus, she was a White Sox fan, the only one with anything to brag about where baseball was concerned.

"Maybe we should call your sister and see how she's doing," Father suggested.

"It has been a while since we've heard from her," Mother agreed. All three of them went into the kitchen and surrounded the single landline phone in the house while Mother dialed the phone number. It rang and rang and rang. Elaine had an answering machine but it wasn't picking up.

"Well, maybe she's with friends," Father said with a slight warble in his voice. It was the first indication to Kyle that either of his parents felt any sort of stress over the situation. To that point, they had taken everything in stride. But now that the possibility existed that the outbreak might have claimed one of their own offspring, cracks began to show in their steely façades.

Mother tried to convince herself that she believed that. "She's no dummy. If there were any problems, she would have gotten the heck out of there. And she'll call us when she has a chance. And if something happens... but I'm sure someone like the sheriff will call and let us know. Until then, there's no point in worrying, is there?" She talked faster and faster, a sign to both Kyle and Father that she was about to explode into tears.

Mother marched out of the house. Silently, the two men followed her to the porch. They watched the dark creep towards them and as the stars began to pop out, Kyle noticed a spot of light moving along the road that bordered the cornfield to the north. The growl of a large vehicle rumbled gently in the distance but grew louder as it approached.

They watched expectantly as the lights turned toward them. They couldn't make out the truck yet but soon enough the outline of a large diesel appeared over the hill and its headlights bathed the neighbor's house to the north in a bright white light.

The big pickup turned into the neighbor's driveway and skidded to a halt. They could hear the gravel crunch as the tires dug in. The driver cut the engine and they heard his door slam. It was quiet enough out here in the country that they were even able to hear the distinct sound of the wooden framed screen door slamming shut as the driver entered the house. Lights turned on and Kyle's Father grunted.

"Damn fool Harrison," he said. "That much light is going to bring them in from miles around, you wait and see. Looks like a damn lighthouse down there."

The night passed without incident, however. No zombies appeared on their doorstep.

In the morning, the pickup truck was still parked in exactly the same spot it had been last night. While there was nothing especially strange about that, the fact that the house lights were still on was a bit strange. Kyle got the sense that things were not alright in the Harrison household.

They went about their normal daily routine, collecting eggs and milk and feeding the animals, keeping one eye aimed at the neighbor's home. At one point, Kyle caught Father staring at the two story farmhouse. "Got an awful feeling of dread," he muttered when he noticed his son watching him.

After breakfast, they checked the perimeter of the property, inspecting the moat for invaders. *Thank God*, Kyle said to himself after their search turned up nothing living or dead.

As the afternoon warmed up, they retreated to the cool shade of the living room and took naps, Mother included.

Kyle awoke to a low grumble which he attributed to thunder. He leapt up and rushed to the kitchen to look out the only west facing window in the house. Mother was already there, cooking dinner.

"Wow, was that your stomach or your father's?" she grinned. "I could hear it from in here."

His stomach growled loudly in response and they had their answer. They laughed freely, but that sense of alarm that Kyle had since last night was still with him.

Later, as night rolled over the land, Kyle couldn't help but notice that the Harrison lights were still on.

"Do they ever turn them off?" he asked his parents.

"They don't hardly turn them on," replied Father in a low tone that implied he knew what was wrong over there.

"What do you think that means?" Kyle asked.

Father didn't respond immediately. "What do you think it means?" he finally answered.

Kyle had a good idea of what it meant but he didn't want to say. Instead he shrugged and feigned ignorance.

Father's head drooped to one side. "It means we might have new neighbors before too long."

# CHAPTER 12

The next morning they awoke to the faint sounds of grunting coming from the moat. Kyle and his Father went to see what it was, guns in hand. They both had the safeties off just in case, but neither was ready for what they saw in the ditch.

"Harrison!" Father gasped. "What the hell are you doing down there?"

The neighbor, obviously dead, was clawing at the sides of the moat, trying to climb out. His skin was mottled purple and blue and his eyes were empty. The skin around his mouth was torn and peeled, like an exit wound after a gunshot. He reached pitifully up at them, catching nothing but air.

"I told you he'd bring the zombies with his house all lit up like that," he told Kyle. "He's been nothing but a pain in my butt since they moved in. His wife is no better and his kids are worthless too. Goddamn little hooligans!"

He wagged his finger at the retched monster in the moat. "And now what the hell am I supposed to do with you? We can't leave you down there, but if I shoot you then your family will be down here with the sheriff just as fast as you can say spit. God damn! Harrison, you surely know how to fuck up a man's day." The dilemma now was whether to leave him alive, so to speak, in which case Harrison would inevitably climb out of the moat and eat them, or to do the smart thing and blast him.

"Damned if you do and damned if you don't," Father growled as he raised his gun to his shoulder. He drew a bead between Harrison's eyes and pulled the trigger. The bullet punched a hole through the center of the dead man's forehead. Pink mist puffed out from the back of his skull as he crumpled to the ground. It took a few seconds for his body to stop moving, during which time Kyle noted that no blood leaked from the massive head wound. He wondered whether the blood of a zombie stopped flowing at death or if it kept circulating. He didn't know and at that moment, he didn't truly care. The thing was dead and that's what was important. Father's moat had saved their lives.

Kyle looked at his father with new eyes. The man might have been a little mad, but he was smart, and he had saved them with a crazy idea. "Dad..." he started to say.

Father glanced at him, saw the emotion in his boy's face, and saved him the embarrassment of saying anything. "I love you too, son. I'm glad you're here." Then he turned away and marched purposefully to the garage and fired up his backhoe.

"Love you too, Dad."

Somehow, as he watched his father drive to the southern edge of the property and dig what a grave, he could not help but notice that the man seemed much older. Even though he was in his fifties and had the graying around the edges that all men of that age acquired, it was something else. There was something about Father that made him old beyond his years.

The grave wasn't as wide or long as a normal grave, but it didn't need to be. Father explained that he didn't want Harrison to be comfortable. "It will be that much tougher for him to crawl out again if he's all balled up in that hole."

"You really think he'll come back? You shot him through the brain."

Father shrugged. "Beats the hell out of me," he answered. "But they all came back once, why not again? A hole through your thinker doesn't cut the brain stem from the spinal cord."

The business of getting Harrison into the hole was more disgusting than Kyle had imagined it would be. Father drove the backhoe over to the moat and drove the serrated edge of the bucket down into the center of Harrison's abdomen. First, he pinched the corpse in half and then he scooped up both pieces individually, drove them to the grave and dumped them in. Intestines dragged the ground. Other unidentifiable organs dangled from both parts of the carcass, dancing crazily as the tractor bumped over the rough terrain. Kyle thought he would lose his lunch at first, but he was able to keep it down, barely.

Father filled the hole and tamped the loose dirt down with the bucket, then drove the backhoe back and forth over the grave until it was as tightly packed as possible. Finally, he returned the machine to the garage.

"That ought to take care of him," Father said. "I wonder how long it will be before we see his wife and those little bastards of his down here." He glanced at the nearby farmhouse as he said it and Kyle could see the wheels turning in his head.

Mother had witnessed the entire incident through the living room window, but she never came out. It was disgusting work, work for men, and her men were more than capable of doing it.

After that, the morning passed quietly. They went about their chores as if nothing had happened. The only real difference was the somber tone with which they worked. Father said nothing until Mother was clearing away the lunch dishes. "You know that if he's a zombie, the rest of his family probably is too. As far as I see it, there's only one thing left to do. We need to go check out the house."

Mother had been afraid he would say that. Kyle could tell from her stoic expression that she expected it. But because she said nothing, Kyle knew that she believed there was no real alternative. If they did nothing then it wouldn't be long before they had a snaggletoothed redneck white trash zombie bitch and her fat no-account devil spawn children coming after them. Nothing could be worse than ending up as food in their bellies. So as gruesome as the prospect was, it was still better to take the fight to them than to risk an invasion of their home. Living with a battle hardened veteran had molded her to think that way.

"Better wear your hunting gear then," she said. "The thicker the better. You don't want one of those little bastards biting you."

They gathered their gear quickly. The sun was at its zenith as they set out. Father's theory was that the undead preferred the dark. "That's vampires, Dad," Kyle told him.

Trying to save face from his faux pas, Father replied, "Still, if you get them when the sun is at its highest, you'll be able to see a lot more,"

"I'll give you that," Kyle smiled.

They used an eighteen foot extension ladder from the garage to span the moat. "Like to see one of those dead bastards do this," Father muttered quietly as he picked his way gently across the makeshift bridge.

Once they were both across, Father dragged the ladder towards them, then hid it in the brush on the far side of the road.

They started up the gravel road toward the Harrison house. Mother laughed as they sauntered away in their heavy outfits.

"You guys look like Ralphie's little brother in 'A Christmas Story.'"

Checking each other out, they had to agree. It was quite comical. They both managed a quick chuckle and then got back to business.

Though the gravel in the neighbor's driveway crunched under their feet, they did not worry that the noise might tip off any zombies. It would have been impossible to sneak up on anyone in the middle of the day wearing hunting gear and carrying long guns, so they didn't bother to try. In fact, Father surmised that if they made enough noise, they would be able to draw out any zombies that might be lurking. Even so, once they reached the front porch, they both tiptoed across the old wooden deck to the large plate glass window.

The interior lights were all on but there was no movement inside. "No blood or bodies," Father whispered.

"That's good," Kyle whispered back.

"No, that means if anyone is here, we'll have to ferret them out," Father corrected him.

"Should we knock?" Kyle whispered, pointing at the front door.

"Are you joking?" Father returned. Then he realized that Kyle was being sarcastic. "Anyway, smartass, everyone here is either dead, undead, or hiding. They're not going to answer."

Father pulled the screen door open slowly. The spring that held it close protested slightly. He turned the knob on the thick wooden door and bumped it open.

No one locked their doors in these parts because no one needed to. Everybody had loud, territorial guard dogs and guns. No one ever dared to break into country homes around here because they knew the consequences.

There was no response of any kind from within the house. No dog barked, no one spoke, no floor boards creaked.

"In we go," Father mouthed silently as he made a military gesture toward the interior. His eyes had a crazed, faraway look to them that Kyle attributed to some sort of flashback.

"Dad, just remember, it's not Vietnam in there," he said quietly. His father shushed him with a pointed finger. He tilted his head toward the living room and quickly charged through the door, startling Kyle with his speed. He'd never seen his Father move that spryly before. One second he was there and the next he was thirty feet away, in the middle of the room, gun at the ready.

Adrenaline flowed through him like heroin. Time slowed again and he was suddenly aware of his heart hammering in his chest. He stepped gingerly into the home.

The Harrison home had the same layout as nearly every other farmhouse built during the same period. There was a parlor or living room at the front of the house with a stair case to the second floor tucked in a corner. The living room opened onto a formal dining room that had a study attached to it. Both of those rooms had doors that led to the kitchen at the back of the house. There was a small pass-through bathroom between the study and the kitchen.

Quietly, quickly, they cleared the front room like a couple of television cops before moving toward the formal dining room. Next, they lunged into the study like a mini S.W.A.T. team, fingers on their triggers.

The tiny little bathroom was empty, though the bowl of the toilet looked like someone had tried to refinish the porcelain with their entrails.

In the kitchen was more of the same nastiness as the bathroom. Blood and shit and lumpy blobs coated the linoleum floor, staining the pastel flower print a disgusting shade of chocolate covered cherry.

"Someone was dragged through here," Father pointed at the floor. "See how there are two streaks heading for the door?"

Kyle saw it but the smell of the gore caused him to gag. He had to cover his mouth and concentrate on not vomiting. Normally he had a strong constitution but the stink of the mess on the floor was enough to turn his stomach. He nodded his response while choking down his lunch.

"Shouldn't have eaten such a big lunch," Father teased. "I expect we'll see more of this, so get used to it." Kyle nodded but knew he would never get used to the smell.

"Stay here," Father told him. Moving to the back door, he shifted his rifle to his hip, pointing it to the ceiling to take the weight off his arm. Bit by bit, he pulled the rear door open and stuck his head out. He grunted.

"Okay, that's one Harrison we don't have to hunt for anymore," he said, staring down at the body of the youngest girl. She was all of six. A thick swarm of flies buzzed around her body. Kyle caught a whiff of her decaying flesh and vomited. This time he did not even bother trying to hold it back.

Father's eyes were moist when he turned away from the body. All parents were linked to children, even ones not their own. It was something that men at Kyle's stage of life could not comprehend and there was no use in trying to explain it. Father almost wished it had been Kyle that had found her because it would not have had the same impact on him. Then again, he wouldn't wish that image upon his son for love nor money.

The one thing that Kyle could comprehend was that his Father was sympathetic to the plight of the Harrisons even though he tried to hide it. Even if his years in the military had taught him to never show emotion, especially when it really hurt, it was more than obvious that he did care.

More easily than his father was able, Kyle pushed the emotion down into his stomach and moved on. "How many Harrisons are there?" he asked. He knew very well that there were three children, two parents and two dogs.

Father wiped his eyes and answered deliberately. "There's five of them total, plus two dogs. We know the dad is out of the picture and so is the youngest daughter, so all we have to account for now is the Mother, the other two kids, and the two dogs."

"Why do we need to account for the two dogs?" Kyle asked.

"You haven't heard those things barking since you got here, have you?"

Kyle shook his head.

"Me either, and they bark all the damn time. What that tells me is that when Pops started to turn, the dogs probably turned on him. If he didn't outright kill them, he may have turned them into zombies, too."

"Seriously, Dad," Kyle grimaced. "You get more stories crossed than anyone ever."

"Well, goddamit son! I'm trying to say that maybe the dogs may came back too and that we're going to have to fight zombie dogs." He raised his eyebrows and shrugged. "Okay, I'll give you that one. Sounds like one of those bad horror movies you like to watch, doesn't it?"

Kyle nodded. "That one's Resident Evil." The thought of real zombie canines attacking him flitted into his brain and the smile faded from his face. "Oh shit. They might be able to jump the moat."

Father frowned. "Yeah. Let's go look upstairs before we go in the basement, okay? I'd much rather get trapped upstairs than be trapped down there with no way out."

Kyle agreed. They walked back to the beautifully polished oak staircase. Seven steps led to the landing, after which the staircase turned and went behind the living room wall up to the second floor. It was narrow, having been built at the turn of the Twentieth Century when people were much smaller. Kyle and his Father were both big men to begin with—they both cleared six foot easily—and so it was tight. Father led the way. Kyle followed closely behind.

"Put on your safety," Father instructed. "I don't want to get shot in the ass." Kyle snickered playfully but did as he was told.

Father stopped when his head was even with the upstairs floor. He peered into the open bedroom, checking for signs of life. Nothing moved. There were no noises. But something felt wrong. He could sense a presence—who or what it was he couldn't say—but it was definitely there. Still, they had to clear the house or risk paying the price later.

The last few stairs creaked loudly under Father's feet as he ascended and they expected something dead to come at them, but nothing did. That suggested that it wasn't the dogs that Father was feeling.

They went from room to room searching through closets and under beds, looking for any signs of life... or death. There weren't any blood spatters or telltale signs that someone had died or reanimated in the upstairs, but all the lights were on.

"Time for the basement, I guess," mumbled Father. There was a nervous quality to his voice that betrayed his steely façade.

Then, they heard a noise from below. A floorboard creaked. Then another and it was louder, closer. Someone was walking through the living room and whoever it was, he was coming towards them.

Kyle's heart thumped in his chest. His father reached out and tugged at the back of his jacket, pulling him backwards. They backed quickly and as quietly as they could up the stairs. Father swapped positions with him and stepped down the stairs slowly.

The steps compressed under the weight of the zombie down below, groaning loudly. A shadow crept up the stairs and across the landing.

It was a strange, low shadow with horns, almost devilish. "Woof woof," whispered Father. Kyle understood instantly. He clicked the safety off his gun and walked around the railing until he was above and even with Father. They both leveled their guns at the landing and prepared to fire.

The dog, in some sort of trancelike state, came slowly up the stairs. It did not look up at them immediately, but as it turned, in slow motion, it showed the same dead eyes that Harrison had in the moat. Its hair was matted and dirty and spotted with blood. Its jowls were covered with thick brown foamy suds and its jaw was clamped tightly shut. A black thing, its tongue maybe, protruded from its mouth.

The dead eyes eventually locked on Kyle and his Father. Slowly again, the dog began to climb toward them, shaking ever so slightly as it stiffly maneuvered its body around the corner. One of the rear legs was gone. Raw meat hung limply from its hindquarter. Maggots crawled excitedly in the open wound.

"Dad, look at its back leg," Kyle gasped.

"I see it," Father replied. "All right, I'm going to put one right between its eyes. If it doesn't stop moving you blow its head off, okay?" Kyle nodded in agreement. Father added, "But there's no point in wasting bullets, either. You never know how many we're going to need."

"Okay," Kyle answered.

Father squeezed the trigger. The resulting explosion was enough to make Kyle jump. The dog, however, did not jump. It flew backwards into the wall of the landing. When it flopped to the floor, Kyle was able to see that the top of its head had been blown off, decorating the wall of the landing behind it with a brackish mix of brain, blood and bone. The unnatural beast wheezed once and stopped moving.

Kyle wasn't sure how long they stared at it, waiting for it to move again, but eventually they realized it was completely dead, not just undead. Cautiously, they crept down the stairs toward the carcass. Stepping over the body, Father disappeared around the corner. Kyle waited as Father made sure the room below was clear before he went down the stairs.

He gagged as he stepped over the animal. It wasn't the brains or the flecks of skull sliding down the wall, it was the smell. Once, a cow belonging to the neighbors to the south of their farm got tangled up in the barbed wire fence bordering the two properties and died. It was so bloated by the time they got the thing loose that it looked like a Macy's Thanksgiving Day Parade balloon. Old Man McGill did his best to carefully remove the poor dumb cow from the fence without gouging it, but he accidentally punctured its stomach and the beast exploded, showering the foulest smelling goo everywhere. The whole area stunk for two days. Now, for once, Kyle was glad he had already emptied the contents of his stomach.

Again they swept through the main floor of the house, heading back to the kitchen. Kyle stopped to open the refrigerator. There was food, still cold, on the shelves. He reached in and pulled out a bottle of grape juice.

"I don't think I would drink that," Father said. "You never know. They could have drunk from the same bottle and spread it to each other."

Kyle stared at the bottle, then slowly replaced it. He knew his dad was right. He would just have to suffer through the rest of the afternoon with vomit breath.

There was no access to the basement from inside the house. That was typical of the homes built in that era. Unfortunately, it meant they would have pass through the back porch—by the body of the dead girl.

The Harrisons had a chest freezer on the back porch against which the girl's body was wedged. Father kicked one of her hips just to make sure that she was dead and stiff. She didn't move.

"Why do you think she was out here?" Father wondered aloud.

Kyle shook his head. "No clue, maybe she was getting something from the freezer."

Instantly, Kyle got a queasy feeling in his stomach. Father got it, too. He motioned Kyle to back up a step or two.

"Shoot whatever comes out when I pop the lid."

When they were both in position, Father counted to three and flung the lid open as fast as he could.

Inside was the other family dog, frozen stiff. There were bite marks along its back and neck. The one inside the house must have turned undead and then attacked the dog that was now in the freezer.

"Doesn't really explain why they put it in here. It's not like they were going to..."

Kyle finished off the thought. "...Eat it?"

Father shrugged his shoulders. "Why not? I guess I can believe that. Maybe Dad turned, attacked the first dog, which nailed the second one, and Pops tossed it in here for later. Still doesn't explain the little girl..."

He peered down again at her scrunched up little body and screeched in surprise. Her eyes were open. She was staring back at him!

He leapt backward, throwing out his arm to push his son away too. The little girl uncurled herself, stretching out her limbs, then took to her feet. She stepped towards them tentatively, a confused look upon her face.

Father called out to the girl, but she simply growled in response. He leaned down, picked up a small rock and tossed it at her. It hit her in the forehead. She didn't even flinch.

"Good enough for you?" he asked Kyle.

"Yeah," Kyle replied. "You want me to handle it?" He knew it wouldn't bother him as much as it would his father.

"No, it's not the same as a real girl," Father said pointedly as he pulled the trigger.

As they stood staring at the remains of the little girl, Father said in a low tone, "That only leaves two Harrisons to account for. Any guesses where they might be?"

Kyle shook his head knowingly. "My guess is that they're probably both in the cellar. If they were alive I would think they would have come out by now."

"That's my guess, too."

They expected the cellar doors to be locked, but not from the inside. Father banged on one of the steel doors but there was no answer. He hollered that they were there to help, but there was still no response. "Well that can't be good," he commented.

In the family garage they found two pry bars and a pickaxe. But before they could even begin to hack through the metal, the doors exploded outwards, revealing a blue-gray woman with matted brown hair and a teenage boy with vacant eyes who looked as if hadn't eaten in weeks. They popped out of the cellar so quickly that both men were caught off guard.

Both the woman and the boy clamped onto Father's arms with their teeth, ripping their heads wildly from side to side like savage dogs, trying to tear the flesh from his bones. The fabric of one of Father's sleeves ripped, spurring him into action.

He whipped around so that he was directly behind them and then raised his pry bar and whacked the woman as hard as he could. The force of the steel smashing into the crown of her head dropped her to the ground. Father noticed a few of her teeth were still stuck in his sleeve.

Kyle yanked his weapon back quickly and smacked the teenager as hard as he could too. But the boy did not fall to the ground. Stubbornly, he clung to Father's arm, gnawing furiously at what he thought was flesh. Kyle hit him again three more times before the tenacious fellow finally crumpled to the ground with the side of his head smashed in.

By that point, the woman was on her knees again and climbing to her feet. Kyle backed up and took another swing at her. But she managed to tilt her head just enough so that the steel bar glanced off her temple, opening a tiny cut in the flesh above her ear.

Father was stunned. He backed away from the scene, chanting "No, no, no," over and over as he probed the tears on his jacket, looking for evidence the zombies had managed to get through the heavy material.

He couldn't see any punctures but he wasn't convinced, so he stripped off the jacket and his shirt. Only when he was naked from the waist up and still saw no wounds did he begin to calm down.

"Phew," he gasped when he realized he hadn't been bitten. He took a few deep breaths and then took stock of the situation. The teenage boy was finished. Kyle was still battling with the mother, but he seemed to have things somewhat under control. He watched as Kyle, who was backing away from the dead woman as fast as he could, still swinging the pry bar, smashed the bones in her left forearm, causing everything below the elbow to hang limply. The woman growled at her sudden handicap but kept after him.

Kyle backed into a tree and had nowhere to go. The zombie grabbed him by the neck with its good hand and leaned in to bite him.

"No!" Father hollered as Kyle screamed for help. Father lurched forward, letting loose a barbaric "yawp" and planted the tip of his pickaxe in the crown of her skull. She slumped against Kyle's chest and for a second, Father thought that he had only made things worse. But she went limp and slid to the ground in a heap.

"Fuck an A, Dad!" Kyle screeched. "I thought I was fucked!"

"I thought we both were!" Father gasped, breathing heavily, Adrenaline pumping wildly through his system. "You okay? The dirty old bitch get you anywhere?"

"I don't think so," Kyle said, checking over his body closely.

"Do you see any?" he asked his dad.

Father checked him over. "Nope, you're clean," he said. "Now check me."

To anyone else who might have stumbled upon the scene, they would have looked like a pair of zoo monkeys checking each other for lice and ticks.

Sucking in a lungful of air, Father sighed. "One more thing to do." He went back in the house and turned off all the lights. He also locked the front door before coming out the back and locking it behind him, too.

"That ought to keep any other damn zombies from using it as hideout. It'll also tell us when someone else has been here."

"Should we burn it?" Kyle suggested.

"No, too much light attracts the moths, remember?"

Later, when they were telling the tale to Mother, they laughed about most of the adventure. They recounted every step and every action, discussing what they could have done differently or better. It was a hell of a way to bond, thought Kyle, but he had never felt safer in his life than at that moment.

CHAPTER 13

The call they had been waiting for came two days later. "I'm okay," Elaine assured them. "Me and some friends are still living at the dorm. We're barricaded in and we're pretty safe." A massive group of zombies had laid siege to their dorm but because there were a number of nerds in her building who were able to immediately identify the problem as a zombie outbreak, they were able to properly secure the building and keep them safe.

"But it would really help if you would come and get me," she told them. "We thought maybe the zombies would shrivel up and die but they haven't. There's more and more of them every day. It's like they have telepathy or something. They must broadcast to the others that dinner is ready to be served. None of us could get out if we wanted to. We've all been trying to call our parents but you're the first family that any of us has been able to reach."

Father was mystified. "Why didn't you call us sooner? You're only three hours away."

"I know," she said apologetically. "But I'm a big girl Daddy. We thought things would get better by now but they haven't and so it's time to call in the big guns. Can you come get us?"

"How many of you?" he inquired.

"Well, me and James, my boyfriend," she started. "I think you'll like him Daddy, he's a lot like you. And maybe a dozen others?"

Kyle leaned back from the phone so that he could see his father's reaction. His jaw was set. He always did that when Elaine informed him of a new man in her life. What was it with fathers and daughters?

"Okay," Father said as emotionlessly as he could. No boy was good enough for his little girl, but he had learned long ago that his contempt for them only made his daughter more interested in them. It was only thanks to Mother pointing that fact out to him that he began to learn to keep his mouth shut and let nature take its course. She had a good sense of which men were catches and which weren't. She always made the right decisions sooner if he left her alone. "Well, we'll figure it out and we'll be there soon as we can. You and James just stay away from everyone else in the meantime. It may take us a while longer than normal, so don't panic if we're not there until tomorrow. Bye pumpkin. I love you."

"I love you too, Daddy. Please hurry."

Father's face turned red as he hung up the phone and his eyes got misty but he did not cry. Instead he sucked in a lungful of air and expelled it slowly. It was cleansing. It was enough to set him right again.

"Do you remember which dorm your sister lives in?" he asked Kyle.

"Yeah, I do. I think I remember how to get there, too. You just take 37 till you hit the sign that points toward the University and follow it in. It's the dorm closest to the stadium and you can't miss it. It's on the main drag."

Father nodded. "Yep, that's right."

It suddenly dawned on Kyle that his Father might not be going with him. "You're not coming?" he asked.

"Well, do you think that we should leave Mother here alone to fight off zombies? Or do you think maybe I should stay here with her just in case?" Mother was a sturdy woman who could take care of herself, but neither he nor his Father would have forgiven themselves if they left her to a hungry herd of zombies who somehow managed to scale the moat.

"You've got the box truck," said Father. "What I suggest is that you drive into town and get a couple of those tubes of Runflat and then beat a path for the Interstate. They should still be pretty open. You'll be able to make it down to I-465 in an hour or two. Then depending on what 465 looks like, it's another half hour around the city and then it's another hour or so down 37. That's assuming you don't have to drive around wrecks or through zombies."

"Sounds like a plan. Any other advice?"

"You might want to get a bunch more ammo if there's still any left in town. You can hit the Wal-Mart by the Interstate if not. They sell it by the crate."

They spent about an hour prepping the truck. Kyle filled a five gallon bucket with water and tightened the lid down so it wouldn't leak. He piled in a small grocery bag of food, enough for three people for two days. Then he put on his hunting gear and loaded the cab like he was going to "road hunt" his way across the state. Finally, he was ready to go.

He kissed his Mother and said his goodbyes to his Father, then unceremoniously climbed down the ladder into the moat and back up the other side, kicking the ladder back to his Father. He waved and went around the driver's side and climbed into the truck. Then he was gone.

As he rolled down the county roads that would take him to the Interstate, he prepared himself for Walmart by replaying old zombie movies in his head. The Evil Dead series came instantly to mind. At the end of "Army of Darkness," where Ash blasted the undead as they attacked him in the aisles of S-Mart, stood out. How ironic that he was about to play out that scene in real life.

But when he pulled up to the doors of the Walmart, he knew things weren't going to go as planned. There were live people at the doors, men with guns, guarding the entrance. He climbed from the truck, careful to take the keys with him, after pulling into one of the handicapped spots.

One of the guards started to hassle him about parking there and he replied, "Since when do greeters carry rifles?" The bald headed, squat little man started to curse at him but Kyle raised his palm to him and said, "Talk to the hand because the brain ain't listening!" He had such disdain for lowbrow people that even though it made him feel physically dirty to behave in such a fashion, he couldn't resist descending to their level when he shopped at the giant chain. That was one of the reasons he didn't like to shop there: it made him feel bad about himself.

"Buddy boy," growled the guard as he grabbed Kyle's fingers and bent them downward until such terrible pain shot up his arm that he dropped to the ground and groaned in agony. The guard leaned in and hissed at him in low tones. "Things are different now. I'm in control here, not you, and I don't take shit from white trash mothers like you. You're the kind of people who give this place a bad name. I could kill you if I wanted and claim you were a zombie about to eat me. I'm God here, do you understand?" For added emphasis, he bent Kyle's hand a bit more, doubling the amount of pain.

He'd been taken completely by surprise by the man's aggression and was incapable of doing anything else at the moment other than agree with him. Tears welled up in his eyes. He grunted and nodded.

The guard wrenched his hand once more before letting him loose. "Now get in there, get what you need and then get home before you get shot."

Kyle thought to curse at him but he didn't want to risk another incapacitation. He skulked away like a whipped puppy. Into the store he went as the guard called out to him mockingly, "OH, and welcome to Walmart!"

He had expected the store to be deserted. He had planned to walk out with everything he needed and not pay for a bit of it, but that wasn't the case. Apparently, after the Apocalypse, there would be two things left alive: cockroaches and Walmart!

There weren't that many workers but there weren't a great deal of shoppers either. Of those shoppers brave enough to be out, most scurried around like insects who knew there was a snake nearby. They got their water or milk, their food staples, their ammunition, and headed for the door.

Kyle noted that true to Corporate form, management had put everything needed for just such an occasion in the main aisles by the front doors. It was like the day before Thanksgiving. It was called "The Blitz" back then, when things were sane. What was it called during a zombie attack? The After Dead Special?

The only things not in the blitz lane were guns. Couldn't have those unlocked, could we? He scoped out the pallets for his type of ammunition, but could find none. *God, hope it's not all gone!*

There was a line at the sporting goods counter. The old man there kept repeating that all guns but the muzzle loaders were sold out, but that he had plenty of ammunition for nearly every type of weapon. As he got closer, Kyle could see a pallet of shotgun shells and bullets for all shapes and sizes of guns behind the old man. There were two workers on either side of the pile, picking out whatever caliber customers asked for and shoveling them forward as fast as possible. They were doing a brisk business. How funny that at least one company was able to make money off the end of the world.

There was an entire stack of 30.06 bullets, just right for the rifle his Father had given him and a massive quantity of .22 boxes, each holding 500 rounds, which he would also need. He was flush on .12 gauge shells, but they had some here too, and it couldn't hurt him to have more.

When it was his turn, he asked for as many rounds of each type as they could give him.

"Two boxes of each, limited to six boxes of ammunition total," the old man said. "We've got to ration 'em out to everyone."

"Two? That's it?" he shot back.

"Two," the old man said, a steely look on his face. He would not be cowed by anyone. "That's four thousand rounds maximum. Unless you're going to kill an entire city, you won't need that many. Well, unless you're a piss poor shot and then you'll get eaten before you can use 'em all. So which is it, Sonny? Are you going postal on a city or are you a piss poor shot?" The old man glared at him, awaiting his response. Kyle was not about to give him the satisfaction of answering. He just winked at the old man and motioned for him to bag his ammo as he handed over his credit card.

Wow, credit works still, too!

I-69 was a good distance from Huntington. It took him a while to reach it, but it was pretty much a smooth ride all the way there. He passed through a couple of little towns, only running over a few undead who stood in the middle of the street like Sun worshippers waiting for the dawn. Other than that, there was no traffic, no signs of life. It was like the entire world had suddenly disappeared into the Twilight Zone, leaving him behind to fight a planet full of zombies. But he knew that behind all of those drawn curtains and pulled blinds, there were people hiding in terror of the roaming evil.

He wasn't really scared of the undead. Of course they were terrifying when they were trying to get you, like back in his apartment complex, but after the initial rush of fear had subsided, it was replaced by something more akin to annoyance. Perhaps that was it—they had disrupted his life but only temporarily. How long could they go on roaming the earth, after all? At some point they would rot away into nothingness or stiffen up with rigor mortis and that would be the end of them. From that point on, it would be a simple mop up job for the National Guard.

Given the fact that it was late July in Indiana, the temperature and weather would surely play a factor in putting down the Corpse Rebellion. *Ooh, I like that. Have to save that one for a book.* He thought again of the bloated cow he'd seen and smelled a few years back. It did not take long in the Midwestern sun for an animal made of solid meat to turn into a puddle of toxic jelly and explosive gases. The thought of that cow exploding danced in his head for a moment, causing him to gag.

"Enough of that," he scolded himself before the clip of the woman he splattered on the front of the truck came back to him.

He hit the scan button on the radio and waited for the tuner to latch onto a signal. He knew there wouldn't be a lot of choices, but he ought to be able to pick up Indy channels before too long. That was assuming, of course, that there were any left. Almost immediately, the radio latched onto the same news channel that he had listened to only a few nights before. The voice of the same broadcaster droned on about the present state of affairs. Kyle hit the scan button again but the radio eventually came back to the same station. It was now the only station on.

"Most of the larger cities have been completely overrun," said the man. He sounded tired, exhausted. Who wouldn't have been exhausted if all they did day in and day out was read depressing reports about the end of the world. Kyle thought he would surely shoot himself if he had that job.

The signal wasn't quite as strong as it was at his parents' home. He was driving away from Ft. Wayne and that meant the farther south he drove the quicker he'd lose the station. He could already hear static creeping up on the edges of the man's voice and he knew it wouldn't be much longer before there was more static than voice.

"Although the rural areas tend to be safer at this point, there are still reports coming in of zombies wandering through the countryside and attacking random farmhouses. Still, authorities are urging people to stay away from the cities as that is where the numbers of zombies continue to increase. National Guard troops have been called out to surround major metropolitan areas in all 50 states. In the Hoosier State, Indianapolis, Fort Wayne, Evansville, and Lake and Porter counties have all been cordoned off. No one may enter or exit those areas without permission from the National Guard."

Kyle worried how he was going to get around Indianapolis with the roads blocked off. The announcer did not list Bloomington as one of the areas that had been cordoned off so he took that as a good sign, but that didn't alleviate the problem of getting there. He knew how to navigate via the interstates but if he had to take state roads or even county roads and sidetrack around Indianapolis, he would be lucky to make it to Bloomington at all.

Deciding that he would keep to the original plan and take the Interstate as far south as he could before worrying about the rest, he settled in for the drive. There were no vehicles traveling in either direction and even when he passed exits or minor roads that crisscrossed the countryside, he didn't see a single car or person. *No animals either.*

"Last man on Earth," he said dejectedly. At about that moment, the voice on the radio disappeared altogether and he was left with silence. Quickly, the movies that he'd spent most of his teenage years watching and now wishing he hadn't sprung into his mind. Reality was bad enough without his imagination adding scary monsters to the situation. Unfortunately, he had nothing to distract him from his own vivid imagination.

"No one gets out of here alive," he said aloud, repeating a line from some movie whose name he couldn't remember. Then he added thoughtfully, "And in this case maybe no one gets out dead either."

With each mileage sign he passed, the adrenaline levels in his system cranked up a notch. Soon he began to see numbered roads, like 216th Street and 191st Street and he knew it was not long till he would hit the beltway around Indy.

Fifteen minutes later, he saw signs for 96th Street—the road just north of the intersection between I-69 and I-465. Bits of wrecked cars littered the sides of the highway for the last twenty miles or so, but as he approached 96th Street the road became cluttered and then completely blocked by charred skeletons of unidentifiable vehicles. It was like all the cars in a demolition derby had crashed into each other and exploded, instantly engulfing everyone and everything within the vicinity.

He let off the gas, allowing the truck to decelerate to a crawl, as he approached the edge of the destruction. The truck glided to a stop only yards from the nearest car. He tried to pick out a path that might lead him through the scorched pile but he saw no clear path. The road was just too clogged. However, he noticed that the median was relatively empty. He might be able to get around the mess if only the incline wasn't so steep. He was afraid the truck would tip over and then he'd be completed screwed.

Maybe though, it was possible to go straight down the incline and up into the northbound lanes. There was a mass of cars over there too, but he knew from experience that the northbound side of this intersection was nowhere near as hectic as the southbound on a good day, so it was worth a shot. He had to try.

"How about that shit?" he laughed upon reaching the other lane. He couldn't have seen from the southbound side of the interstate that there was actually a wide open lane right down the middle of the wreckage but now as he was facing it, anyone could see that a nearly perfect trail had been bulldozed through the center of the chaos. It had to have been either National Guard or Army that did the job, not that it mattered.

He drove cautiously down the lane, fully expecting some corpse to jump out of the charred wreckage and try to eat his face, but it didn't happen. So he pushed the accelerator down a little bit farther and cruised toward the massive cloverleaf intersection. As he neared it, he could see that there were a number of military vehicles at the bottoms of each ramp and atop the overpass. There also appeared to be live soldiers stationed at regular intervals along the beltway.

A flash of light appeared somewhere in his periphery and a second later he heard the report of a high velocity rifle. "Dudes, I'm alive," he howled.

Suddenly there was activity all over the interchange. Men were running about, taking up defensive positions, and aiming guns at him.

Rolling down the window, he stuck his arm out and waved it frantically up and down so as to let the soldiers know that he was in fact alive and not a hungry zombie out to get them. He crept along at barely fifteen miles an hour, waving and honking the horn, until he was close enough he could hear someone shouting over a loudspeaker.

"You in the truck, halt where you are. Get out of the cab and lay face down on the ground."

Apparently he did not respond fast enough because someone fired another warning shot. He slammed down the brake, accidentally killed the engine, and leapt out of the truck. Down on the ground he went. *Hot pavement!*

A group of soldiers approached with guns drawn. Before they reached Kyle, they barked commands at him. They were all jabbering so fast that he had trouble understanding what they were saying. He didn't know what to do so he clasped his hands behind his head and started repeating his name, job, and phone number over and over.

The first soldier reached him and kicked him sharply in the ribs with the toe of his boot. The cold steel of the soldier's gun barrel poked into his cheek. "I don't suppose you guys have safeties on?" Kyle inquired calmly.

The soldier who had kicked him in the ribs chuckled. "Hell no, buddy. The way things are these days, if your safety is on you're a dead man."

"Or undead," Kyle returned, hoping that the guy had a sense of humor.

"Yeah, that would be funny if I hadn't heard about 10,000 times already. Now why don't you tell us what you're doing here?"

He told them how he came to be there and where he was going. The soldier appeared disinterested in Kyle's story until he reached the most important part. "It's my sister, man. She's all of 19. She's a scared little sophomore at IU and she said her dorm is surrounded by zombies. If I don't get down there soon, she's going to die."

Shaking his head, the soldier replied, "And if I let you go any further, you'll be the one who dies and then what kind of help will you be for your sister? My men will shoot you if you turn into one of *them*."

One of the other soldiers came up to his buddy. "Sergeant, I think this fellah can take care of himself. He's got an arsenal in the cab. Nothing illegal, just rifles and shotguns. That sort of thing."

The Sergeant scratched his head and thought about Kyle's situation. He was a Hoosier too and not without feeling. He was just doing his job—trying to keep the vast majority of the population safe. "Do you have a picture of her?"

"Of who?" Kyle asked, not realizing what he meant.

"Your sister, man," the Sergeant answered, "Do you have a picture of your sister?"

Oh, so that's what it's going to take, huh? The guy was a creeper. "Yeah, it's not a very good one but I've got one of her and me at her graduation last year. It's in my wallet. You want to get it out or shall I?"

"You get it. And you can get up," the Sergeant said disaffectedly.

"Wow!" he exclaimed once he got a peek at the picture. "Is she single?"

"Yeah," Kyle knew how to play the game. Maybe she was, maybe she wasn't, but whatever it took to get past this guy and to his sister.

"She's damn hot," the Sergeant smiled. He removed his helmet and handed back the picture. "Is she seeing anyone?"

"No, not that I'm aware of," he lied. "All she said on the phone earlier was that I needed to come and get her and a couple of friends. I can't speak for her, but she does tend to like strong men who know what they want out of life and who have a good job. At the moment I'd say you've got about the best job there is."

The Sergeant, who looked to be about 25, thumped himself on the chest like a gorilla. "Yeah, that's what I'm talking about," he grinned. He got on his radio and told his troops to pass the word that the box truck would be allowed to drive around to Highway 37 unimpeded.

"Now, you know that 37 looks a lot like what you saw back there at the top of the rise, don't you?" the Sergeant asked him. "You're going to have to pick your way through burned-out cars and bodies. It's not secure. You might get attacked along the way and there's nothing anyone can do for you once you're off 465. So if you're sure you want to do this, I would suggest you take all your safeties off all your guns and keep all your ammunition at the ready."

Kyle nodded. "Dude, it's my sister. I'm not going to let anything stop me." The Sergeant motioned for his men to follow him back and then turned away. "We'll move our truck and you go on up. If you see any zombies along the way, don't stop. We've got guys stationed every 300 feet to shoot anything that moves. If something does get on the road, run it over but don't stop. Got it?"

Kyle nodded again. "Good," said the Sergeant. "One other thing…" He fished out a tiny notebook from his chest pocket and jotted something in it, then ripped the page out and handed it to Kyle. Kyle knew what it was even before he looked at it.

"That's my phone number," the Sergeant grinned. "If you don't see me here when you come back, then you have her call me at that number. Otherwise, I want to meet her before you head back north."

Kyle nodded once more as he neatly folded the paper and stuck it in his pocket. The Sergeant thrust his hand out and grabbed Kyle's, shaking it vigorously.

"All right brother," he smiled. "Let's get you out of here so you can save that fine looking sister of yours."

Kyle climbed back in the cab of the truck and cranked up the engine. Their Humvees had already moved away from the ramp. For a few seconds, the machine gun mounted atop the unit pointed in his direction, worrying him that someone didn't get the message. Still, he couldn't stop. He gave the truck some gas and zipped up the ramp. There was another squad of men in another Humvee at the top of the ramp blocking the way, but they moved long enough for him to pass. He cruised onto the Interstate and floored it.

As promised, there was a lone soldier stationed on either side of the highway about every hundred yards. All were equipped with automatic rifles, each had large boxes of ammunition, food and water stationed with him. It didn't seem safe to him to defend such a structure as the Circle, but the road was elevated in a lot of places and that gave the soldiers the high ground. He felt bad for the men who were stationed in the low, flat spots or where homes and businesses butted right up to the highway but that wasn't really his concern at the moment.

Surprisingly, the roadway was free of the debris that had littered I-69. There were cars in the median and shoved into the grass but the asphalt itself was remarkably devoid of wreckage. The only time he had ever seen the road so deserted was during the Indianapolis 500, the actual race that is, when everyone was at the Speedway.

Since he didn't have to worry about accidentally bumping into anyone, he spent a lot more time looking out at the skyline of Indianapolis than he would have in regular traffic. Here and there wisps of smoke curled up into the air before collecting into one yellowish gray cloud that drifted lazily off to the east. *Funeral pyres?*

Although the roadway was originally built a good distance from downtown, Indianapolis had grown virally outward until what had originally been a bypass now cut through heavily populated areas. As the truck climbed up the overpasses, he was able to look out into the neighborhoods. From time to time, he caught glimpses of bodies. Some lay in the streets or yards as if they had been shot down where they stood. Every so often he caught sight of birds pecking at bodies and was disgusted. *Do you suppose the birds are spreading the disease?*

At one point, just before he reached a major intersection, he saw a wisp of smoke curl into the sky that appeared close by. Slowing down to take a look at it, he could make out yellowish orange licks of fire poking above the tree line. There were too many trees obscuring his view to see the source of the fire, so he put the truck in park and climbed out of the cab. He wandered toward the guardrail but the National Guardsman who was stationed on his side of the road came running over, yelling.

"Sir, you need to get back in your vehicle and continue moving. All you're doing by being out here is attracting those flesh eaters. Please get back in the vehicle." The young man, who couldn't have been more than twenty, sounded angry.

Kyle shrugged his shoulders and turned his palms outward. "I don't understand. What's the big deal?"

Now the soldier was close enough that he was within arm's length. He reached out and grabbed Kyle by the shoulder and forced him back to the truck. "Sir, this area is still heavily infected. We've already had to battle one batch of the bastards off of the ramp this morning and that was just because somebody sneezed. There was so damn many of them I thought we were screwed. And the worst part is that once you start firing off of one side of the road, the zombies on the other side hear the gunfire and they start coming towards you. It's a lot of work for all of us and if you hadn't noticed, we're wearing full gear in the middle of July in Indiana. It does not make us happy."

"Sorry," Kyle apologized. "I just wanted to see what that fire was over there. I've seen a bunch of them as I've been driving down the road here. That's all I wanted to know."

The soldier let him go with a final shove. "Well, sir, I can tell you that," he said. "Once we kill them we throw them into a big pile and we burn their bodies so they can't come back again."

"Does that work?"

"So far," the soldier answered. "Now please get in your truck and get moving. That's an order."

It was the first time the Kyle had ever felt old. Here was this young guy who was probably only eight years younger than himself calling him "Sir" like he was the kid's uncle. He suddenly understood why old folks didn't like being reminded of their age. He didn't feel or act old, and to tell the truth he didn't believe that anyone under thirty was old, so he didn't appreciate being made to feel that he was already over the hill.

"Dude," Kyle protested as the soldier pushed him towards the truck. "I'm not even thirty yet. I'm not old and I'm not stupid, so don't treat me like I am. I live up in Monticello and I've made it this far without getting killed and up until a couple a days ago I didn't even have a gun, Mr. Big Macho Stud!"

He slammed the door behind him and fired up the engine, blowing a huge black cloud of smoke behind him that enveloped the soldier. He watched in the rearview mirror as the young pup tried to wave away the sulfurous cloud of poison.

"Revenge is sweet," Kyle chuckled.

He made his way down the east side of Indianapolis with very little drama indeed. But as soon as the road began to swing around to the west again he realized that there were going to be problems. The road was clogged with cars, some of them burned out, some not. For the most part, he could get around the wreckage by driving on the shoulder, but a few times he had to drive down the incline and along the ditch.

There weren't as many soldiers in this corner of town, for some reason. Here they were spaced about a quarter of a mile apart. The road was at ground level, not atop a built up hill, so the soldiers had been forced to create little forts within the wreckage of vehicles.

He waved at every one of the soldiers as he went by, hoping to keep some goodwill alive and knowing that he would have to pass them on his way back. Most of them waved back but a few of them gave him the finger. He took it in stride and drove on.

One soldier looked like he was about to fire his weapon on the truck and Kyle could see that the guy was cursing him out. *Oh well, can't expect them all to tow the party line.*

Then he realized the soldier wasn't cursing him. "Oh, he's waving."

The soldier was waving his arms wildly, pointing and shouting for him to keep going, but Kyle thought he wanted him to get off the road. He slowed the truck down to talk to the guy but that only irritated the soldier. He started running towards Kyle with his gun raised. Kyle floored it and roared off down the highway even as the soldier started firing into a line of trees on the south side of the road.

A herd of zombies had stormed the highway and was lunging towards the soldier. He was firing on the crowd, dispatching them as quickly as possible.

"Brave soul," Kyle remarked as he watched the man advance steadily towards the crowd, firing the whole time. As Kyle got farther away, he could see that some of them had gotten back up and were again lurching toward him. He watched the soldier reload his weapon. The young man was quick but the zombies weren't far away. One of them was nearly to the end of his barrel before he was able to open fire again, blasting a hole through the zombie's torso.

Kyle turned back around and drove faster. He couldn't bear to watch what he thought was surely inevitable. *I'll deal with the regret later. Besides, what could I do?*

Presently, he reached Highway 37. The soldiers at the top and bottom of the ramp expeditiously moved their vehicles for him. At the bottom, he stopped for a second to tell them that he was headed to IU to get his sister and that he would be back as quickly as he could.

We know, we all work on the same channel," one of the soldiers replied. Irritated, he waved Kyle through. "I'd get a move on before you attract some of those bastards to our position." Kyle obliged him.

Highway 37 was a two lane divided highway, just like an Interstate except for the fact that there were intersections along its length, unlike the ramp system used by its cousin. There were seemingly hundreds of red lights along the route to Bloomington, and as it was the main thoroughfare from the capital to the college city, it was very busy before the outbreak. Unfortunately, it seemed to have been very busy during the outbreak, too.

There were burnt out vehicles and corpses everywhere. He couldn't go more than a tenth of a mile without seeing at least two pairs of smashed up wrecks. College kids still thought they were invincible. *Doesn't take much to turn into a fireball when you hit something at 80 miles an hour.*

The scene grew even worse when he was only a mile or two from the intersection that would take him toward the IU campus and straight to his sister's dorm. There was wreckage of all kinds, both human and machine, strewn across the roadway. Although it was hard to tell a rotting zombie from a rotting non-zombie, some of the corpses were obviously victims and others were not. The attackers had not been ripped apart and eaten.

Though he was getting uncomfortably used to the sight of decaying humans, what didn't sit so well was the sheer quantity of bodies lying about. The closer he came to the intersection, the more bodies there were. It was like a war scene. On one side were students, on the other the zombies. From appearances, the zombies had won an overwhelming battle. No doubt some of the fleeing students had turned zombie themselves and attacked their compadres. The stink was unbelievable.

He idled the truck, taking stock of the situation and trying to pick out the cleanest path amongst the fallen. *Bodies everywhere!*

It was disturbing to think that friends and roommates must have turned on each other in the grisly attack, or boyfriends on girlfriends and vice versa. He noticed a few tiny bodies in the rubble and that was even worse. Until that moment it hadn't occurred to him that babies would not have been immune. He hadn't given them any thought whatsoever. He could not imagine what it must have been like to be one of those parents who were forced to watch their helpless infants murdered in front of them before they were eaten themselves. It made his stomach turn. At that moment, he was glad that he was alone because the insanity of it all finally brought a tear to his eye. How could God have allowed such a horrible thing to happen? Where was God when things like this happened? How could he allow even babies to die such undeserved deaths? There was no silver lining here, no redemptive lesson—only death. If no one lived through the melee, how could have anyone learned anything from it?

All the emotional stress pent up in him from the last few weeks came blubbering out in the form of a hysterical laughing cry that, if anyone had seen him, would have caused them to think him insane.

Unfortunately, or fortunately, depending on one's viewpoint, he didn't have anymore time to devote to letting it all out because one of the bodies started to move. Then he heard a 'thunk' from the rear of the truck. His laughter died instantly.

A male and female zombie were creeping up the driver's side from behind the truck. There were three others coming up the passenger's side.

"Fuckers!" he screamed at them, gunning the engine until he was far enough ahead that he could see all five zombies in his rearview. Then he slammed on the brakes, shifted into reverse, and backed towards them as fast as the truck would go.

The truck hit them with a flat 'thud.' Their bodies crunched under the tires with the same noise coons or opossums made when you hit them.

Before they could get back up, he jammed on the brakes again, dropped it into drive, and shot forward again. He didn't care that he might puncture his tires. He was too angry to care.

He didn't look back this time. Instead, he kept driving. Looking back would do no good. It would just make him angry and he would end up spending more time here killing the bastards than he should. He needed to focus on the goal: Elaine.

The road curved slowly to the right. Soon he saw the tops of dormitories above the trees lining the road. He was close. The dorms moved around until they were directly in front of him. He was still maybe a half mile away but they so huge that they seemed much closer.

As he got nearer, he began to notice clumps of people moving about the base of the skyscrapers. For a few seconds he felt joyous. He couldn't understand why all those college kids were out running around in the middle of a zombie attack, but then again he knew better to wonder why college kids did anything. They could find amusement in the dumbest things, even apparently in the middle of the end of the world. But as the truck closed the distance, he realized that those college kids were not what they seemed. By then, they were rushing towards him across an expansive parking lot.

CHAPTER 14

At first, the group flowed towards him leisurely like a wave far out at sea rolling toward the shore. But all too soon the wave turned into individuals, some of them in a dead run.

"A dead run, ha," Kyle snorted. At least he had not lost his sense of humor in all the chaos. In fact, he seemed to have really gotten the hang of making smart comments in the midst of tragedy.

The road he was on skirted two sides of a giant parking lot nestled against the dorms. The quicker moving zombies were already half a dozen cars deep into the lot and moving fast.

He calculated that he might have one minute before they reached him, which gave him just seconds to determine the best course of action. He was no strategist but his instincts told him to keep to the pavement. If he went into the gravel lot, he was likely to lose traction and that could be the end of him.

There was a T intersection at the end of the road where he did a U-turn. The zombies turned to follow him and that bunched them up again.

Hmm, that gives me an idea. He drove back down the road, all the way to the other end of the lot. His thought was that if he did enough round trips before they reached the pavement, he could trick them into bunching up in a cluster. Then he could mow them down.

It worked. He made three or four passes in each direction, picking off the quickest of the rotting bastards in short order. The rest of the advancing horde had clustered together just as he had hoped. So when they finally reached the asphalt, it was simple enough to gun the engine and make a mad dash through them. With enough speed, he was able to use the large bumper of the truck as a cow catcher, knocking them out of the way or dropping them to the ground. Of course he worried that he might puncture a tire, but he had guns. If he could mangle enough of the rotting, stinking shitbags with the truck, taking out the rest would be no issue. It was obnoxious work, but with each pass of the truck, the crowd of flesh eaters shrunk. *Like driving a bush hog backwards through a forest!* he thought to himself.

"Maximum Carnage" was how he defined the strategy in his head. He hoped that his luck would hold out for the whole group but as he looked out over the torn faces of those who wanted to devour him, he wasn't so sure. Some of them were getting back up even after he hit them dead on. One sorry woman had been ripped from her t-shirt, baring her disfigured chest to the world. If the steel bumper hadn't caved in her ribcage, Kyle reckoned that she would have won any wet t-shirt contest she entered. But the impact had flattened her breasts and smashed them so far apart that they nearly unidentifiable. Still, he looked.

Two or three more passes should get them all. The truck and the tires were holding out. *That's all I need.*

The sound of bodies bouncing off the front of the truck was a bit unnerving and though Kyle would never admit it, he closed his eyes each time at the moment of impact. But none of the buggers came through the windshield and none of them had managed to grab hold of anything protruding from the sides. The last thing he wanted was for some lucky stiff to get a hold of one of the rearview mirrors and hoist himself up into the cab.

No sooner had he processed the thought than a dead teenager latched one hand firmly onto his door handle. The momentum of the truck drug him through the crowd, turning him into a humanoid bowling ball.

It was comical until the kid realized that there was fresh meat inside and began banging his head on the window. As the intensity of the banging grew, so too did Kyle's fear that the fiend might actually get in.

"Hey, do you know any guys in Lafayette, buddy?" Kyle grinned sarcastically at the teen. He sped up until he was very nearly at the end of the road and then slammed on the brakes. The zombie lost his grip on the door handle and flew off the truck. Kyle watched as the kid slid face down along the asphalt, leaving a maroon trail studded with hamburger sized chunks of meat behind him. He waited for the kid to get up. He knew the nasty thing would. He waited.

Just when Kyle decided that maybe the kid wouldn't get up, there was motion. A leg twitched. Then an arm. Then the kid was up on his feet, tottering while he regained his balance. He examined his surroundings, looking for dinner.

"Think you're smart, don't you?" Kyle called out. "Let's see what kind of a swinging dick you really are."

The zombie tried to leap out of the way of the truck as it suddenly roared towards him. The problem was that his brain and body were no longer synced with each other and all he could manage was to open his mouth just as his face sunk into the grill of the truck.

Though Kyle had somehow become used to the sound of skulls bouncing off the truck, this time there was no 'pop.' The zombie's head cracked open like a ripe watermelon and spilled its contents into the tightly woven heatsink of the radiator.

Kyle spun the truck around to face the group still in the access road. He was completely unaware that the teen was still hanging from the front of his vehicle. He just assumed that the dragging sound he heard meant the little shit was hung up on the undercarriage.

Others were fumbling toward him, dumbly gathered into a tightly bunched group in the middle of the drive. Kyle put the pedal to the metal and charged through them again. The dragging noise became more pronounced, especially once he plowed into the crowd. When he was through them and far enough away from the remaining zombies to climb out of the cab without fear of instant death, he idled the truck.

"Disgusting!" he cried, grimacing at the sight of the mashed skull wedged in the grill. The body of the college boy, still connected but disintegrating quickly, hung limply underneath the truck.

Given a safer situation, he would've tried to pluck as much of the boy out of the grill as he could. But considering the fact that there was still a small batch of hungry, gory college kids after him, he dispensed with the formalities.

He grabbed a tire iron from the cab and slid it between the kid's neck and the grill. As he quickly pulled the steel bar backward, there was a wet crack noise and the body dropped to the ground. The head remained in the grill.

"Oh, Gawd!" Kyle exclaimed, immediately losing his composure and his stomach contents.

"Sumbitch," he cursed, wiping vomit from his lips. The kid's neck meat was nearly black with coagulated blood but the smell of it was worse. It was overpoweringly rancid, like a dumpster behind a fast food restaurant in a heat wave. Kyle vomited again. He staggered away from the corpse, still gagging, and crumpled to the ground next to the truck. A few more retches and soon he was empty. It became impossible to separate the stink of the dead kid from the smell of stomach acid.

"Errrrgh," groaned a zombie. The last batch of predators was close enough that he could hear them. That helped to distract him from his fit.

One more pass was all it took to dispatch the rest of them. A few who weren't completely destroyed dragged themselves along with whatever limb was still usable. But their gang had been decimated to the point that there were no real threats, and so he drove right up to a door at the base of the tower and parked. He strapped a rifle over his shoulder and grabbed a shotgun for good measure.

"Finally," he sighed, taking stock of his situation. He counted about a dozen crawlers still moving, but no walkers.

Something caught his eye. In his periphery someone was coming toward him from around the corner of the dorm. It was another clump of zombies! They moved slowly at first but the breeze carried his scent towards them and it didn't take long for them to figure out that he was dinner on the hoof.

A male and female began to run at him. They were moving very fast, almost too fast for zombies. He waited until they were only about 40 yards away before raising the rifle to his shoulder. He squeezed off a shot, aiming for the male's head, but hitting him in the shoulder. The force of the bullet smacking into him caused him to spin around before sending him to the ground. The fellow let out a scream and started cursing.

"Oh! What the Hell! He shot me! He shot me!" Only then did Kyle realize that the man was not a zombie.

"Oh Jesus, a live one," he mumbled sadly. In his defense, no one else would have waited any longer to shoot either, and from a distance the dirty man with the matted afro could have been a zombie. But it didn't help to alleviate any guilt.

The girl that was with him had stopped running and dropped to the ground, screaming as she coddled her companion. She peered up at Kyle, who still held the gun as if to shoot again. In a panic, she screamed again.

"Oh please God! Don't shoot me! Don't shoot!" She pressed her head against her friend so that if the invader shot her, at least she wouldn't see it coming.

"You're not zombies?" Kyle asked dumbly.

The girl peeked out from under her arms, slowly realizing that the man did not intend further gunplay. She tended to her friend, trying to stem the flow of blood from his shoulder.

"Hell no!" she spat. "Do we look like a bunch of undead bastards to you?"

"Well," Kyle started, stopping before he could say anything dumber than what he'd already offered.

"What the hell did you think you were doing just firing indiscriminately at us?" the girl whined in between a pair of extremely long obscenity filled comments on his lineage. Kyle shrugged apologetically.

The girl kept cursing him and everyone who had known him. Her slurs were almost laughable. But when she denigrated his sister, he snapped out his daze.

"Hold up there, bitch. Don't you say a fucking thing about my sister. And while we're on it, didn't you see me plowing down zombies? And you still came running at me like you did? Who's the stupid shitbag? It sure isn't me. Your friend's just lucky I missed his head and you're lucky he screamed or you'd both be dead right now."

"We thought you were here to save us, not kill us," she bawled.

Out of the corner of his eye, Kyle saw another group approaching. They were more cautious, having witnessed Kyle's reaction to the couple.

They were alive, Kyle noted, but that didn't mean they weren't a threat. He had shot their friend, after all.

"Kyle!" called a familiar voice from the crowd.

He knew that voice. "Laney!" he shouted back. The group parted like the Red Sea and his sister popped out. She bolted over and flew into his arms, squeezing him like he was a soldier returning from war.

"You made it!" she sighed.

"Of course I did, Laney," he answered, hugging her as tightly as she was him. "There was no way I could leave my little sister to a bunch of bloodthirsty zombies."

They let go of each other, but she took his hand and held it tightly. "How are Mom and Dad?" she asked.

Kyle started to tell her but the fellow on the ground groaned loudly and cursed.

"Do you think you sons of bitches could get me to a hospital or something? I'm bleeding to death over here."

A couple of people rushed over to him and pulled him to his feet. Two men took off their shirts and plugged the entrance and exit wounds with them. Then they half walked/carried him towards the door he'd seen from across the lot. A man inside pushed the door open, held it while everyone went through, then closed it behind them, making sure to lock it. As the wounded guy was helped to whatever medical facilities they had, Kyle watched some other students pile up a tremendous barricade against the door.

"Won't help," he called out to them. "Didn't at my house."

One of the men replied, "It's worked so far."

"Touche."

They led him to the main floor lobby, which was actually up on the second floor. They could look through massive windows onto the front lawn below. A single lookout perched in a corner of the lobby, keeping an eye out for anything of importance. A skinny, attractive girl, he noted. Thin cotton tanktop, no bra. Even in the heat of July, her nipples poked at the fabric. *She can't be cold. Must just be intent on her job.*

The rest of the group gathered around Kyle like a messiah, plopping down at his feet to hear what he had to say about the outside world. It made him feel a bit like a messiah, too. He'd never felt like that at any point of his teaching career. *Curious.*

He told them of Lafayette, Huntington, Indianapolis, the voice on the radio. He answered their questions as best he could and when he was done he asked for a drink of water.

"The water's off," someone said. "So is the electricity. That was the first thing to go."

"Yeah," someone else said, "I heard that some stupid intern down at the power plant got himself bit by a zombie, then killed everyone there before he managed to electrocute himself in a transformer. Shorted out the whole county, he did."

"You British?" Kyle asked him. Kyle was a bit of an Anglophile and whenever he ran into an Englishman, he would begin to act like one. It was unintentional but there it was.

Somebody in the crowd sniggered. "He ain't British, he's white trash Hoosier. He just likes to pretend he's high class."

The entire group chuckled. Kyle couldn't help but feel a smidgeon of pity for the guy. It was obvious he was an outsider, a low class fellow with aspirations of becoming someone better. Kyle could appreciate that and quickly took offense to their laughter.

"Shut your fucking mouths!" he commanded. The laughing stopped immediately, except for one character, but when Kyle marched over to him and puffed up his chest, the fellow shut up. Kyle was a good foot taller than the kid and when he saw Kyle meant business, he pretended to be distracted and looked away.

Elaine inserted herself into the drama. "My brother," she said, standing up, "teaches teenagers with emotional problems. He doesn't take kindly to bullying. He's very protective." She wrapped her arms around her brother and escorted him away from the group. In a loud voice, for the benefit of all who were listening, she told him, "If you want water, you'll have to go up to the third floor. That's where we have the water stored."

As she walked with him, she told him how they had arranged things in the first days of the outbreak.

"There was a paraplegic guy up there who was getting ready to take a bath when the power went out. Luckily, he didn't drain the tub or we would have all died of thirst a long time ago."

From the middle of the crowd behind them, someone corrected, "No, the lucky part is that they didn't do the plumbing right in this piece of shit dorm. All the water that was in the system has just been sitting there in the pipes. There's no more water available in the top four floors of the building. When we get down to basement level, we're screwed. I reckon we have about four more days at best."

Whoever it was that spoke sounded like they knew what they were talking about. The rest of the group murmured in agreement, trusting in their colleague's assessment.

"What have you been doing for food?" Kyle asked them, suddenly hungry.

A tall, brawny blonde man told him, "We're not hurting for food. The dorm kitchen was stocked the day before the attack. There is enough food in there to feed 800 people for a week and there are only about a dozen of us."

"Yeah but you're forgetting the fact that most of that food is in the freezer," someone sneered. "And every time we open that freezer we let a little bit more cold air out. Pretty soon that whole place is going to smell like a slaughterhouse in July."

"You mean like the parking lot right now?" a joker hollered out. Most of the group groaned. A few of the women complained how rude and immature the commenter was.

Before they vanished up a stairwell, Kyle peered out a window at the squirming mass of mutilated zombies writhing like worms towards the building. There were a ton of them. *All my handiwork* he thought proudly. It would take them quite a while to reach the dorm at worm speed but none of them were going to be able to get into the buildings anyway, so he dismissed them with a snort and followed his sister up to the third floor.

Later, when his thirst had been quenched and his hunger satisfied, he sat in the expansive lobby and took in the state of affairs. The front of the building was almost entirely glass. There was no security to speak of. They did not even have a barrier in front of the doors to keep any attackers out, except for the one that led to the parking lot.

"Oh my God!" Kyle wondered out loud. "Are you guys crazy? You've been living here in the midst of a zombie attack with no protection or anything? It's a wonder you haven't all been killed already."

The smart aleck in the group, the one with all the answers, piped up. "A couple of years ago they replaced all the glass with extra thick plexiglass. It was during the overhaul after the 9/11 scare. They called it an 'invisible safety feature.' There were other things they did, but those are secret. I seriously doubt that you could drive your truck through these windows. If you look close enough at the frame, you can tell that the glass is about two inches thick."

"Like two inches of plastic is going to stop the undead from getting to you," he chortled. Indiana was a world-class university but it wasn't really renowned for its engineering and technology programs. Besides, Kyle knew from some of the more public experiments and YouTube videos that two inches of plexiglass wasn't going to stop a bomb nor would it stop a hellbent terrorist from finding a way to get a large truck through them. But he also knew that if people perceived they were safe, they would go about their business, effectively taking the 'terror' out of terrorism. It was cheaper than actually putting up real, effective barriers and it even created jobs. It was a capitalist solution to a collective problem and it was very effective.

The sun was beginning to set when the group dispersed. Some people paired off as they headed for the various wings of the building. Commonsense told Kyle that they should've remained together on one floor as a way to protect themselves. There was strength in numbers. But Liberal Arts majors and Humanities people were not strategists. They didn't care about such things. They were idealists and dreamers who thought that if they wished hard enough, they could make the bad things in the world go away. Most of them were unwilling to give up even the smallest of comforts, such as their own bed in their own little dorm rooms in the face of overwhelming disaster. It made no sense to him. All he could do was shake his head as he watched people head up the stairs to their rooms.

Elaine was no different in that aspect. She was an art major, at least for the moment, because Kyle suspected that once she realized there was no money in art she would change her mind. She liked the finer things of life and vowed that she would never return to her parents' farm once she had a regular job. She was a city girl at heart and was civilized and elitist. So when she led him up to the fourth floor, where no one else seemed to be, he was more than a little miffed at her, but he knew better than to say anything to her.

Hers was a typical girl's room. It was decorated in pinks and purples and had lots of frilly stuff in it. Kyle had never met Elaine's roommate but he hoped that the frilly and lacy underwear draped on the furniture belonged to the roommate and not his sister. To him she would always be 15 years old, still a girl just on the cusp of becoming a woman. He did not want to think about her as a woman but one or two specific pieces of underwear implied the owner had a happy sex life.

She gestured toward a bean bag. Then she dug around in one of the large floor to ceiling closets that flanked the door, eventually producing two bottles of water. She handed one to Kyle and cracked the other one open for herself. She raised her bottle to him and made a toast. "Here's to my big brother coming to my rescue one more time. Cheers, big brother."

He tipped his bottle toward her then sucked down the whole thing at once. She took a few sips and put the lid back on. Then she climbed into one of the beds and lay on her side. She gathered a stuffed animal from its place on her pillow and mashed it to her chest.

"It's been so scary," she said in tiny voice. "Everything just went haywire. People started attacking each other. I didn't know what to do so I ran up here to my room and locked myself in. It was horrible." She closed her eyes tightly and stopped talking momentarily as the events of the last few days replayed in her head.

Kyle sat down next to her and put an arm around her. "I know," he said consolingly. "Lafayette was the same way. In fact, I had literally just met a girl and we were hitting it off really well and then all of a sudden she turned into a zombie and like, just took off. Then I had to kill a whole family…"

Elaine gasped.

"No, they were all zombies. Then I stole a car just so I could get back to my apartment without getting eaten. My whole apartment complex was drenched in blood and guts. It looks like someone just came in with a fire truck full of chum and sprayed it everywhere."

She stared at him, wide-eyed and slack jawed.

"You met a girl?"

He huffed in amazement. "That's what you take away from that? I killed a family, stole a car, my home looks like a slaughterhouse, not to mention the fact that Father and I offed the neighbors, and you stick on the 'met a girl' thing? Damn Laney, only you."

"Yeah, tell me about her," she said enthusiastically. He tried to deflect her but he knew it would be impossible, so after a few minutes of trying to tell her about the rest of the events leading up to his arrival on campus, he gave in and retold the whole sordid story.

"You bit her on the ass?" she grimaced. "Gag, too much detail," she said. "I don't want to hear the sex details, moron, just the good stuff."

"That is the good stuff," he replied indignantly.

"Not for your sister it isn't."

He skipped over the juicy parts of the story and answered her questions about April as bet he could. The more she asked, the more he realized that he knew nothing about the girl except that she was great in bed. He started to feel bad, like a scolded child, when she asked him why he didn't know certain things about her.

"If you really liked her for more than a toy, I'd think you would know this stuff," she commented innocently.

"Damn, Laney, you make me feel like a douche bag sometimes."

She shrugged, "Sometimes you are a douche bag."

He told her about his trip to Mother and Father's farm and the incident with the neighbors and then he told her about the soldiers on 465. She listened, sometimes with her eyes clamped shut and other times giggling wildly at the sheer incredulity of his tales. They were only funny because of the way he told the stories. She had always loved his stories. When they were younger, she would curl up on his bed and make him tell her a story every night before she went to her own room. That had been their nightly ritual until one night she went into his room later than normal and caught him pleasuring himself. She never came back after that and though they never talked about it, it was still there, like a white elephant, as far as he was concerned anyway. Who knew? Maybe she had forgotten the incident. He would never be able to. It was too embarrassing.

Anyway, she had the same sense of lowbrow humor as he did and so when he talked about things like the Mexican's brain popping out, she chuckled even though it made her sick to her stomach. To her it was just another of his gruesome bedtime fiction.

By the time he finished retelling his recent history, the sun was almost completely gone. That meant it was close to 10 p.m.

"I'm so tired," Elaine yawned. Kyle yawned too.

"Stop, you're making me yawn," he groaned. Then a thought came over him. "I don't suppose that you guys lock up the kitchen at night, do you?"

"No, we haven't had to ration yet, but some of the guys have started talking about it."

"Is there any security between here and there?" Kyle asked.

"Such as it is. They post one guy at each of the four entrances to the building at night. The doors are locked but the sentries are one landing up from them so they have the high ground if anyone tries to break in. So far we've been lucky. We've only had a few zombies try to get in, but none have been able to do more than crack open their skulls on the plexiglass. Luckily, they haven't figured out that all they have to do is break one of the windows in a first floor dorm room and they're in. We can't guard all those rooms, so we just blocked off that floor entirely. Apparently, the zombies don't see people down there so they just assume it's not worth the effort. That's why they stand outside in the parking lot and stare up at us. They have no clue how to get to us."

"Christ Almighty," Kyle moaned. He couldn't believe that they were so vulnerable. "We've got to get the heck out of here! Whatever you do, don't tell Mom or Dad about how unprotected you've been down here. You'll give them a heart attack."

Elaine snickered and yawned. "If a zombie attack by their neighbors doesn't kill them, nothing will. You going to get something to eat?"

Kyle thought about it and chuckled. She was probably right. "Yeah, want anything?"

"No thanks. Watching my weight."

Having worked in the kitchen of his dorm in college, he was familiar with the typical industrial layout and immediately discovered the walk-in freezer in Laney's kitchen.

He was surprised to find that the door handle was only locked with an ice pick, which he assumed was just to keep it closed. It took little effort to pull it out, but when he yanked the thick steel door back, he got the shock of his life.

Staring back at him was a tall man with wide eyes and gaunt face. Kyle yelped in surprise and nearly pissed his pants. In the instant before he slammed the door shut again, he was able to take in a perfectly detailed photographic memory of the man. He worked frantically to replace the ice pick before he realized that the chap was frozen and blue and therefore dead. He looked rather normal otherwise, not like he'd become a zombie before getting the Han Solo treatment.

He wondered if the guy had been bitten and chose that way out. *He must have asked them to freeze him to death so he couldn't finish turning. Suicide.*

The shock was enough to cause Kyle to forgo any nice dinner he might have planned for himself. Instead, he took three apples from a bag on a counter, though he didn't believe he would actually be interested in eating anything for quite a while.

He found his way back up to Elaine's room and lay down in the unoccupied bunk, which smelled of lavender, and tried to go to sleep. After an hour he managed to relax enough to drift off.

CHAPTER 15

By the time Kyle and his sister reached the cafeteria the next morning, the rest of the group was already eating elegant breakfasts of steaks and eggs along with multiple refrigerated desserts. Although he didn't bother to ask, Kyle guessed that none of the food was coming from the walk in freezer.

A young Indian man stood up after Kyle and Elaine had filled their plates and taken a spot at one of the two tables nearest the serving line. He raised his hands above his head and waved them back and forth and whistled until everybody was paying attention to him.

"Friends, Romans, countrymen—lend me your ears," he shouted. Everyone but Kyle laughed.

"Why is that funny?" Kyle asked his sister softly.

"He's an English major. Who knows?" she replied in an equally quiet tone.

"It seems like it has been forever since this horrible outbreak began," he started, "but it's hard to believe that less than three weeks ago we were all going about our daily life worrying about midterms or job interviews or whatever else was going on in our lives. Now we're in the midst of the End of the World and it was looking pretty bad there for a while. But now a Savior has come." He paused and gestured toward Kyle. The group clapped politely and someone cheered once for him, then the Indian went on. "I just think it would be great for everyone to take a moment to say a proper goodbye to each other before we pile into Mr. Williams's truck and head for home. Chances are that some or all of us will never return to our beloved alma mater, so I think it would be a fitting gesture."

There was general agreement, but Kyle thought it was ridiculous. He shook his head but said nothing. Some people needed emotional outlets.

"I think it would be better if we all stood up one at a time right now and did it," added the young man, "so that we can all be ready to go that much faster."

"Gay!" someone coughed. Someone else threw a sausage at him. In the span of three seconds he went from clean laundered young man to a slimy pile of food. Disgusted but surprisingly accepting of his fate, the young man grimaced and bore it. He nodded his head and said, "Fine. I just thought it would be nice for us to know who we've been hanging out with, whom we managed to survive this terrible dark night with."

Kyle was never much one for fanfare. He hated all manner of pomp and circumstance. That might sound a little strange for a high school teacher since they were generally perceived as people who thrived on that type of stuff, but Kyle was somewhat the rebel in that regard.

He gobbled down a good solid breakfast, then stood up in the middle of a speech being delivered by a sorority-type girl who thought the Indian's idea was good. "Well, I don't know how I became the bus," he said, "but seeing as how I'm driving and I have to be back at work in a few weeks, then I guess as soon as my sister is done eating the bus is leaving. I don't care who's on it except for her. So when she's ready to go, we're out of here." He shot Elaine a wicked smile. She popped a piece of top sirloin in her mouth and washed it down with a glass of milk.

"I'm done," she announced smartly, shooting back her own wicked grin at her brother.

Shocked and dumbfounded, everyone in the room stared at Kyle. Joking? Maybe? Hopefully?

But when Elaine got up from the table and slapped her palms together twice and raised her hands above her head to signify that she really was done, they decided it was not the time to risk it. Some of them choked down the rest of their food as fast as they could. Others grabbed handfuls and ran out of the cafeteria like their asses were on fire.

"Can we bring anything with us?" one boy asked calmly as he finished his breakfast.

A sinking feeling came over Kyle as he stared at the nerdy little guy. These people were as bad as the teenagers he taught on a daily basis. They were going to pester him over every little detail until he gave them an answer. He guessed it was better to set the stage now than later.

"I don't care how you work it out but when I hit the gas, that's it." Then he looked up at the clock over the entrance to the dining room and announced to the entire group, "Forty five minutes and the bus rolls out of here with or without you."

Those who were still left in the room dashed out in a mad rush to pack up their stuff before the truck left.

"You're such an asshole sometimes," Elaine laughed. "You know I'm not going to be ready that fast. Why did you tell them that?"

Kyle made his point by waving his arms around the empty room. "If I tell them forty five minutes, every single guy will be at the back door bashing his way through the zombies in twenty minutes or less. None of the women will make it on time but they'll be screaming out the windows for one more minute. It will take them an hour and a half to get all gussied up and get all their shit together and another fifteen minutes to drag it out to the parking lot. That's two hours. Do you think you can be ready to go in two hours?" he asked knowingly.

She punched his shoulder. "You think you know me that well, don't you? Well you don't. You don't know what I went through the last few days. My fiancé turned into a…" she broke off her statement in midsentence. Her face went ashen.

"You're what went what?" Kyle inquired. Elaine bit her lower lip. She sighed deeply and lunged toward her brother.

She gripped him tightly and sobbed into his chest, "You heard me." As near as he could tell, the rest of the conversation went something like this: Elaine's fiancé turned into a zombie. She didn't get to kiss him goodbye or anything. She was supposed to meet him after class at some little grassy area outside some building but he never showed up. She couldn't find him anywhere. The whole time the zombies were eating people and killing everyone. And then he showed up at the front doors of her dorm, dead, trying to get in. It was horrible. He was all blue and purple and looked like he just crawled out of a storm drain.

Kyle didn't know what to say, so he just held her. Experience had taught him that was usually the best course of action when dealing with upset women—just listen, don't speak.

Then she suddenly stopped crying and stared him directly in the eye. "Not only did he become one of them, but the worst part is that you ran over him when you showed up here yesterday. I watched from the window. You hit him head-on and he stuck to the grill." She burst into tears again.

Kyle's jaw dropped open. "Aw shit, Laney, you've got to be kidding!" She wasn't.

"Jesus, Laney!" he gasped. He tried to apologize but she stopped him.

"Just don't say anything," she said, putting a finger to his lips. "You probably did me a favor but I don't really want to talk about it anymore. I don't think they're too many people in this world that didn't lose somebody. There's no need to discuss it. We just have to get on with life. At least I know that my family is safe."

She burst into tears again and like a good big brother should, in times of crisis, he held her tightly and let her cry it out.

"I'm so sorry," he repeated. If he had known who the kid was…" He didn't know how to finish that sentence. What could he say? "I might have been a bit gentler when prying his head loose from the grill?" No, there was nothing to say that could make it any better.

"No way you could have known," she whimpered with a hitch in her voice.

She cried for a solid five minutes, then took a deep breath and wiped her eyes. "Okay, goddamit, I'm done crying. Let's get you a new shirt and get the hell out of here."

Exactly two hours later Elaine was ready to leave, just like her brother had predicted. Also just like his prediction, all the men were ready to go way before that and had cleared a path from the dorm to the truck. They used shovels and rakes to dispatch the crippled undead that had gathered at the doors. Most of them were the ones that Kyle had run over the day before, so they were still crawling on their bellies, but there were a few others—walkers—from somewhere else.

He didn't like what the walkers represented. "Smoke and fire," he muttered. Where there were a few, there were surely others.

Where there were new zombies, the group of men surrounded them like wolves around a sick lamb and bashed them to pulp.

Kyle watched the gory festivities from a hallway window in the elevator lobby on Elaine's floor. It was much like watching a Jackie Chan movie he thought, where Jackie was surrounded by bad guys and had to kick and punch his way to safety. The zombies, playing the part of the bad guys, never stood a chance. They took their fatal beatings and slumped to the ground, never to rise again.

When the battlefield was relatively still, one of the college boys came and asked if Kyle would loan him the keys so that he could bring the truck around to the front entrance.

"It will make things easier," he suggested. Of course Kyle refused, but not because he was afraid that one of them would try to escape without bringing the rest of them along, but because he couldn't. He was still using the hotwire method to start the engine. If any of those college boys had looked closely enough, they would have seen that not only were the doors unlocked but the ignition wires hung down from the steering column. As the kid who asked for the keys wandered away, cursing under his breath at Kyle, Kyle shook his head disapprovingly and muttered under his own breath. "Stupid college kids. Think they know everything but can't see the forest for the trees."

When Elaine was finally ready to go, Kyle had her wait at the front door while he brought the truck around himself. The handful of men who had taken it upon themselves to act as sentries in case of further attack walked out to the truck and piled into the back.

It only took a few minutes to load everyone up. The Indian man had drawn up a map and a driving plan for Kyle so that he knew which roads to take and who they were dropping off first.

"Turns out we had a lot of time, waiting for your sister," he sneered suggestively. Impressed by the man's organizational skills but not his attitude, Kyle took the map in hand and studied it for a few minutes. He had not anticipated having to drive around what appeared to be the entire central portion of the state before heading home. He had only come to save his sister, not the world. And as he looked at the spiderweb on the map he began to wonder just what he had gotten himself into.

"So I'm supposed to start here at the center of this crap and drive like this?" he asked, tracing the path around the map. "And then we end up right back here before heading north? And then we're supposed to go all over Indy?"

The Indian nodded, proud that he had done such a wonderful job of organizing the trip.

"This isn't going to work," Kyle shook his head.

"Why not?" the Indian asked indignantly.

"Well, you haven't seen Indianapolis have you? I have," Kyle replied smugly. "The National Guard has everything inside 465 roped off. They're going from house to house, neighborhood to neighborhood doing cleanup, if you follow me. There is no way any of us are going to get off this truck inside the Circle."

The Indian started to say something but Kyle cut him off. "You can either get on the truck or you can stay here and find your own way home, but I'm leaving and that's the end of the argument. Whoever it is that has to go downtown Indianapolis can get dropped off at 465 and make their own decision about whether they want to continue or not. But you'll see what I mean when we get there, so stop arguing with me and get in the truck. Or don't, I really don't give a shit." With that, he climbed up on the tailgate and started to pull the door down. The Indian jumped up on the bumper and crawled inside the truck before the door banged shut.

They cruised through the southern half of the state, dropping people off as indicated by the map. By the time they returned to Bloomington there were only about three people left. Along the way, Kyle and Elaine caught up on their personal lives.

Elaine talked about her fiancé, the things that she loved about him as well as his quirks. And she told him how school had been going and how she finally settled upon one specific career. "Bet you thought you'd never hear that, huh?" she grinned slyly.

"No, I figured you'd end up as some artist or something, floating from job to job just to pay for your canvases."

She went on until there was no more to tell and then she asked Kyle about his life. She wanted to know specifically how teaching was.

"I never thought you'd end up as a teacher," she told him. "I guess I always thought you would end up as some sort of professional athlete with a crap load of endorsements, a huge house, a trophy wife and perfect little children. Oh, and a big pool in the back yard. In-ground, of course."

"What in the world would have made you think that?"

"Life was always easy for you," she said jealously. "You were always the big stud athlete, the great student, and always had women crawling all over you." With a flourish she added, "Women want you and men want to be you."

She idolizes me. The revelation came as an epiphany to him. There were eight years between them and he had always seen her as a little girl, but now he saw her in a new light. When he was a senior in high school her little friends were always around making googoo eyes at him, but he never took notice of any of them. They were all still built like little boys. But Elaine had been paying attention. She had been paying attention and keeping score. She resented his popularity even though she herself was just as popular and pretty and smart as he was.

By the time he was in college and beginning his teaching career he wasn't around her enough to make an impression on her friends, but she had still kept score even then. He had no idea that even after he left the house, she still felt like she was living in his shadow. He knew that he was good looking and that women were easy—if you just acted like you didn't need or want them— and that's how he managed to outdo his male friends. He knew some of them were jealous of his success with women. He just didn't know that his sister was also jealous of his success—his general success with life, that is. It made him feel bad, but at the same time he now had a newfound understanding of his sister.

"I'm not that good looking," he said, trying not to smile. "Well, I am that good looking but I never thought that other people actually saw me that way."

She frowned at him. "Oh you're so full of crap. You know you're hot. All my friends ever talked about was 'oh your brother is so hot I just want to jump him' or how they'd like to do nasty things to you, with you, or for you. It was disgusting. I hated it so much, even though it made me popular. But now that I'm older and nobody knows who you are down here, I was just beginning to feel like myself, like I had an identity of my own, and now the world comes to an end and everything just totally sucks and then to top it all off, you come swooping in like a knight in shining armor to save all my new friends. Life's just not fair for some people."

Kyle's jaw dropped open. He was at a loss for words.

Then, as an afterthought, Elaine added, "I really should be pissed at you for killing my fiancé."

"Whoa!" he exclaimed. "I thought you said you *weren't* upset about that. You said I was doing you a favor by killing him. Remember, he was already dead when I killed him, and it's not like I knew who he was. He didn't jump up and say, 'Hey dude, I'm your sister's fiancé. Please let me eat your brains.' If I had known which one was your fiancé, I never would've run him over. You're my baby sister and I love you and I would never do anything to intentionally hurt you. You have to know that."

She crossed her arms and looked out the window. "I do. I'm just very upset about the way my life is turning out right now. I was finally going to get that Hallmark greeting card sort of life that I thought you had."

He snorted at that. "My life is *not* that great," he huffed. "I get so obsessed with stuff that I can't live a normal life. My credit is so crappy that I will probably never be able to buy a new car or a house because I can't remember to pay the damn bills on time. I can't tell you how many of my school loan payments I've missed just because I never open the bill when it comes. It's not that I'm lazy. It's that I spend all my time grading, coaching, or writing. And to be perfectly honest I only have one good friend and he got eaten on the first day of the Lafayette outbreak."

It felt like there was something important that needed to be added to that statement but his brain wouldn't let it pass his lips. He wasn't sure exactly what it was but in the back of his mind something was there. Maybe he just couldn't admit it to himself or anyone else, even Elaine, that he really did know something more about Brad's death.

"There's more," he said, his mouth suddenly going so dry that he had to lick his lips. *Is it going to come out?* "But I don't want to change your impression of me. I like the way you think of me as a good person. So let's just leave it at this, I'm not as good a person as you think. You're better than me and if anyone ever disagrees, I'll have to pound them."

There was an awkward moment of silence before she leaned across the bench seat and kissed him on the cheek. "This is getting to be too much like an after-school special or something," she said. "So let's change the subject, shall we Joe Dirt?"

"Yeah let's," he laughed, writhing and groaning as if he were making love to someone. "You're my sister!"

"I'm your sister!" she repeated before bursting into laughter. There was nothing like a Joe Dirt reference to send them both into hysterical laughter. It was definitely low brow humor, but they both loved those kinds of movies and Joe Dirt was their favorite.

They dropped off another person along 37 as they headed north toward Indy, leaving just two fellows in the back of the truck. The National Guard troops were still there and they greeted the truck with hoops and hollers. They knew what the truck's return meant and they had nothing to do during the stretch of time Kyle had been in Bloomington but build up Elaine to Goddess status.

"What the heck is all the fuss?" Elaine queried her brother as the truck slowed to a stop.

"Oh, that," Kyle grumbled, aware that it was now time to pay the piper. "I had to show them a picture of you to get them to let me through and they all apparently fell in love with you." He waited for her to chew him out but was surprised to see a bit of a smile creep across her face. She was flattered by the sight of a half dozen strange men cheering for her from just a single photo.

"Stay here a minute," he told her as he put the shifter into Park. He climbed out of the truck and wandered tentatively over to the soldiers. Elaine watched intently as her brother talked to the men, wondering what he was telling them. Every one of them had come running over to Kyle and as near as she could tell, every one of them was grinning like an idiot. They stole glances at the truck, trying to pick out Elaine. They were all alpha males, so by their reckoning, eye contact counted as consent.

Kyle pointed at the truck, the city, and back towards Bloomington a few times. The head soldier made nearly the same gestures, but he wasn't smiling anymore. He shook his head a few times as he gestured toward downtown Indy.

A few minutes later, the entire squad approached the truck. Her brother came to the passenger's side of the truck and opened her door. The squad leader brushed past him and thrust out his hand.

"Nice to meet you, Miss," he said ever so politely. Elaine smiled and took his hand. She climbed down from the truck and he escorted her, hand in hand, toward the back of the truck, making small talk. Kyle followed behind like an overprotective third wheel. They had guns on them. His was in the truck.

This could end badly.

At the back of the truck, the squad leader commanded one of his colleagues to raise the lift gate and help anyone left back there to get out. Once the door was open, however, the soldiers discovered that there were just two college boys and they lost all interest in the truck. They didn't bother to help the two men but it didn't matter anyway. The two men thanked the soldiers and chucked their duffel bags to the ground then climbed out under their own power. They hadn't expected any other type of treatment from male soldiers.

Everyone's attention turned back to Elaine as they drifted toward the front of the truck. They were all in predator mode: They were sure Elaine would see through their leader's bullshit and figure out which of them was the real catch. Like peacocks fanning out their beautiful feathers, the soldiers puffed themselves up to look more important. They overemphasized every movement and word. The key for soldiers was to look heroic and at the moment they were as heroic as they could possibly be.

Kyle's last two passengers were shocked to see the destruction of their hometown. They glided towards it, enthralled and saddened by the pillars of smoke rising from the skyline. Here and there they could see tiny, bright licks of fire curling into the atmosphere.

"Son of a…" one of them whispered.

The other could only agree. "Yeah."

To Kyle, things hadn't changed much since he had driven through it just yesterday. The only thing he did notice was that one of the taller apartment buildings, one of at least twenty stories, was burning out of control. It looked like a giant torch burning in the heart of the city.

One of the students asked Kyle, "Is this what you meant when you said we wouldn't be able to get back in?"

Kyle nodded. The squad leader overheard the man's question and assumed a defensive posture.

"Sorry sir, but nobody goes back in the city. As you can see, the city has not yet been completely cleared of zombies and anyone who goes in is not likely to come out alive. It's for your protection." He enunciated every word so clearly and precisely that Kyle became painfully aware of how intent the men were to impress his sister.

"But my family lives downtown," the college boy returned. "What am I supposed to do?"

The soldier shrugged his shoulders and unsympathetically answered, "If your parents were downtown at the start of the outbreak they might've gotten out okay, but if they didn't get out right at the beginning then chances are your parents are dead or worse."

Though he said it without emotion, there was a look of sorrow on his face that implied that he had lost someone important himself. Who hadn't? Even Kyle had not escaped unscathed. He'd lost his best friend and a potential love interest. Silently, he counted his blessings that his family was still alive.

The other college boy shrugged and picked up his duffel bag, turning back toward Bloomington. Elaine called after him as he marched off.

"Where you going?" she yelled.

The man shrugged and kept walking, but glanced over his shoulder and yelled, "I always wanted to see the world, I guess now is as good a time as any to start. I guess I'm off to Machu Picchu." He smiled confidently and turned away. There was a slight bounce in his step, Kyle noted.

Kyle envied the kid. *Now that's freedom.*

All he wanted was to get back to his little cubbyhole in Lafayette and write stories. All he ever wanted was to write stories. He wanted to have a book in the Library of Congress just so that he could have his assigned LOCC number tattooed on his arm.

As they watched the guy saunter down the road, the other student was getting more upset. He was walking in circles, pounding his head with his palms and moaning and groaning. Though Kyle wasn't sure if the man was frustrated or just beside himself with grief, it was plain to see that he was about to explode. It was like watching a train rolling inexorably toward a stalled car on the tracks. You could see it coming from a mile away but you couldn't stop it.

The whole time the man was growing more frantic, the squad leader was busy trying to get Elaine's phone number. He was really chatting her up. Kyle's gaze drifted from the soldier to the enraged young man and then back to his sister again. Either situation was interesting but for wildly different reasons.

Right about then the upset guy let out a mangled roar and bolted towards downtown. Immediately, the soldiers responded to him as a threat. The squad leader broke free from his trance and started yelling at him to stop, as did the others. But the sentries stationed on the other side of the interstate who had not been privy to the conversation were unaware of what was happening. They spun around to see someone rushing towards them in the shadow of the overpass and their fellow soldiers screaming at him. They assumed he was a zombie attacking from the rear and opened fire.

Bloody mist sprayed from the top of the crazed man's head as bullets ripped holes through his skull. The bullets missed the motor control center of his brain and his body kept moving forward even though his consciousness had fled its mortal container. The same sentry who hit him the first time flipped his rifle to automatic and peppered him with bullets. The college boy took a few more steps and then collapsed, hitting the ground with a sickening thud.

"Godammit!" the squad leader hollered. "No one gave the order to fire!" He took off in a half run, screaming at his men, leaving Kyle and Elaine staring after him.

Kyle leaned over and quietly told his sister, "I think it's time we get out of here."

Shocked, she nodded in agreement. They slipped into the truck and fired it up. The squad leader was so engrossed in the moment that he didn't really notice the diesel motor fire up, nor did he notice when they drove up the on-ramp and headed east. There was no sentry at the top of the ramp as the one there had pulled to the opposite side to defend his comrades.

They drove around 465 in silence. Specifically, Elaine was silent. From her outward appearance, she seemed to have assimilated everything in stride. But she stared emotionlessly across him at downtown

Indianapolis. She took in the smoke and the occasional fires as if they were something that she saw on a daily basis. She made no comments, she passed no judgments, she just stared.

He reached over and patted her leg. "I know it sounds cliché, but everything is going to turn out okay." He was afraid to take his eyes off the road for fear of running into something or driving off the road surface, but he wouldn't have looked at her even if he could have. It wasn't his way. Whenever something emotional came up that needed to be discussed, he generally stared into the distance so that he wouldn't have to face the other person. As long as he avoided eye contact, nothing affected him. He remained coolly detached. Plus, he wasn't sure that he was telling the truth. He couldn't swear that things were going to be alright. Elaine knew when he was lying.

His sister was a bright girl and she knew his behaviors well, so she just nodded silently. Besides, she wasn't really interested in rehashing anything that had happened in the last few days. She was sure Kyle had lived through equally horrendous events. She saw no point in commiserating. The fight ahead would be just as rough as it had been to this point, so why dwell on it? She was going back to the farm—a place where her father and brother could protect her and where her Mother would provide all the comfort she needed to make it through the coming dark days.

When they drew closer to the intersection of I-69 and 465, Kyle told her what to expect. "We're going to have to talk our way through the soldiers the same as we did with the others. Hopefully the same guy that let me onto the interstate won't be here because he was all gonzo for you and we may never get away. After that, we have to wander our way through a bunch of wrecks and there are a bunch of dead bodies in there, so you should prepare yourself for that. But after that it's pretty much smooth sailing until we get home. We've got plenty of food and drinks and probably enough gas to get home, so I don't plan to stop anywhere."

It went just as Kyle said. The soldiers wanted to inspect the back of the truck and make sure they weren't looting anything or transporting any zombies. The guy who was interested in Elaine was in fact on duty and greeted Kyle with a salute and a smile.

"I really didn't think you'd make it back alive," he grinned. "I sure didn't think you'd make it back with your sister. Congratulations, sir."

Kyle shrugged and saluted him back. "We do for our own, right? And I have to thank you for making the roads safe for us. I don't think I could've made it all the way around Indianapolis if you guys hadn't been protecting the highway. My hat's off to you guys and I hope that you and all of your family members will be safe too. Godspeed!"

The head soldier tried to make time with Elaine but she cut him off. She held up her hand and pointed to her engagement ring. The smile melted from his face. "Oh," he said, dismissing them with a wave. "You're free to go. Good luck." He shot Kyle an angry glance.

Kyle shrugged. "I didn't know."

They drove down the single lane through the rubble. There were fresh bodies littering the path and as the truck bumped over the occasional limb or torso, it rocked from side to side. Kyle tried to make it a smooth ride by driving over them like they were speed bumps. Each time he hit one, he checked his to see if Elaine would disintegrate into tears but to his surprise, she instead burst into laughter.

"What's so funny?" he inquired as the truck thumped and bumped its way over putrefying corpses.

"Oh nothing," she giggled. "I shouldn't be laughing but for some reason the whole thing is just funny now."

He started to chuckle a little bit too. "Are you going to share? I could use something pretty funny right about now."

"Well, you'll think I'm really twisted," she started.

"I thought that a long time ago," he smiled. "Remember, I've lived with you since you were a baby. I know the crazy Elaine better than anybody." She was still in shock. It was obvious.

"I guess that's true. Okay fine, just remember you asked for it," she taunted. "There was one fat-ass bloated corpse back there on my side of the road and I knew you were going to hit it. I just knew you couldn't avoid it. You probably hit it on purpose, but when you nailed it, it exploded and slimy crap shot all over the car next to it. It was like smashing tomato worms with our bikes. Oh my God! It was so disgusting!" Then she started giggling again, which turned into a real belly laugh, and finally she roared loudly for several minutes. When she finally calmed down enough to go on with the story she looked over to see his reaction.

Kyle was thoroughly lost. "How is that funny?" he asked, repeating himself until she finally sighed heavily and stopped laughing.

"It's funny because the splatter of slime on the car looked exactly like that painting you made in the eighth grade of your little girlfriend at the time. It just cracked me up!" And then she burst into a new round of laughter that lasted for another several minutes.

"WTF Elaine!" Kyle took offense to her comment. He recalled that picture. He did it all in red paint with a wide brush and what he thought was to be a wonderful tribute to the beauty of his thirteen year old love turned out to look more like a portrait of the creature from the Black Lagoon than anything else. Everyone in the class laughed at him and for the rest of the year they called his girlfriend "The Creature" and hounded her mercilessly. Of course he was mortified and she would have nothing to do with him after that. But still he took that picture home and hung it on the inside of his closet door, where he thought it was hidden from the world and where he could enjoy it secretly. He should have known better since his sister liked to go into his closet after his shirts. She wore more of his shirts to school than he did. Unfortunately, although at the time she was too young to fathom his connection to the picture, she found it so scary that she painted a SpongeBob SquarePants over the top of it.

"I loved that picture and you ruined it!" he sniveled.

She laughed at him. "It was the scariest thing I'd ever seen. I was always afraid it was going to come to life and eat me. Spongebob kept me from having nightmares about it." He wrinkled up his face in anger, but it was a little funny. Soon they were both laughing about it. It felt good to laugh.

CHAPTER 16

Because the farm was so isolated, it was easy to slip back into their old lives and August quickly passed the Williams by. It was just the four of them in their old routines, living life as if the rest of the world never existed. Father milked the cow and Kyle fed the other animals. The women did housework and the cooking and when everything was done they spent their free time playing euchre or sitting on the porch reading and sleeping. The only thing that really even reminded them of the sorry state of the world was the deep trench around the property line and even that had come to be a normal part of the daily routine. They never found any zombies and rarely did they find anything else, even rabbits or coyotes, in it either.

Life had become so idyllic that soon Kyle began to enjoy his life again. He had no desire to go back to work, nor to his hermetic life as a writer in a cramped apartment. He even began to wish for the world to stay as it was– quiet and peaceful. If the outside world never again intruded upon his beautiful little life he would be fine with that. He knew that was probably a pipe dream, since there would eventually be more zombies fanning farther out into the countryside in search of food. That meant that sooner or later they would see waves of the undead.

Even though Father did not care to have the TV or the radio hooked up, he did help Kyle one morning to reconnect the house cable to the one that ran up their TV tower. It had been damaged a few years ago when a tornado rolled through and cut the line with a random piece of flying debris. Father had no use for television once "Frasier" went off the air so he had never bothered to fix it. Everything they got came through the small rabbit ears that sat atop the TV, but since all the closest local stations were gone now, they'd have to reach a little further to get a signal. It was only when Elaine sweet talked him into it did he bother to make the repair.

"Don't forget to look around while you're up there and check to see that none of those dead bastards are running around nearby."

"Yes, Dad," Kyle moaned. The bit of broken cable was only about thirty feet up the fifty foot tower, but it was high enough for him to look out over a good deal of the surrounding countryside. It was also just high enough up to make Kyle nervous.

When he arrived at the broken end of the cable, he noted a plume of smoke rising into the sky from the general direction of town.

"Bad sign," he said, not quite loudly enough for Father to hear him clearly.

"Huh?" Father shouted back.

"Nothing. Just smoke coming up from town, is all."

"Damn," Father muttered, crestfallen. That meant the zombies were still nearby.

There was nothing to be done about it, so Kyle set about repairing the line. When it was done, he squirreled down the tower and went in to check the set.

There was only one channel broadcasting and surprisingly, it was out of Kokomo. The Williams' household was at the edge of that station's broadcast signal and even though the tower was just tall enough to receive it, it was still quite a fuzzy picture.

Normally, the station showed reruns of sitcoms and played local sporting events such as college basketball or football, but in the midst of a global crisis, the station had begun to run hour-long news broadcasts in the morning, at lunch, and in the evening. Between news, they still ran I Love Lucy and The Brady Bunch and various other oldies, but the news thing was new. They never ran news on that channel. It was the anti-news channel. That's how they got an audience.

Unbeknownst to Kyle and his family, the reason the Kokomo station ran any news at all was because all the stations in Indianapolis had been overrun by hordes of hungry corpses. Just like the Lafayette channel, the news had literally eaten itself. Only word-of-mouth reports from various reporters who bravely, or stupidly depending on your point of view, managed to sneak their way past the National Guard and reconnoiter downtown with small hand-held cameras and voice recorders.

The Kokomo station showed some of those clips but most of the reporting was actually replays of the national news which was broadcast from Chicago, New York and Washington. Officials thought they had finally begun to get the better of the outbreak. With the help of all branches of the military and civil services they were able to enforce a curfew that slowed down the spread of the infestation and then they went from door to door clearing individual problems.

The CDC published their best guess solution for stemming the spread of the disease but it was to no one's surprise that it involved staying clear of other people's bodily fluids and washing one's hands. That was their answer to everything: soap. They also claimed that the time of transformation from healthy adult to the walking undead varied from person to person. Some people turned within minutes while others took up to a week.

"Whoa, that means you're still not clean," Kyle teased his sister.

She punched him in the shoulder and spat back, "Neither are you, dirtbag."

"Ouch, I'm hurt," he teased.

Another week went by. More reports came in that indicated the worst was over. The announcer claimed, "Although there are still reports of new zombie outbreaks occurring all over the globe, here in America the problem seems to be slowing. Authorities believe that within a month life may begin to return to some form of normal. Of course, people are being urged to follow the new guidelines regarding handling of the dead, though they read like something out of a horror movie and not normal daily life." The announcer went on to explain the procedures but Kyle only half listened. He got the gist of it—leave them where they dropped and burn the body and whatever they were touching.

That night as they were sitting on the porch, weapons across their laps, Kyle repeated the announcer's prediction.

"In another month, we'll all be able to go back to our normal lives," he said. Father and Mother nodded slightly but Elaine burst into tears. She still hadn't told her parents about her fiancé and his dreadful ending. Kyle knew that's why she started bawling.

Politely, Mother asked her what was wrong, to which she mumbled something unintelligible.

"Darling, I can't understand you," Mother prompted with a subtly irritated tone.

Elaine mumbled something not unlike Pidgin English. Mother shook her head and repeated, "I still didn't get it, sweetheart. What's the matter?"

Kyle could take it no longer.

"I ran over her fiancé when I went to pick her up the other day. He was a zombie, though, and I didn't know he was her fiancé."

Stunned, both parents stared dumbly at Kyle, then Elaine. Neither knew where to start. Finally, it was Father who said something.

"Why didn't you tell us sooner?" he said softly.

"I don't know Daddy," she sobbed back. Then she burst into tears again. Father got up from his chair and hugged her tightly.

While Father was comforting his daughter, there came a noise in the night that caught their attention. Something was scraping the gravel in the road. Immediately, Kyle stood up and readied his rifle. He looked through the scope in the direction of the noise but it was too dark to see anything.

"Don't suppose you have a night scope around here, do you Dad?"

Father pointed at the scope on his gun, which he'd laid on the floor by his chair.

"Figures," Kyle smirked. "You gave me the cheapo gun."

"What's the matter, son?" Father sneered, "Eyes ain't what they used to be?"

Kyle shook his head. "You can't see any farther than I can."

While they were busy ribbing each other, they heard the noise again, but closer. This time there was much more gravel, more scraping, more crunching. It sounded as if there were many feet coming their direction.

Mother stood up slowly clutching her rifle in one hand. She looked like John Wayne for a moment, the way she stood so self assured. No one alive, dead, or undead would ever take her or any of hers. She would see to that.

"Elaine," she said coolly, "you can go back in the house if you want. Me and the boys'll take care of this." But Elaine was having none of it.

She had a great deal of anger towards the undead for ruining her life and this was the time to take some vengeance. She grabbed up her rifle, jumped off the porch and ran into the darkness toward the approaching horde.

She reached the moat in seconds and stopped cold in her tracks. She could smell them now. The stink of death grew as they came towards her. Silhouettes loomed out of the dark. They were definitely human.

"Time to die, you fuckers," she hollered at them, raising the butt of her gun to her shoulder. Father was instantly at her side. He squeezed her shoulder firmly and commanded, "Let me do the talking. Don't shoot till I say." Then he called out to the people on the other side of the trench.

"Hello out there! Are you alive or dead?"

They stopped moving but did not answer.

"I'm going to count to five," said Father sternly, "and if you don't answer by the time I get to five we're going to start shooting. And I have to tell you, we have two rifles and two shotguns and we don't miss." Still there was no answer so Father began to count.

"One...two...three...four..." Father paused an extra moment, then loudly instructed his family, "I'm going to fire one shot up into the air. Keep an eye. If you see zombies in the flash, open fire."

Elaine responded determinedly, "Okay. Fire away Dad."

"Okay, here we go," Father replied. "Five!" He fired into the air. The flash from the muzzle momentarily lit up everything within thirty feet. It was immediately obvious that their visitors were in fact zombies. Kyle counted six rotting, pockmarked, staring corpses before the light was gone. One of them had a missing jaw. Kyle could see the zombie's tongue dangling down the front of his neck.

The monsters, who had been navigating by scent, suddenly sighted fresh meat in the bright blasts and advanced toward them, unaware of the moat. Two of them fell in even as they took bullets to the chest. Kyle and his family kept firing until they could see no more of the rotten bastards standing.

Kyle then stepped to the edge of the ditch to finish off the two down there, one of which was the zombie with no jaw. But the recoil from firing nearly straight down caused Kyle to lose his balance and one foot slipped out from under him. Down he went, into the ditch.

"Oh shit!" he screamed as he fell. It seemed forever before he hit the bottom of the trench, but the zombie was immediately upon him, ripping at his shirt. It clawed at him, but Kyle rolled away from its grip like he was on fire, got to his feet and started to run away. He was no more than a dozen steps down the moat when he heard a shotgun blast and saw a flash of light. Stunned and deafened, he jumped into the air, froze, and fell stupidly to the dirt. Instinctively, he jumped up again and ran the entire length of the ditch, only stopping when he literally hit the corner.

He turned back to face the oncoming terror, fully expecting to be face to face with the damn thing, but there was only the dark.

His ears rang from the noise of the last shotgun blast still reverberating in his ears. Eventually that went away and he began to hear crickets chirping in the night.

"Kyle! Kyle! Where are you!" he heard his father calling excitedly. He sounded far away.

"Down here," Kyle yelled back. "Hurry, come help me out of here! Quick!" He had no idea where the zombie was, or if there were more in the darkness. With every passing second, his fear grew exponentially.

Father kept yelling as he approached. "Don't worry," he shouted. "I blasted the other sucker good! He won't be bothering you! Okay?"

That was quite a relief, but it still didn't completely assuage his fear. For all they knew, the rest of the undead posse might have crawled into the moat. They might be coming for him this very moment and neither he nor the rest of his family would know it until it was too late.

Heavy footsteps approached but Kyle couldn't tell if they were the footsteps of the jawless fiend coming for him or his father up above. Just to make sure he was the only thing moving around down there, he fired a shot along the ditch. Unfortunately, he hadn't warned his father before he fired. There was an almost simultaneous blast from up above, followed by a string of curses.

"Jesus boy!" Father shouted after his heart started beating again. "You nearly gave me a heart attack! What the hell did you do that for?"

"Just making sure," he replied.

Father's face appeared above him and his hand stretched down. "Don't trust me?" he asked as he pulled his son up from the black hole.

"Don't trust them to stay dead, more like," Kyle replied.

They left the zombies in the ditch till morning and went back to the house. Only after another hour or two of setting on the porch in absolute silence did they all begin to believe they were safe once more. The women went in the house and readied themselves for bed.

"Hmmm," Kyle heard his sister say, "Looks like I got a little something on me."

Kyle and his father panicked. They ran inside to see what she was talking about.

"Shew," Father sighed. "Just looks like dirt."

"Thank God," Mother said, wiping a hand across her forehead. "Glad it's not blood. Still, maybe we ought to get out the rubbing alcohol and do a wipe down on everyone."

August mornings in Indiana are hot and dry. It was already seventy seven degrees by the time they were finished with breakfast and over eighty and climbing when Father climbed into the backhoe. He headed for the ditch where last night's leftovers were waiting. Kyle walked alongside the machine, rifle in hand, to help out. His sister Elaine wanted to tag along, though they tried to dissuade her.

"Considering all you've seen, and your fiancé and all," Father tried to tell her, "Don't you think you've been through enough?"

But she was adamant. She wanted revenge for the wrong done to her and every zombie she helped put in the ground gave her a bit more closure. They couldn't convince her to let it go, so they acquiesced and headed for the ditch together.

Dropping the engine into idle as he rolled up to the moat, Father climbed down from the tractor and joined his children at the edge. To his surprise, there were no zombies visible in the ditch at all.

"See, told you," Kyle warned.

"Well, they can't have gone far, can they?" Father replied. "Let's go hunting."

There was just enough of a lip on the seat of the tractor that each of his kids was able to wedge one ass cheek onto it. Father dropped the vehicle into gear and they were off, bouncing roughly along the moat. What a sight they were, too.

Rednecks, Kyle laughed to himself as they drove through the yard on the big green tractor with guns over their shoulders.

Eventually they reached the southeast corner of the ditch. Kyle climbed off the tractor and stuck his head over the edge. "Nope, not here," he called out. They drove to the southwest corner and Elaine climbed down, repeating her brother's statement. "Nope, not here."

It was the same at both of the other corners. The zombies had disappeared. The worry became that somehow they had managed to climb out. After one more entire trip around the perimeter, Father sent Kyle to check the garage and the barn and Elaine to check the house with Mother while he spun the backhoe around the other direction.

"It's possible they're just wandering along in the same direction as us, at about the same speed, and we're just missing them," Father suggested as he searched for an expectation. Under his breath he added, "God help us." He gave the tractor some gas so the kids wouldn't hear the rest of his prayer and headed back down the ditch.

Kyle and Elaine ran toward the house, yelling for Mother to come out, which she did.

"What's wrong?" she answered worriedly when she saw the kids running toward her. "Where's your father?"

She could hear the thick chugging of the diesel but it was nowhere to be seen. Beginning to panic, she dropped the metal bowl she was drying and ran towards them.

Just as she reached the pair, the backhoe appeared from behind the barn with Father perched atop it. "Oh my God!" she sighed. "Don't worry me like that! I thought something terrible had happened!"

"Sorry," Elaine apologized. "But we can't find those two zombies anywhere and they might have escaped. Dad sent us to check the buildings. We just didn't want you in there alone... just in case."

She looked at her brother, who nodded in agreement. "Stay here," he told them, "I'm going to check the garage."

Like a soldier sneaking stealthily up on an enemy, he entered the garage with gun drawn. He flipped on the overhead fluorescent as quickly as he could, hoping that if the bastards were inside the garage that he could blind them long enough to blow them to Kingdom Come. No zombies.

He looked all over the garage but couldn't find any trace of them ever having been there, so he hurried back outside.

"Dad told me to go search the barn and have you guys search the house but I think it's probably better if we all work together. So, Mom, you stay at the door and watch to see if those old buggers come out of their hiding places. Sis, you come in with a shotgun and stand at the bottom of the stairs while I check upstairs. If you see either one of them, start blasting and get out of the house. Once I get the upstairs clean we'll do the downstairs and then the basement. After that you can come stand guard for me at the barn while I check it out."

Both women did as they were ordered, which surprised him since neither was generally the submissive type. But Kyle had not even made it all the way up the stairs before the engine of the backhoe cut out and Father could be heard screaming, "They're here! They're right here!" A few seconds later the boom of a .12 gauge rang out twice.

They raced outside and there was Father standing on the edge of the ditch looking down. They ran over to him and peered down into the ditch. Mother and Elaine nearly gagged at the disgusting sight before them. Kyle gagged too but he tried to hide it so as not to appear wimpy.

"That's right you sons of bitches," Father cursed as he waved his finger at what was left of the zombies. "Nobody gets across my moat without getting their head blown off!" He wasn't kidding either. In a very literal sense, he had blown their heads completely off. There were only bloody, pulpy stumps where their heads had been.

Father stood over his handiwork, cursing at them. He might have been reliving some moment from the war or just genuinely angry, but he kept hounding them even as the rest of the family tried to keep their meals down.

After a while, when they had all adjusted to the gruesome headless corpses rotting in the hot ditch, they were ready for clean up. Mother went back to the pile of dirty dishes in the house while Father dug a hole with the backhoe near the spot where he had buried the other zombies. After that, he came over and scooped up the bodies with the loader. Kyle and Elaine walked alongside, guns at the ready in case the two corpses came back to life.

The first body dropped into the hole with no problem, but the second one didn't seem to want to come out of the bucket. It was a fat woman, so fat her clothes barely stretched over her massive belly. At first, the back of her shirt got caught on one of the bucket's teeth, forcing Father to bounce the bucket up and down, which made the dead woman dance a horrible jig. Her limbs flopped to and fro like a marionette and thick syrupy blood sprayed in every direction. A couple of spots actually hit Kyle and Elaine in the face, which they quickly brushed away. Kyle told his sister to rub dirt on any spot where the blood hit her.

"What the hell is that going to do?" she asked him quizzically.

"I don't know, maybe none, but I remember going to the doctor for having poison ivy really bad as a kid and he told me to rub dusty dry dirt on any part of my body that had touched poison ivy. He said if I did it as quick as I could I probably wouldn't get it because the dirt would soak up the oil. I was just hoping that maybe the dirt would soak up whatever infection is in the blood, too."

"You're insane," she said, shaking her head at him. "Still…"

She quickly grabbed two handfuls of the soil at her feet and rubbed it all over her face. Kyle laughed at her, even though he was doing the same thing she was.

"You look like a freaking dust bunny!" he laughed wildly.

She started laughing too and said, "So do you! No, you look like one of those aborigines from Australia!"

Father was still wrestling with the fat lady. She did not want to come off the bucket. Finally, he lowered it as far as he could and then quickly flipped it upward. Just as he hoped, the shirt finally came loose. The hulking body cartwheeled up into the air.

Unfortunately, it didn't come down exactly the way he expected it to. The bitch twisted in midair, coming down belly first on the edge of the grave. The pressure on the abdominal wall was too much and it popped like a balloon, spraying rotted guts and slime twenty feet in any direction. Kyle and Elaine were showered by the gore. Elaine immediately vomited and then began to wail plaintively.

Wide-eyed, they stared at each other, not knowing what to do. Then, like a schoolboy, Kyle yelled, "Stop, drop and roll!" and dove onto the ground. He rolled over and over, trying to soak up enough soil to cover his entire body. Elaine did the same but both of them knew it was to no avail. There was simply too much goo on them to use the dirt trick effectively.

Elaine didn't want to tell them that some of the slime had gone into her mouth and the taste of it was what made her throw up. She kept that to herself, hoping and praying that she had expelled all of the rot and that she wouldn't turn into a zombie when it was all said and done.

Father let out a string of expletives when he saw his children doused by the zombie's last revenge. "Get to the fuel tank! Now!"

They ran to the garage as quickly as they could, Father barking instructions at them the entire way. He also yelled at Mother, telling her to crank up the shower and get out the bleach. When they reached the tank, Father commanded them to strip down. He grabbed the hose and blasted them with gasoline. Mother came out with a bucket of bleach water and a pile of washcloths. She wiped them both down, then hustled them into the bathtub together and cranked up the shower as hot as they could take it.

Brother and sister stood back to back, completely naked, as the water rinsed the outer layers of gangrenous gunk and dirt from them. Mother ran out of the room and came back with a scrubbing brush that she used on the floors when she was a younger woman. It had thick nylon bristles and a wooden frame and the sight of it coming at them made Kyle and Elaine groan. Mother dipped her brush into the bucket, pulled it out and started scrubbing her children— hard.

It was almost too much for Mother, who knew exactly what the slimy mess could mean for them. Hysterically, she yowled at Father, "Don't just stand there! Go in the broom closet and get the other brush!" Father knew better than to argue with her. Together they scrubbed at their children until their skin was red and raw and the water was on the cold side of tepid. Only then, when they were as sure as they could be that they'd gotten every bit of them, did they allow the kids to get out of the shower.

Mother handed them a couple of large bath towels and they wrapped themselves tightly. She disappeared again as she went to lay out clean clothes for them in the kitchen. Father took the cleaning tools and the towels out into the yard and burned them.

Although they had seen each other naked throughout their childhood, it was still uncomfortable for Kyle and Elaine to see each other naked as adults. However, the event had been so traumatic that neither of them gave a second thought to their sibling's nudity as they stood side by side putting on the fresh clothes their Mother had picked out for them. Silently, they sat side by side on the couch waiting for their parents to come back. Neither knew what to say.

When Father returned, he slumped down into his favorite chair and cradled his head in his hands. Mother, on the other hand, spent an hour cleaning the bathroom with bleach. It sounded like she cleaned it twice, something she rarely did since her first cleaning was usually deeper than anyone else's. But finally she joined them in the living room.

Normally a quiet woman, she was unable to contain her fears. "So is this it? Is this the end for all of us?" Father did not reply. She kept babbling about the end of the world and crying incoherently until he finally yelled at her.

"I suspect it is Mother," he hollered angrily. "And if it's true that this thing spreads through bodily fluids, then I suspect we're all in trouble. At least we'll all be together when the end comes."

Dumbfounded, Mother stared at him as if the whole thing was his fault. He glared back. "What?" he demanded angrily. "You think this is my fault? How could I have known? The only reason I didn't get soaked in that mess is because the tractor has a windshield on it. And besides, you and I both got our hands in it when we were watching the kids down. We're all in this just as deep as each other. You ask me if we're going to die? I'd say yes. If not now, then later when the food runs out or a whole pack of those bastards overruns the moat."

Elaine started to whimper. The end seemed inevitable.

CHAPTER 17

In a normal life, Kyle knew that his parents would precede him in death, so the thought of them passing was hard but not unmanageable. But to picture a life without his sister was impossible for him. They had been each other's playmate since Elaine had come out of the womb.

They had done stupid things together, like jumping out of the hayloft into a fully loaded wagon twenty feet below. It was great fun until Kyle snagged a foot in the twine that held together one of the bundles. He flopped over the side of the trailer, pulling the hundred pound hay bale over on top of himself. It knocked him out and nearly crushed his ribcage. Elaine had given him mouth to mouth, screaming for her parents. He spent a week in the hospital for that one.

Then there was the time when they'd been teenagers and he had tied the legs of two chickens together with a rope and threw them over a fence. At first it was really funny but when he went to separate the birds they clawed the shit out of his arm and one of them almost pecked his eye out. Elaine had been the one to dress up his wound and help him hide it from his parents. He still had a tiny little prick mark in the corner of his eye socket—a constant reminder of how stupid he could be and how Elaine had always saved his ass.

The more he thought about it, the more he realized that he was always the one in trouble and she was the one saving him. It was never the other way around, the way it should have been. He was the big brother and she was the kid sister. Why had he been such a dufus?

Another embarrassing memory came to him. Once he'd caught her masturbating in her bed and tried to blackmail her. She could have turned it around and tattled on him for doing the same thing, but she didn't. She let herself be his slave until she dreamed up a wonderful revenge for him. She dumped an entire tube of Krazy glue in the bottle of hand lotion that he kept hidden in the back of his closet for his own sexual purposes. Then the next morning when she walked in bright and early and he was still laying in bed with one hand under the cover, she asked sweetly, "What's the matter? Not feeling good? Do you want me to go get Mom?"

She didn't give him time to answer. She hustled out of the room despite his hushed protests and called loudly for Mother. She knew Mother wasn't in the house but Kyle didn't.

He begged her not to call Mother but she kept yelling, louder and louder. He offered to release her from her bondage if she'd just shut up.

She kept yelling. "Okay, okay," he wailed. "Whatever you want!"

"Twice the slavery you made me do," she grinned.

Only when the deal was sealed did she break out her finger nail polish remover for him. He never blackmailed her again after that.

Of course there were happier times when they weren't torturing each other but none of those came to mind at the moment. Why was it so hard to remember even the simplest happy moments but yet he relived the bad ones on a daily basis?

He had to force himself to recall a good memory. Some stupid boy had broken Elaine's heart and she cried for hours on his shoulder as they sat and watched the sun set over the corn. He had the urge to tell her that she was too ugly for any man and that she would die a lonely old spinster but he kept it to himself, as hard as that was, and he always been glad that he had. He still remembered the deep rich colors of the evening sun and the slight breeze that kissed their faces as the swing swayed gently back and forth. He could still feel her cheek on his shoulder as she cried and begged him to tell her why that boy didn't like her. And he remembered the way she kissed him on the cheek and gave him a bear hug when he told her later that he'd beaten the boy's ass and spread the rumor that Elaine dumped him because he was fond of goats.

Maybe that wasn't the stereotypical sweet moment, but as far as Elaine cared, at that moment he was the perfect brother.

As the day wore on, Elaine became erratic. When she wasn't at the table soaking her skin with moisturizer she was getting cool water from the tap and sucking it down like she'd spent a week in the desert. Her face grew redder and the pupils of her eyes seemed to get bigger. Once, Kyle had been to the eye doctor and they put something in his eyes to dilate his pupils, which made them as big as platters. He looked pretty scary for the rest of the day and was too sensitive to the light to drive home. That was how Elaine was starting to look now. Her pupils were stretched as wide as they could go. She looked wild and lost.

By dinner time, she'd lost her appetite and was more unfocused. She was in her own world. Kyle had an autistic boy in class who was in his own world most of the time and Elaine was beginning to present the same behavior. Mother and Father chalked it up to the dramatic events of the day but Kyle knew better. Something was seriously wrong with her. Deep down he knew she was in trouble but he wasn't sure how to help her.

Mother and Elaine turned in early that evening while Father and Kyle sat on the front porch with the guns across their laps. They rocked quietly. There was no need for words. Men could go for long stretches of time without ever saying anything to each other, unlike women. It didn't mean that anything was wrong, as women believed when their conversations hit the inevitable silent moment. Quite the opposite in fact, it meant that they were both quite content and that everything was good, or at least as good as could be expected given the circumstances.

The rest of the evening passed without incident. Finally Father yawned and stretched and said he was going to bed. Kyle stayed up a bit longer and then he headed for bed too, although he spent an hour reading by candlelight before he finally turned the light out.

Kyle didn't sleep well. He tossed and turned and kept checking to see if it was morning yet. It was hard to tell with blackout curtains on the windows. He had to keep getting out of bed, pull back the curtains a bit, and peek out. He must have checked a dozen times before he saw any light at the horizon.

It was that moment just after first light when he heard a noise that woke him. He couldn't pinpoint where or what the noise was but it sounded like one of the cows slurping up water from a mud puddle. The longer he lay there trying to decipher it, the more annoyed he became. Finally, he rose nervously from his bed and went to the window to look out. There were no cows in the South pasture and no animals anywhere in view.

He walked into his sister's room and looked out her window. The cows were out there by the barn but they were too far away to be heard while eating. As he turned back around he noticed that his sister's bed was disheveled and empty. Perhaps she'd gotten up early and was downstairs sucking down more water. After all, there was nothing like a gasoline bath followed by a bleach shower to make a person thirsty as hell.

Still in his underwear, he padded softly down the steep, narrow stairway which crackled and popped beneath his weight, and emerged into the living room. There was Elaine, squatting over something. It was hard to tell what it was because the light wasn't yet strong enough. But as his eyes adjusted, he realized it was another person on the floor.

The slurping noise was overwhelmingly loud. It was definitely Elaine making the noise. Kyle struggled to wrap his brain around the meaning of what he was seeing.

Elaine was still in her nightgown, which was white and which made her flesh look darker and more discolored than he knew it should be.

"What the hell's going on?" he muttered to Elaine. "Who is that on the floor?" She didn't answer.

"Elaine," he whispered at his sister. She didn't respond. She was focused on the person on the floor. Had one of their parents had a heart attack in the night? Was she giving mouth to mouth?

"What's happening, Laney?" he said a little louder.

A horrible thought gripped him. It was too horrible to comprehend.

"Lane? Is that Mom on the floor?"

She still didn't reply.

Kyle's brain began to wrap around the details of the scene. The slurping noise seemed to coordinate with the rhythmic movement of his sister's head.

"Lane," he repeated sternly. The slurping. It was… and the legs of the person on the floor. They were…

Elaine's arms were much darker than they should have been. They were mottled. He could tell that even in these low light conditions.

"That's Mother, isn't it, Lane?" he demanded.

Lane's head snapped back; at the same moment there was an elastic pop like a rubber band snapping. In that instant that her head whipped backwards, Kyle had all the answers he needed.

"Shit and Shinola," he gasped. The gray light of the morning suddenly turned gold and grew stronger, letting enough light creep into the living room for him to make out the whole grisly scene. The dark spots on the wall weren't shadows, they were blood. And Elaine appeared to be lapping up something wet that was oozing from Mother's upper chest and neck. Kyle was horrified. He was a deer in headlights.

Elaine leaned in close to Mother. Her jaw opened. After what seemed like forever, Kyle managed to scream out. "Dad!"

His father replied quietly, "I'm over here, son."

Kyle looked around. There was Father squatting against the wall next to the television stand. He held his head with both hands, pulling at his hair. He rocked gently back and forth as he stared at the nightmare before him.

Kyle pointed at the women and demanded of his father, "What the heck is going on?"

Father continued rocking and tugging at his hair. He didn't answer.

It's all me. I'm the man, now.

Kyle rushed across the room and kicked his sister as hard as he could, burying his toes in her rib cage. She lost her balance and toppled to the floor, ending up on her back.

"Shit!" he cried.

Elaine's face was drenched in blood and her eyes were black and dead. Her teeth, dark orange in the golden light, were bared like an angry dog's and he could see bits of something stuck between them.

His eyes went to his Mother, whom he suddenly realized was still somewhat alive. Blood pulsed up from the holes in her chest and throat. Her eyes were open and her mouth opened and closed ever so slowly.

"Oh Jesus!" he whispered. Elaine rolled over and climbed to her feet. She stared at Kyle for a second, as if she was trying to determine how best to attack him, then lunged at him. But he was faster than she was. He punched her right in the nose, knocking her down again.

Elaine was gone. She had been replaced by a—a doppelganger—and was gone. His rifle was at the back of the house where he'd left it last night. He went into survival mode and rushed from the room.

"Shit," he cursed himself. He wished he'd taken it to bed with him, but Mother wouldn't have allowed it anyway.

Mother was dying, Elaine was dead, and Father might as well have died too.

With one hand on the barrel of his rifle, he flipped the safety off and headed back to the living room. Elaine was again lapping up Mother's blood like a dog. Kyle kicked her over onto her back and put the mouth of the barrel against her forehead. He started to squeeze the trigger but stopped. He couldn't do it. She was still his sister, and while part of him knew that that it was just her animated corpse in front of him, he still had trouble separating her body from her soul in his mind.

Father lamented from the corner, "I couldn't do it either, son." He dropped his head back into his hands and began to cry. "If you've got any strength left in you, then pull that trigger. She's not your sister anymore. And when she's finished with your Mother she's going to kill us too. Do it, if you can!"

Kyle was stunned. There were so many things wrong with Father's statement that he didn't know where to begin. And as he stood there watching his Father sob, anger boiled up within him. He tried to squeeze the trigger again, but still couldn't do it.

Elaine was beginning to writhe under the barrel. She twisted and turned, trying to get out from under the weapon. She moaned lowly. The unearthly sound made the hair on the back of Kyle's neck stand straight up.

He looked away but kept the barrel of the gun butted up against her forehead. He still had it in his head that she was his sister and not a predatory corpse and try as he might, he just couldn't squeeze the trigger. Finally, he just gave up and went into the kitchen and sat at the table.

Like Father, he cupped his head in his hands. Mother was dead, or soon would be, and there was nothing to be done about it now, but Elaine was still a problem to be dealt with. If his father couldn't do it, and he was the strongest, most steel willed man Kyle knew, how could he expect that he would have the intestinal fortitude to go through with it?

He had no idea how long he'd been sitting at the table when the slurping stopped. As he looked up, he saw his sister leap across the room toward Father. Father growled in despair but the sound was cut short by a gurgle.

"Oh good God!" Kyle gasped as he leapt up from the table. His sister was on top of Father, munching away on his neck.

"Kill her son, kill her!" he gurgled at Kyle. "Hurry, before she gets you too."

"My gun," whispered Kyle, realizing he'd left it on the kitchen table.

He quickly retrieved the gun and marched back into the living room. Father was still alive, reaching out to him.

"Do it, son, don't worry about me," he gasped. "And don't let me turn either. Put a couple in me after I pass just to make sure."

"I can't Dad," Kyle replied. "I can't do it."

Father managed to croak at him, "I'm already dead son. If you don't finish us off, I'll come back and kill you. I can't bear the thought of it, so you've got to do it. Your sister is already dead, too. So do it."

But Kyle wasn't strong enough. He stood trembling as the husk that pretended to be his sister continued the attack on Father. He wanted to do it but he couldn't. To kill his Father… it was incomprehensible. And even though his sister was no longer human, she was still his sister.

So there he stood watching his sister rip the soul out of their father and deriding himself for not being man enough to do what had to be done. *Just do it, just close your eyes and pull the trigger. Be a man.*

A real man would see the compassionate side of murdering what was left of his family, he told himself. One shot could end all their misery, yet the larger part of him was just too afraid to do it. His conscience refused to yield to the necessity of the situation.

Then it was too late. Father started twitching, went into convulsions and then finally stopped moving. Elaine gnawed on him for a while longer before the aroma of living flesh began to wear away. It wasn't long before the smell of her live brother overpowered the stink of her dead parents and she turned her attention to him.

She came at him with outstretched claws. Kyle's heart pounded in his chest. Even faced with his own mortality, he still couldn't pull the trigger. He backed away and she stepped quickly towards him.

He fell onto the couch and she dove at him. Instinctively, he did what his conscience would not allow him to do consciously. The gun came up and a loud, bright blast blinded him. She was in mid leap when the buckshot hit her, knocking her to the floor. She landed in a crumpled heap at his feet and didn't move. The paralysis gone, Kyle jumped up, spun around and leveled the gun at her. Her limbs twitched. He put another load into her temple.

Then he slumped to the floor, inches from his sister, and tried to comprehend the carnage. "What the hell?" was all he could manage to say.

A half-hour passed, then an hour. He still hadn't moved. Nor had he come to grips with his situation. But then, out of the corner of his eye, he noticed Father climbing to his feet. He was just as dead as Elaine, but he had a more malevolent look on his face. He locked onto Kyle and stepped stiffly towards him.

"Shine's off the apple, Dad," he sighed as he raised the barrel of the gun and fired two shots into his Father's chest. Father flew backwards into the massive console TV. The force of the concussion bent him backwards at such a strange angle that Kyle actually heard his father's head smack the thick oak casing with a hollow "thunk."

That wasn't enough to stop Father. He got back up and stepped towards him again, but Kyle wasn't shell shocked anymore. He set the stock of his gun against his shoulder, coolly lined up the shot, and fired into Father's face. The center of his face, from his mouth to his eyes, disintegrated into a steamy red pulp that splattered on the wall behind him.

As if things couldn't get worse, Mother started to twitch again and then sat up. Her head swiveled around and her dead eyes locked onto him. He trained the gun on her and squeezed the trigger. Nothing happened.

He pumped the dovetail and fired again, but with no effect. He hadn't kept count of how many shots he'd fired. The gun held five shots and as he recounted, he still couldn't remember exactly how many times he'd fired.

Mother was lifting herself to her feet. Her eyes remained locked on him.

"Christ!" he swore. He pulled the dovetail back far enough to check the chamber, which was of course empty, and then quickly got to his feet. He sprinted towards her with the gun raised above his head like an axe. He brought it down into the bridge of her nose so hard that she instantly dropped to the floor. Then he ran into his parents' bedroom and grabbed Father's rifle. As a test, he fired haphazardly into the wall.

"Good." It was loaded. He went back into the living room and lined up a shot. As he squeezed the trigger, he closed his eyes because he couldn't bear to watch.

When he heard her body hit the floor like a sack of potatoes, he knew it was finally over. Shielding himself with a hand so he wouldn't burn a final image of the massacre into his brain, he tiptoed through the living room and went upstairs to gather up some things. When he was done, he exited through the kitchen door, carefully not to look into the living room.

He dragged his stuff over to the ditch, near the box truck, and then went back into the kitchen and gathered up a number of water pitchers and milk jugs. He grabbed all the guns and all the ammunition in the house, except for the ones that were in the same room as his family, and added them to the pile, too.

Next, he hooked the garden hose to the gas tank in the yard, cobbling the two pieces of disparate equipment together with duct tape. Then he took the business end of the hose into the house and chucked it into the living room. He went outside again and opened up the spigot as wide as it would go. Little spurts of gas shot out from between gaps in the duct tape, but for the most part the gas went into the house.

When there was no more gas left in the tank, he went to the back door. There was a noxious amber puddle spreading across the kitchen floor. He found a box of matches above the coat rack in the entry way and lit one up.

He lobbed it toward the puddle, but it went out well before it reached the pinnacle of its trajectory, and it fell far short of the gas anyway.

"Dammit." He would have to get a lot closer to the puddle to get a fire going. The smell of gas was so thick, though, that he worried the ensuing fireball would incinerate him as well as his family.

There was a yellowed stack of newspapers in the back of the entryway. Kyle rolled one up into a tube and lit it. The paper, a decade old if it was a day, burned quickly. He would have to get rid of it quickly before his hand caught fire.

"Double dammit," he cursed. He tiptoed toward the kitchen, unsure of how close he could get without igniting a massive fireball. The heat from the makeshift torch was getting uncomfortably hot.

Surveying the creeping puddle, he decided the best method of lighting it without killing himself was to toss it like a bouquet and run for dear life. So that's what he did.

Even before it hit the actual liquid, the vapors caught fire and fingers of flame shot in every direction. He flung himself toward the back door, just managing to hit the tiny vestibule before the shockwave slammed the door shut behind him like an angry poltergeist.

There was a "whump" and the next thing he knew, he was lying face down in the gravel driveway.

The entire house was engulfed in flames before he was even able to sit up and take stock. Wood crackled as the old timbers quickly caught fire. Glass tinkled as windows overheated and popped like balloons.

Already the heat was so intense that he had to shield his eyes from it.

He crawled backwards, watching as the house suddenly fell in on itself. Like a massive bellows, it exhaled embers and ashes.

The fire grew more intense as it swiftly consumed the century old lumber. Every few minutes he had to back up a few more steps because of the mounting heat. Finally, he just stood up and walked over his pile of stuff.

"Damn," he sighed, realizing that there was now officially nothing left for him here. No family, no home, no nothing but the garage and barn and who really gave a shit about them? He didn't.

He drank in the last few images of his childhood home and then climbed down the ladder into the ditch.

After a few minutes idling at the intersection where his parent's road met the highway, he turned off the engine. There wasn't any point in wasting fuel if he couldn't decide where he wanted to go. The entire world was open to him again, like it had been when he first graduated from high school and then again when he graduated from college. He was educated and intelligent and had a good work ethic, at least when he was interested in the work. He wasn't tied to Indiana anymore. The sudden loss of his family made him aware that they were the real reasons he hadn't pulled up the tent stakes and headed for points further south, like Mexico. But now that they were gone it was as if he were seeing the entire world in a new way. Where should he go? What should he do?

There wasn't any telling how long the plague would last and that meant that fuel and other provisions would probably become more and more scarce, even though the most recent reports said that life should soon be returning to normal. Perhaps he wouldn't even have to decide where he wanted to go as the fuel issue might dictate his destination. He knew that the truck had a range of 200 to 300 miles and from where he was he would only be able to get into the neighboring states before he would have to refill the tank.

He did not care much for Illinois. He didn't know much about Ohio and Kentucky held no interest for him. But Michigan was a beautiful place and was less than a hundred miles away. If he had to live somewhere, Michigan would have been in the top five on his list. Then again, winter would soon be marching southward and who knew if there would be any power this year? What would be the point of going north to get away from all the horror he had recently witnessed just to end up freezing to death in the wilderness somewhere?

A little voice told him that Monticello was the easy answer. He tried to put it out of his head, but the more he thought about it, the smarter a decision it seemed. He had a job there already and the place had a small amusement park that brought in tourists from all over the region. Once the zombie plague had subsided, people would need distraction and that meant that people would attack amusement parks and other such venues like the zombies had attacked the living. He could make money in Monticello. It was guaranteed. The other thing he knew was that the twin lakes of Freeman and Shafer both had dams that generated electricity. Even in nasty storms, when other areas lost power, Monticello never did. It was clean and continuous energy. There was no coal or natural gas supply to worry about. As long as it rained and kept the lakes full, there would be power. Power meant that he could continue to write his stories and live the same lifestyle he had lived all along, well, maybe as close to it as he would ever again get.

It was the obvious choice. South held too many unknown variables and any farther north was just stupid right now. He fired up the motor and headed toward the sleepy little resort town he called "home." And somewhere up the road, the radio even began to pick up a radio station that was playing music. The song was "Highway to Hell" from AC/DC, but it was still a sign that things were improving.

CHAPTER 18

By the middle of September, the outbreak had been contained and by the end of October, which was a quarter of the way through a normal school year for Indiana, the Government officially declared the end of the plague. Gradually, life began to return to normal. TV and radio stations began to broadcast things other than plague updates again and sitcoms and other types of escapist shows ruled the airwaves. People needed a laugh, Kyle reckoned.

Still, it was strange to be watching reruns of Cheers knowing that he had personally murdered his entire family and had run over countless numbers of people as he wandered across the Hoosier state. Even the ride home from his parents had been a death race. By the time he got back to Lafayette it had become second nature to aim the truck at anyone lingering on the pavement for more than a few seconds. He'd honk the horn and if they got out of the way, he kept going. If they didn't move, he smashed them. He considered it a public service to eliminate as many zombies as possible.

He left the TV on nowadays, even as he wrote. In his earlier days that would have been sacrilegious. But these days were different. It was the closest thing he had to comfort in his life, and it was really of no comfort at all. He guiltily enjoyed hearing the adventurous retellings of redneck posses wandering the countryside killing the undead and sometimes being swamped themselves. It was horrendous to derive entertainment from things like that, he knew, but it made him feel connected to the rest of the human race. He had lived through many of the same things those rednecks had. He had faced death. He had also caused many deaths, if you could call them that, and he enjoyed hearing how others were coping with the stress of it all. In the old days, he hadn't had much sympathy for anyone. But things were different now. He wanted to be close to someone. He needed a human connection.

Am I Alex? he would say to himself sometimes when he saw happy families in the grocery stores. It was a reference to the last chapter of "A Clockwork Orange," where murderous Alex grows out of his violent lifestyle and begins to wish for a family like everyone else. Was he finally a real adult? Had it taken the near extinction of the entire human race for him to realize that he was just like them? That he had always desired the same things as everyone else? Was he, then, not superior to everyone else as he had always believed? It was something he grappled with on a daily basis now.

The news reports weren't all good, of course. There was still some looting and rape in the major cities and a few even more horrible perversions in the countryside. But Kyle expected nothing less than the worst from humanity and so he wasn't shocked at those reports. History had borne witness time and time again to the great atrocities that one group of humans could perpetrate on another. Slaughter was the norm for humans, as far as Kyle could tell. The ghastly outbreak of zombies was nothing less than a modern rendition of the Mao's Cultural Revolution, or for that matter, any revolution in which the peasants rose up and attacked oppressive elements in their societies. Had he not been on the receiving end of so many attacks, he might've even cheered for the zombies but events being the way they were, he was prejudiced against them. He did not want them to take over. He was better than they were.

Had he thought about it a little more, he might have made the connection to his personal dilemma: he still believed himself superior to everyone else, but in reality he was only middle class. Had he been truly superior, he would have had an extra layer of insulation between the zombies and himself. He would have had people to deal with the zombies for him.

Up to ninety percent of the entire human population had been annihilated over the course of the outbreak, which meant that there were fewer idiots out there. There were also a lot less intelligent people out there, since the meek had suddenly disinherited the earth. When it came to fighting off zombies, brute strength and steel wills were what was needed, not IQs of 140. Some super-smart people survived, but only because they holed up during the entire struggle and let others do the heavy lifting. There again, Kyle did not make the connection to his true station in life, choosing instead to believe that he was higher up the food chain than he really was.

Eventually, the local newspaper resumed publication and although he had never bothered to read the rag before, he now found it surprisingly interesting to read. It seemed that Lafayette had been at the heart of the outbreak and had not fared well at all. Monticello, only twenty five miles north, had not fared much better. In the summertime the town, which normally had a population of 5000, swelled into a city of more than 20,000. Since the zombies struck in July, the damage was much worse than if it had hit any other time of year. According to the paper, at least two thousand people immediately lost their lives in the area. That was bad news for Kyle as it meant that student numbers were sure to be lower and that meant the need for teachers would be down. Layoffs were a possibility.

The amusement park had been a focal point for the zombies. Authorities postulated that someone from Lafayette came to the park not knowing they were about to turn into a zombie, died at the park, and then wreaked havoc. A witness described how she saw a woman laying on the ground near the Sea Dragon get up and attack three people who were tending to her.

"I thought she was having a seizure," the woman said, "but then she bit those people who were trying to help her. When I saw her jump on top of a man and bite him so hard he started bleeding, I just ran."

It was a beautiful day and thousands of people were at the park. The storywriter said that patrons "laughed like bees flitting about a field full of flowers. It wasn't long before the entire park was drenched in blood and guts." The zombies killed everyone in sight and then marched across the parking lot into the campgrounds. Eventually, they ate their way south toward town, killing motorists who were stuck in the weekly traffic jam that marked the start of the weekends at the park.

If it hadn't been for one heroic sheriff's deputy who radioed ahead just before he was killed, the damage would have been much worse.

Monticello proper was a town full of older folks, something like a gigantic retirement community. It had a small hospital in the center of town and there were numerous old folks homes nearby. One newspaper report quoted the deputy as having said, "You got to get everybody out of the north side of town. Bring every gun we've got and get ready to start shooting. Kill anyone coming south from the beach. They ain't alive!" The dispatcher telling the story said that she then heard gurgling and a scream and then the deputy's walkie-talkie went dead. The story concluded with a footnote that the deputy himself was later shot in the head as he stumbled toward town, a zombie himself.

Normally, Kyle would have found the news revolting because all outlets, television and newspapers especially, pandered to their audiences. They liked to showcase the worst in humanity and he didn't buy the excuse that they were simply mirroring society. They were a massive part of the problem, not any sort of a solution. But the zombie outbreak was a major event in the history of humanity and no one could escape from the coverage, nor did they want to. That included Kyle. He had lived it, like everyone else, in a fragmented way. He saw bits and pieces, but he could not see the whole pie. To peruse the news was to make sense of it all and he found himself compiling stories like a historian might. He scrapbooked the pieces and began to assemble them into book form. It might just be the ticket to getting published.

He had nothing better to do with his spare time than to work on the book since school would not be back in session until after the New Year, according to the Governor. Schools would be allowed to make up their minds how they wanted to handle this particular school year, but in August it would begin again as if nothing had happened, excepting that there would be fewer kids and fewer teachers. Kyle thought it was a mistake. He thought they should have taken more time to look over the system and to revamp it. It was a perfect opportunity to reboot the entire system from scratch. They could fix what was wrong with it, not just continue with the same old mistakes. Kyle even sent the State Superintendent of Schools a number of letters proclaiming the value of using this opportunity, but all he got back was a thank you note from one of her advisors. It was the same type of rejection letter that publishers sent him when they rejected one of his pieces.

"So be it," he exclaimed after opening the fourth rejection letter. He decided it wasn't worth fighting. He would just try to influence his own community to do things differently, to tailor education to their community and to forget about what the state had to say. It would be his own private little rebellion. In the meantime, he worked on the book.

So he spent the fall and early winter compiling stories into a book. He did it the right way —he contacted all the people in the articles and asked if they would give him an interview. Most of them said yes because they suspected that it might be their only shot at fame. He had them sign release forms and told them that he was writing a nonfiction book about the entire event. A few people did not want their real names used. Some of them were embarrassed and humiliated and even though they wanted their stories told, they could not stand the scrutiny that would inevitably be brought to their doorsteps by the publication of his book.

There were so many people with such different takes on "The Event," as he began to call it, that it seemed as if he might be shaping up an entire series of manuscripts. He tried shopping around his premise to a couple of agents and publishers and to his surprise he promptly received letters of interest from three publishers. When the first one came, he let out a crazy "Whoo hoo" of excitement. By the time the third one had come, he just smiled smugly. He'd finally found something to get his foot in the door.

There was only one wrinkle. Kyle wrote fiction and if he got published as a nonfiction writer, it was entirely possible that he might have to stay in that vein for a very long time. Writers were usually pigeonholed, like actors. Readers did not want their romance writers writing horror stories or science fiction or whatever. If a writer managed to write in two different genres it was because they used a pseudonym. Kyle was willing to take that chance. He had more than enough material from the collection of stories to write a least a handful of books. Once he was published it wouldn't be hard to find someone to publish his fiction.

Maybe there's a silver lining in "The Event" after all. The moment the thought popped into his brain, the image of Brad and April accompanied it and he immediately felt shamed. *How can I profit off my friends' deaths? But they would have wanted their stories told, wouldn't they?* It's the least he could do for them—make them immortal. It would be his tribute.

When school began the first Monday after New Year's, Kyle's life was looking decidedly upward. For the first time in a long time, perhaps since he was a boy, he began to see that he was approaching the finish line of his protracted race to become an author.

Class sizes were a lot smaller and when they held the first staff meeting, the vice principal, who had become the de facto principal because his predecessor had been murdered by a zombie at the city park, read the list of faculty and staff members who had passed away. The staff was down 25% and student enrollment was down a like number. As it turned out no one had to be laid off. Kyle wondered how many of them went home breathing a sigh of relief over the fact that the zombies had managed to cull just the perfect ratio of teachers and students. He suspected most of them. He did.

So into his classroom Kyle strutted that morning and with great aplomb, began to instruct his students in the ways of the world.

As he noticed throughout the day that his class sizes were more manageable—smaller classes always were—he also noted that unfortunately, a disproportionate number of good kids were gone and in their place were more of the idiot kids who had no respect for themselves and others. He found himself wishing that more dirtballs had been chomped and less of the good kids. It must have had something to do with the fact that the dirtballs were already survivors before The Event and the good kids never had to worry about survival before. How ironic.

He didn't get very far into his first lesson before the kids wanted to talk about The Event. He tried to steer them away from it but it was nearly impossible.

Oh well, at least they're tying our terminology to it, he thought at last. So he caved. They spent the rest of the week talking about The Event and about the impact it had on their lives. He gathered a lot of great stories from them, careful to ask for permission from their parents to reprint their tales. They were happy to oblige because even though it was their children's moment, parents always claimed part of their children's success as their own.

CHAPTER 19

By the second week of classes, Kyle had discovered that he had one of Brad's children in class. His stomach turned when he saw the name on his roster and made the connection. The images of her father lying dead behind his couch and under a brush heap in the woods rushed back to him. Every day after that, when Brad's daughter walked into class, Kyle's stomach would do cartwheels. He tried to ignore it by minimizing his interaction with her, but it didn't help. Every time he looked at her pretty little face he was reminded of her father. It would nearly send him into an anxiety attack. Did she know? Could she see it in his face? It seemed like she had to know.

Why hadn't he just turned over the body to the authorities? Why? Would it really have been as bad as he thought? He was a big boy. He could have handled the punishment.

No, the Universe had this in mind, didn't it? His punishment was to have Brad's adorably smart daughter in class every day, reminding him of what he did.

She had the same sense of humor as her father and as she was very outgoing. She said things the same way he did, made some of the same faces, even walked the same way. That just made it that much worse. It killed him that he was the only one who knew where her father was and what had happened to him. Each day, the knot in his stomach got tighter and the tiny little dagger of pain grew. He was giving himself an ulcer. He just knew it.

There were times when Paige would tell such a riotous story about her dad that he found himself laughing his head off. A few times he almost laughed so hard at her tales that he nearly threw up on the carpet. Then he would recall the image of Brad's chewed up face and the dagger would stab him again.

Though he tried to avoid talking about his personal affairs with his students, they kept after him. "We've told you all our stories," they coaxed him, "it's only fair that you tell us what happened to you." He offered the excuse that it wasn't professional and that he was paid to teach them, not to tell stories, Brad's daughter said, "My father said the best way to learn was to have something modeled for you." Medium sized dagger.

"Fine," he answered with some trepidation. Being careful to leave out the part about Brad and edit the more adult portions of the story, he told them his tale. It left him drained when he was finished, but thankfully it was the last period of the day. As the kids filed out, he pondered his life.

"Mr. Williams? Can I talk to you for a minute?" It was Paige. He had his back to her but when he heard her voice his stomach did a flip flop.

"Sure..." he replied nervously. The moment of truth. *This is not going to be pretty.* "What's up?"

He tried to say it as calmly as possible. He didn't want to let on that she made him anxious.

She dropped her gaze to the floor. "Can we close the door?"

"Do we need to? What's this about?" If he was lucky, she would just have a crush on him and this wouldn't be about the other thing. *Please GOD, let it be a crush.*

"I'm a bit embarrassed to say this with the door open," she mumbled sweetly.

"I'd really rather not," he said to her. "It's a professional courtesy type thing."

She looked at him strangely. "Um, okay. Whatever. I just wanted to ask you if you wanted to come to dinner some night. My mom is lonely, too, and she just wants to meet you. She knows that you and my dad were really good friends and she really misses him. I was thinking maybe you guys could tell stories about my dad and get to know each other."

Mentally, he sighed. *Thank God.* It was neither a crush nor the other thing.

"Uh, uh..." he stammered. "Let me think about it and I'll get back to you, okay?"

At first, Paige accepted his polite brush-off and turned to leave. But when she reached the door, she spun around and screwed up her face with a half angry look. "No, I'm not going to take no for an answer. Almost every day you make some comment about how lonely you are and how you're working on this book and that's the only thing in your life. But you also tell us that *we* need to get out and experience life. Right?"

She paused for an answer. He nodded. She was trapping him.

"Fine then, you come to my house Friday night at 6 p.m. Here's the address," she said, handing him a slip of paper with a phone number and address on it. "You better not lose it and you better show up."

It felt like two wolves were fighting over the dagger in his stomach. As emotionlessly as he could and with a hand on his stomach, he replied, "And what if I don't?"

"Then you'll be sorry," she responded doggedly. She raised her eyebrows and stared sternly at him. He could turn her down, but the pain in his stomach intensified. If he answered with an "Okay," would it go away? And anyway, what did he have to lose? She wasn't trying to date him herself. She was setting him up with her mother.

"Fine," he muttered. The stomach pain mercifully subsided. He had just been blackmailed into dinner.

As Friday approached, he became so nervous about the situation that he almost skipped work just to avoid Paige and her mother. How could he face Brad's wife knowing that it was his fault that she didn't have a body to bury? Had he simply placed one phone call and owned up to a hard night of drinking, he would not have all this stress. He would not have to relive the images of Brad laying there, rotting, every time his daughter walked into his classroom.

Guilt racked his whole body. He wanted to back out of it, but every time tried to muster up the courage to tell Paige that he wouldn't be coming, he melted. She always had the same determined look on her face, a motherly look that meant she knew what he was thinking and was not going to let him out of it.

What exactly have I done wrong? The whole world went nuts and a lot of families had no body to bury, not just Brad's. What he did wrong, he knew, was that didn't give them Brad's body when he damned well could have. He could have blamed it on the Mexicans and no one would have been the wiser. The Mexicans were dead and they wouldn't have cared even if they were alive.

Nah, I'd still know. It wouldn't help.

He went to the dinner. It was tough, even though Brad's wife was very beautiful, which should have made it that much easier. But the fact remained that he had done the family an injustice and every time he looked at any of them, Brad's wife or daughters or son, he saw flashes of Brad's body lying in the woods just waiting for the wildlife to come by and have a free meal.

Finally, the discomfort in his gut forced him to excuse himself.

"But it's early," Melissa—Brad's wife—complained.

"Yeah, but I've got papers to grade and my stomach doesn't feel so good right now."

Melissa thanked him timidly for coming and offered a polite hug. He slapped her rather mechanically on the back and then broke away from her.

"Thanks for dinner and thanks for the company. Maybe we can do it again sometime," he said unconvincingly. He had to get the heck out of there. He would explode if he didn't.

"Well, how about next Friday?" Melissa insinuated. "The kids are all going to go to the basketball game so it would just be you and me for dinner..."

Kyle noticed a slight flush to her cheeks. Could it be that she wanted something more than just dinner? Was she really hitting on him?

"Uh, I'll have to see," he answered anxiously. He couldn't come up with any excuses not to. Part of him wanted to jump on her right then and there, but the rest of him wanted to run. "How about I call you on Wednesday and let you know for sure if I can make it or not?" He trotted out a fake smile.

"Well, okay," she said cheerily, obviously missing his body language. "If you don't get me at home, just leave a message on the machine. I've got bus driver duty after school pretty much everyday."

"I didn't know you were a bus driver," he said.

"Oh, not for the school. Just for my own kids. I have to drive them to all their after school stuff and then pick them up later. I spend about two hours every weekday in a van driving all over town. But it keeps my mind off of…things." Her chin sank onto her chest. If he didn't get away at that moment he would not get away at all. He took the opportunity to thank her again and bolted for the door.

The next few days went by quickly as school got back into the swing of things. It seemed as if the horror of last summer was so far in the distant past that it hadn't really happened. The human mind was a great thing. It blanked out the most horrible events and smoothed out the parts that it couldn't blank. It was about the only thing that made life bearable sometimes. Strange, he thought, how only days ago he'd been bitching how he could only remember the bad things.

Brad's daughter completely ignored Kyle in class the entire week. She didn't look at him, talk to him, or participate in class even though she took copious amounts of notes and her grades actually went up. He suspected that she was probably just trying to avoid embarrassment. *Well, that takes care of that, doesn't it?*

On Wednesday, she showed up once again after the last bell. "You *are* going to call my mother, aren't you?" she demanded. "She had a really good time Friday. I haven't seen her as upbeat since Dad disappeared."

Kyle could see that her lower lip was trembling. *So you're not as strong as you let on, huh? Finally a chink in your armor.* Then he realized that this opportunity was a chance to make good for his sins. Maybe he should give the thing with Melissa a real shot. He knew that Brad would never return, so he need never worry about a nasty confrontation between them.

"Mr. Williams?" Paige prompted, jolting him out of his little fantasy world.

"Tell her I'll call her about eight, okay?"

She smiled politely at him and her eyes lit up with excitement. "No, I think you should call her at nine. The little ones will be asleep by then and I'll be in my room with my headphones on, so you guys can talk." Then she spun around on her toes and skipped out of the room.

"Oh my, what am I getting myself into?" He was about to start dating a single mom with three children, one of them a teenage girl, and she was the widow of one of his best friends whom he... *what? What did I do?*

A little voice inside him set him straight. *She's beautiful and she single. She doesn't know what happened and you didn't do anything wrong except not call somebody. Maybe you can fix that anyway. So go call her. Maybe you'll get lucky.*

He answered the voice: *A man does have needs,* and he hadn't taken care of those needs in months.

He made the call. They set up a date for that Friday night, while the kids were away at a basketball game. Things were looking up.

When the time came and he was finally at her door, he knocked a bit more aggressively than he would have if she were some strange girl. Melissa opened the door so fast that it seemed as if she must've been peering out the peep hole. "Please come in," she breathed eagerly.

She was picture perfect. Kyle was floored. "Wow," he exclaimed. "You're beautiful." He felt the stirring deep within himself that he hadn't felt since his time with April. There was a momentary twinge of guilt but his conscious mind reminded him that she was a widow and therefore fair game.

"Thanks," she grinned.

"Sorry, didn't mean to sound like a teenager, but…" He didn't know how to end that sentence without sounding more like a love struck kid. Thankfully, Melissa saved him.

"It's okay. I think you're hot, too." She blushed and it was all he could do to keep from jumping her that moment. She had on a tight little dress and her hair was pulled back to expose her neck. He couldn't tell if she was wearing makeup or not, but he knew she was. She knew exactly how to make it accentuate her features without overdoing it. He could see why Brad loved her so. She was gorgeous when she was dressed up and pretty cute when not, too.

The dinner was fantastic but the conversation was awkward. Melissa was a wonderful cook, so he was able to focus on the food. For dessert, she brought out a chocolate mousse that was spectacular.

He stuffed himself. When he'd had enough, he leaned back in his chair. Instinct compelled him to reach for the top button on his jeans, but he caught himself. He clapped that hand to his belly, which forced a bit of food toward his throat. That made him realize what he'd done. It would be hard to do anything with a full belly. He'd sabotaged the rest of the evening.

"I'm glad you like it," she said. "It was Brad's favorite, too." Suddenly, the tone of the evening turned. She teared up and he didn't know what to say so he sat there silently, both hands on his full belly, nodding. Finally, deciding that maybe a little misdirection was all that was needed to salvage the conversation, he suggested, "Maybe we could go in the living room and relax a bit. I'm so stuffed." He patted his gut.

He hoped that would help her forget about Brad, at least for the remainder of the evening. But he should have known better. She was a grieving wife and mother who hadn't gotten a proper chance to analyze her situation because she had to survive the moment. Now that she had some private time with another adult, there was nothing to keep the tears away.

They sat next to each other on the couch. He could smell her perfume. *Lilacs.* She sniffled once and then started crying. Not knowing what else to do, he pulled her close and let her cry on his shoulder. She sobbed for about ten minutes, completely soaking the left side of his shirt with tears and makeup. When she was finally able to compose herself, she disengaged from his embrace and noticed the mess that she had made of his shirt. She chuckled tearfully as she tried to apologize.

"Oh my God, I'm so sorry. I got makeup all over your shirt," she whimpered. He looked at it and chuckled too.

"Did you ever see that episode of the Drew Carey show where Mimi wiped her face in a rag and when she pulled the rag away there was an oil painting of her face left behind? I think that's what you just did to my shirt." He laughed harder. Even though she was embarrassed, the fact that he laughed it off made her burst into laughter. She relaxed for a just a second and that was long enough to awaken something inside her. He was kind and easy going, something she loved in men. It aroused her.

"Take off your shirt," she suggested as innocently as she could.

As he unbuttoned his wet shirt, revealing his chiseled abs beneath, he watched her look him over. He felt a tingling sensation deep down and he slowly, teasingly, finished unbuttoning his shirt. He stood up to pull it out of his pants and then handed it to her. She was still sitting on the couch but looking up at him with a certain longing and he knew exactly what was going to happen next.

She scooted forward on the couch and reached for his belt, loosening it up and undoing his pants. She yanked them down. He offered no resistance. She removed his underwear quickly and took his member in her mouth and proceeded to give him the most vigorous blow job he had ever had. Just when he was about to climax, he moaned, "I'm going to cum," and tried to pull away from her. Personal experience had taught him that women did not find it appealing at all for a man to blow his load down their throats. But Melissa reached around and grabbed a butt cheek in each hand and pulled him tighter. It was a pleasant surprise but there was nothing he could have done by then if he'd tried. He had already reached the point of no return and he came so forcefully down her throat that his knees buckled and he got dizzy. Melissa held him tight until she could tell he was done. Only when he collapsed onto the couch next to her, breathing heavily, did she let go of him.

"Oh my God!" he exclaimed. "That was fantastic!"

"Brad loved it that way, too," she said as she took a Kleenex from a pocket and wiped her lips. "I was a swimmer in college. I could hold my breath an extra long time. Came in handy for catching Brad. Now, are you ready for the main course?"

"Huh?" He wasn't exactly sure what she meant since they'd just eaten dinner, but he suspected she wasn't talking about food. She smiled at him seductively and began to remove her top.

Immediately his member became stiff again. He pawed at her clothes until they were both naked. Then he spun her around and pushed her down onto the couch and guided his cock into her wet and waiting vagina.

Groaning with excitement she spat out dirty, filthy comments that got him so worked up that he came again after only thirty seconds. Surprised and a bit disappointed she said, "Please tell me you're not done. It's been a long time and the motor is a little rusty. You're going to have to work a little bit more than that to get it going."

"No problem," he answered. He pulled out of her and immediately buried his face between her legs. He was no stranger to that method of pleasing a woman. In fact, he was somewhat of an expert at it. Within two minutes she was screaming and writhing as the first orgasm washed over her. Then, as she was just about to climax again, he got up on his knees and jammed his stiff member in her, sending her over the edge. She arched her back, screamed and collapsed.

"Oh shit!" she gasped, the words stretching out as her vagina exploded. Eyes closed, with a little smile on her face, she rode the waves of electric fire until the last one dissipated. Then she cooed, "I almost blacked out."

"You okay?" he asked her.

"Great," she cooed. "Never better. And I mean never."

She lay naked, half-on half-off the couch, breathing sharply. After a few more minutes, she opened her eyes and smiled at him. He was relaxing at the other end of the couch, his cock as stiff as when they'd started. It'd been a long time for him too and he had a least one more good orgasm in him.

"Not done?" she asked, delightedly surprised.

He shook his head. "I could go again."

"Fine with me," she replied. "How about we move this party to the bedroom?" He nodded and they stood up together. He pulled her close and kissed her. She wrapped her legs around him. He hoisted her up high enough so he could get his dick in her and then carried her across the living room and toward the hall where he assumed the bedroom was.

She pulled her tongue out of his mouth and told him, "Last door on the left." Down the hall they went, Kyle trying not to drop her or bash her into a wall as she ground herself against him.

They actually went a few more rounds. Normally Kyle would have kept count to make sure that she had at least as many orgasms as he did but she was already well past him. It was important to his ego that his lovers have more orgasms than he did during each session. It's how he rated himself as a lover.

By the time she told him that she had to go pick up the kids he had had at least five orgasms, something that hadn't occurred since he first discovered masturbation as a teenage boy. He had no idea how many she had.

"I could use a quick shower," he told her.

"I could use one too," she agreed.

"You wanna share?" he suggested playfully.

"Sure," she answered lightly. "I just want to make sure none of your swimmers are running down my leg while I'm getting the kids,"

They fucked once more in the shower because he was so turned on by the water cascading down her luscious curves that he couldn't help himself. She seemed to enjoy it as much, if not more, than he did.

Half an hour later they were both ready to leave. She asked if he wanted to come with her but he politely declined. "I don't think I could look your daughter in the face, right now. She would know immediately what we've been up to."

Melissa laughed. "Oh, you think? She's the one that set this whole deal up, remember? She's been on me to do something like this since about two weeks into the whole zombie thing. She was the first to realize that her dad wasn't coming back. Every fight we had, which wasn't a lot because she's a pretty nice and thoughtful girl, she kept yelling that I needed to go get laid. Who would have guessed that she was right?"

They both laughed at that. "It really did me well, too," he agreed. "So do you think this was a one-time thing or...?"

She took a deep breath, which to him was an indicator that it was a one time thing. "Well the thing is, I really don't know if I'm still married or not. I wouldn't have done this if I truly believed Brad was still alive. He is my husband and I do love him, but I also know if he could get back to us he would have done it already. All I know is he was going to your house and that's the last I heard from him. Did he ever make it to your house?"

And there it was—the $64,000 question. His heart leapt up into his throat. It was the moment that he had dreaded for months. None of the words he had practiced came to mind. He was suddenly blank.

His head involuntarily shook from side to side as if to say no, but when he opened his mouth all that came out was, "Ah,ah,ah."

"Well I guess it doesn't matter anyway," Melissa said brushing it off. "The fact remains that he's probably not coming back. I just wish I had some closure. I just want to know what happened to him."

Kyle shrugged. He was afraid to say anything for fear that the wrong thing would come out of his mouth. Melissa stared at him for a moment and then smiled lightly. Did she see it in his face that he knew more than he was letting on?

She went on. "I really would like it if we could do this again, but I don't want to force you into anything, considering the circumstances. I mean, you worked with my husband and were buddies. I'm pretty sure he would understand given the fact that he hasn't returned for months. Hell, he might even ask us if we had any videotape because sometimes he's a little perverted like that. If you're okay with the possibility that he might come back and that I would have to go back with him, then yes I would love to see you again."

Well, I won't have to worry about that, will I?

He knew it was horrible to take advantage of her like he was, but his hormones sometimes got the best of him. "Yeah, I can live with that."

She stepped into him, slid her arms around his waist and squeezed him tightly. She kissed him gently on the chin and laid her head on his shoulder. "The kids go to pretty much every basketball game if it's here and if there is a fan bus, they usually go to those, too. If nothing else, I can talk them all into spending the night at a friend's house and then we can really have some fun." She looked up at him with her soft brown eyes and added, "And I mean I'll try just about anything. So whatever you want to do, all you have to do is ask." She kissed him again, on the lips, just hard enough to let him know that she meant what she said. At the same time, she stroked his member through his jeans.

"Oh my," she purred. "Ready again?" He nodded and leaned in to kiss her but she pushed him away. "Let's save something for next time, huh?"

Like a love struck puppy he stepped after her even as she giggled and backed away. "I have to go," she said coyly, leaving him standing on her doorstep with a raging erection. Quickly she got in her car, before she could be tempted again, and was off.

"Yes, there will be a next time," he said as he watched her drive off. "You have no idea what kind of an athlete I really am!"

He had a momentary pang of guilt—he had violated his friend's trust and marriage but when the little voice reminded of the situation it went away.

Dude, Brad's marriage ended the moment he died in your apartment.

CHAPTER 20

It was easier to seem less interested after he had sex since the urge wasn't clouding his mind anymore. The romp freed him up to deal with the other things on his mind. Getting published was at least as important as sex and since he was unburdened of his load of testosterone, he was able to focus on the book better. In fact, he got so wrapped up in it that he forgot to call Melissa at the appointed time.

Friday, a week after their tryst, just as he was about to go to bed, the phone rang. It was Melissa.

"The kids are asleep and I thought I would just call you before I went to bed and tell you how much I enjoyed last Friday."

"I had a good time too," he said sleepily.

"Oh, just a good time?" she shot back playfully.

"No, a great time is what I meant," he said defensively. Suddenly he realized that he hadn't even made an attempt to contact her since last week. Her call was her way of reminding him of that. "Ah, I'm sorry I haven't called before now. I..."

"Don't worry sweetie, I figured you were waiting for the next game to call me but since that was tonight..."

"Yeah, I meant to call a couple nights ago. I just got stuck on my book and lost track of time." When in doubt, the truth was always the best way out. He only hoped she'd believe that he was telling the truth.

"Oh," she replied with honey in her voice. "I thought maybe you were playing some head game, trying to make me so horny for you that I would call you. I suspected you liked to be chased. By the way, it worked."

"What worked?" he asked.

"Your little game of waiting me out worked. I'm so damn horny I can't wait to see you again. You want to come over right now?" Her breaths grew heavy and his inner animal responded.

"What about the kids?" he asked.

"Asleep, and Brad had the master bedroom walls insulated so the kids wouldn't hear anything they shouldn't."

"Fifteen minutes," he told her.

When their libidos had both been satisfied they whispered to each other about plans for Tuesday night, when the next basketball game was to take place. If there was one thing that had not changed in Indiana, it was basketball. Come hell or high water, Hoosiers would have their basketball. Kyle didn't get the appeal, nor did he care for the game. But if it was going to get him laid on a regular basis, he loved it. Melissa made him agree to a real dinner, though, not just sex. Then they whispered a few sweet goodbyes and he went home.

Brad's daughter was absent on Monday but Kyle thought nothing of it since kids were always sick. They were like little germ collectors, always bringing home some new disease like it was a stray puppy. But when she missed Tuesday, Kyle worried that she might have the flu. If she did, it meant there would be no dinner and no dessert. It would give them something to talk about on the phone, a conversation starter. Relationships that started with sex normally didn't last very long and he thought he might want to pursue this thing with Melissa, so perhaps Paige's illness might end up being a good thing.

He didn't get angry when he called Melissa later and there was no answer. Perhaps she had the flu, too, and couldn't come to the phone. He left a message on her machine and went back to his book. But he found his mind wandering. He pictured himself a few years down the road, married to Melissa. In the daydream, he saw himself with her and her three kids and maybe one or two more of his own, all happy and living like a family.

Scary thought. How would I be as a stepfather? Oh well, it wouldn't be many years until her kids were out of the house. Then he could treat them like he treated his own relatives.

About an hour later, he dialed her number again. The phone rang once, then again and again. No answering machine picked up, not even after a dozen rings. Thinking that maybe he dialed the wrong number he hung up and went to get the phone book. He copied it from the book number by number just to make sure he had it right. Still no answer.

"Well, don't want to be a pest," he said as he hung up the phone. He decided to wait until bed time before trying again.

When it came time to try her again, he had already dressed for bed and climbed into his favorite recliner. He was wearing lounge pants his sister had bought him as a Christmas gift two years ago. They were thin cotton with a bit of spandex thrown in so they could stretch and give. Besides a couple of books and a handful of pictures, they were the only things he had left from his sister.

Again the phone rang repeatedly with no answer. Surely one of the kids would have picked it up, if not Melissa. No one, especially kids, could ignore a ringing phone.

"Strange," he said into the mouthpiece. Maybe something terrible had happened. Nah, she had three kids and no one to lean on for help. If she was sick, or one of the kids was, then she was probably so preoccupied that the phone was the least of her worries. But the answering machine should have picked up. *Maybe it's not working.* Or maybe she had unplugged it during the outbreak. Maybe it was her way of making sure the zombies outside didn't hear a voice on the machine and come looking for dinner. It made some sort of sense, he guessed, and it appeased the voice in his head, so he let it go. He would just wait for her to call him.

That settled, he went back to his office in his new home, which was a two room apartment in one of the oldest buildings in Monticello, and went back to work on his book. At some point he wore himself out and fell asleep on his keyboard.

Paige showed up to school the next day, looking a little pale but otherwise fine. Kyle wanted to say something to her, but he waited until class was over so as not to embarrass her. It was tough. He found himself staring at her throughout class, but he managed to leave her alone until the final bell rang.

She must have known he wanted to talk to her because she was slow in leaving when the bell rang. All the other kids ran out the door but she was still putting away her pen and closing up her folder. Once the last classmate was out the door, she said without looking at him directly, "I know you were supposed to talk to my mom last night but she's been really sick. She couldn't get out of bed yesterday and she is still sick today. She told me not to answer the phone and she threatened to beat the boys senseless if they picked it up too. She just felt so bad that she was afraid to talk to you."

He nodded dumbly. "I figured something came up," he tried to pass off nonchalantly.

"Well, don't worry Mr. Williams. She really does like you," she grinned weakly. "I can tell from the way that she acts when she talks about you that she's really into you. I shouldn't tell you that, but I love my mom and I actually want to see her happy. Not like the other girls around here who hate their mothers."

He nodded again, not saying a word. It was better to be perceived as intelligent and knowing than to open your mouth and prove that you weren't.

Paige stood up and adjusted her skirt. "She'll call you when she's feeling better, but if that's not for a couple of days don't worry. Just do me one favor."

"What's that?" he asked.

"I'm not a dumb little kid and I'm not a virgin. I can tell by the way my mom's acting that you guys did it. So try to keep the gross little comments and PDAs to a minimum when I'm around, would you? In return I promise that I won't try to blackmail you for a better grade." She grinned sarcastically and strutted out of the room.

"Deal!" he called out as the door closed behind her.

Well, there it was. Melissa was interested and sick. The weight of his worry and the frustration of not knowing vanished. He was happy and alive again. He gathered up his stuff and headed for his car.

"Either I'm a little sissy," he started to tell himself as he drove away, "Or the things that they say about love are really true." *Oh shit, did I just say that? I can't be in love with her after just a couple of dates. I'm acting like my students. Geesh!*

Even though it was the dead of winter, the sky seemed bluer and everything just seemed better. He knew it wasn't true, which meant that his perception of the world was affected by the happy news that his love life was about to get hotter. He hated to admit it, but maybe mainstream fiction was right about how good love could make you feel.

"Bah," he bellowed, dismissing those thoughts. Love was not the be-all and end-all of human existence. If anything, it was more like putting sprinkles on top of a cupcake—it was just a little extra something that brightened up the day but you could live without it.

By the time Friday rolled around, he still hadn't heard from Melissa and he was getting worried. Although Paige had been in class every day and kept telling him that her mother was still sick, it was starting to sound like a lame excuse. But when the final bell rang on Friday afternoon, she told him that her brothers were now as sick as Melissa. "One of them threw up and the other one just lays there and says he has a headache. Whatever Mom has, she gave to them. I know I'm next and that's going to suck. I haven't been feeling well this entire week, so maybe I already have it." She added that even though Melissa wasn't feeling good that Kyle should call her Sunday evening.

"I'm sure that she'd love to hear from you. Maybe that would perk her up a little, even."

On Sunday evening when he called, she did answer the phone and they talked for probably ten or fifteen minutes, but Melissa's voice was hoarse and she wasn't her normal charming self. She sounded stoned. He asked how the boys were doing and she said that they seemed to have recovered fairly quickly.

"But I feel like death warmed over," she said in a raspy, scratchy voice.

Then he surprised himself by blurting out, "I really don't care how bad you think you look. I would really like to come over and see you. I can help out with things around the house, too." He heard her gasp and he held his breath. That wasn't like him to offer to help out around anyone's house. He didn't like to clean his own apartment, let alone help out with three kids in a house where somebody was really sick. He was still somewhat of a germaphobe.

194

"No," she said, politely declining his offer. "I really don't want you to see me looking like this. Paige has been taking care of the house and the kids and me, so it's okay. She's a wonderful girl. I keep waiting for the day when she decides that she hates me but so far it hasn't happened. I just love her so much. I used to think that she got that from her father."

That was another little stab in the heart for Kyle. Every time she mentioned Brad it felt like a knife in the guts. Strangely though, the pain hurt a little less with each passing conversation. Either he was growing used to the idea that there was nothing he could have done differently with Brad's body, or he was becoming numb to it. Melissa seemed to have accepted the idea that her husband was one of the millions slaughtered during the plague and so maybe as the pain subsided for her, it was also subsiding for him.

"Kyle? Are you there?"

"Oh yeah, sorry. I just got to thinking about something else."

"What?" she asked in a monotone. He pretended as if he hadn't heard her.

"I said I got to thinking about something else. It's really nothing," he said. "Well, I guess I should let you go. I just want you to know that when you start to feel okay, I would love to come over. Even if it's just sitting together on the couch and watching TV. I...just miss you."

"Oh that's so sweet," she said in the same monotone. "I really miss you too. I'm sure I'll be over this in a couple more days and then we can do whatever you want. And you know what I mean."

Like a horny little schoolboy he drooled back his reply, "Yeah, okay."

"All right," Melissa said drowsily. "I think my NyQuil is beginning to kick in. So if it's okay with you I'm going to hang up the phone now."

"That's fine," he replied. "I'll talk to you soon." Kyle went to the bathroom and immediately spanked his monkey. Then he returned to his office and picked up where he left off in his book.

CHAPTER 21

On Sunday, Kyle went to a florist, bought a dozen roses and drove directly to her house. It was a gray day and the temperature was somewhere in the thirties, so the two inches of snow that had fallen during the early morning hours was melting and the trees were dripping water. Everything was slushy and wet.

He rang the bell. No one answered. He banged on the door. Still no one answered. He banged a few more times. Nothing. But he could hear the muffled sounds of a television playing inside the house, so he knew that someone must be home. He tried the doorknob but it was locked.

Something thumped loudly inside. Maybe that was Melissa getting out of bed to come and answer the door. He waited for the telltale footsteps but none came.

"Melissa?" he called out, loud enough for anyone on the other side of the door to hear. There was no response. It worried him. What if they had all come down with her virus and none were well enough to answer the door?

Now worried that they were all on the verge of dying, he went from window to window, peering in. Most of them had the blinds drawn, but the one over the older boy's window was partially open. He could see the shape of a child in the bed. He rapped on the window but the kid did not move.

None of the other windows allowed any insight into what was going on inside. As he returned to the front porch, he wrestled with the decision about what to do. If he broke in and nothing was wrong, Melissa would drop him like a hot rock but if he called the police and nothing was wrong, would it be any better? Probably not, but she'd forgive him. He could leave it alone and wait for her to call, but the unmoving child worried him into action.

"The cops," he said aloud. "Best play."

He didn't have a cell phone— he didn't need one when he had the internet—so he went next door and rang the bell. There was no answer there either. He approached a dozen other houses on the street and none of them answered. It was weird, but it was still before 5:30pm, roughly dinner time in the Midwest.

"Looks like my choices are limited," he told himself as he went back to Melissa's house. "Hope she forgives me."

He went around to the back door. It was the kind of door that established a boundary but did not offer any real true security. It had a large window that took up most of the upper half of the frame, which could easily be broken and give any criminal access to the home. But in a small town like Monticello it was enough.

Things were a little different since the zombie plague of last summer but most people figured that if a dead man wanted to get in no door would stop him. It wasn't going to stop Kyle either. He jabbed his elbow through the window and in a few seconds was standing in the middle of Melissa's kitchen hollering out "Hello."

The only thing he heard was the TV in one of the kids' bedrooms. He walked into the living room, his eyes darting to the couch, checking to make sure that history had not repeated itself. There was no body there, or anywhere that he could see, but something was amiss. He could feel it.

"Anyone home?" he called out again. "It's me, Mr. Williams." He waited for an answer but none came. Slowly, he made his way down the darkened hallway that led to the bedrooms. The first door was closed and locked. But the second was open a little bit and that's where the television sounds were coming from.

He rapped lightly on the door and as it was a hollow core door, it swung wide open. There was a blue glow radiating from the television, but no signs of life otherwise.

Someone was in the bed. It was one of the little kids.

"Hello?" Kyle called. The child did not move. *Run!* His brain told him. *Leave it alone and run!* But he had come this far. He had to know. His heart thumped in his chest. *Run, goddamit!* He ignored it.

In the middle of the bed, with covers drawn up to his neck, was the youngest child. He was dead.

Kyle pulled the cover back a bit to get a better look at the boy. His throat had been ripped out and he had been disemboweled. His stomach was ripped wide open and hung halfway out of his body. There were dried rivulets of blood down the side of the bed and a splash on the wall behind him.

The position of the boy's body suggested that he had been asleep when he was attacked. He lay peacefully on his back. His eyes were closed and there was a trace of a smile still on his face. He looked peaceful. Kyle felt like vomiting.

Who could have done such a thing?

The hairs on the back of his neck stood up. A chill crept up and down his spine.

This can't be happening again.

His instincts told him to leave well enough alone, to call the police and let them check out the rest of the house but he had to know if Melissa was alright.

He went back out into the hallway, checking the next room on his way to the master bedroom. It was unlocked. He played with the idea of skipping it but thought better of it. Inside, the scene was much the same as the first room. Paige's throat and chest were ripped wide open. She had the same peaceful look on her face as the youngest boy did, and just like him her body was positioned as if she had been attacked while sleeping.

There was blood everywhere. When he caught sight of her intestines snaking down the side of the bed, he had to leave the room.

The horrid scene made him dizzy and he lost his balance and tumbled into Melissa's bedroom door, knocking it wide open. "Oh Lord," he whispered as he climbed to his feet and stared into the pitch black room. *If she's in here...*

The curtains were drawn and the shades pulled down. Very little light reached that corner of the house on a good day, since it was on the northwest corner of the building and shaded by a pair of squat bushy

198

maples. But since it was cloudy, even less light filtered through what appeared to be black plastic trash bags hanging on the windows.

He steeled himself for the expected gore and flipped the light switch. Immediately, the entire room blinked into focus. No Melissa. There was no blood or guts either. The bed looked like it had been slept in but other than that the room was immaculate. He poked his head into the master bathroom. Melissa wasn't there either. Where could she be?

The little voice in his head knew the answer—the locked room. It was the only place he hadn't been in.

He tiptoed down the hall and put an ear to the door. There was the faintest sound of a fan whirring within, but nothing else. He knocked gently on the door and listened for any movement beyond. There was a faint scrape, which could have been anything from a paper blowing in the breeze of the fan to a cat moving around. He hoped that's all it was but the longer he stood there the more convinced he became that it was something he would rather not see.

He stepped back to examine the doorknob. It had the little hole in the handle which meant that he could force a screwdriver into the opening and pop open the lock. So he went to the kitchen and rooted through the drawers until he found something that would do the trick—an ice pick. Then he went back to the door and stuck the tip of the pick into the opening. He had to give it a solid thump with his hand to force it deep enough to pop the lock, but it worked like a charm.

Prepared for almost anything, he pushed the door open quickly and raised his ice pick above his shoulder, ready to defend himself. The room was dark, like the others. Inside, a closet door choked off his view of the room. He had to push it shut before he could see more.

Strangely, amidst all the drama, Kyle noted that each of the children had a television in their bedroom—something he found irritating. After all, Brad was a teacher and he should have had his children's best interests at heart. Having a television in each kid's room was not responsible in the least. They should've had bookcases full of books and a night light next to the bed in case they wanted to read while preparing to go to sleep. Teachers knew better. No teacher's kid should ever become a couch potato.

A tiny white glint caught his eye. He stepped past the closet, flicking the light on as he went. Something huge and white, hanging from the light, blinded him momentarily. He shielded himself while his eyes adjusted.

The first thing he saw, after the light ceased to blind him, was the oldest boy curled up in a ball in the far corner of the room. His neck had been ripped out the same as his brother and sister, but it was obvious that unlike his siblings, he had been awake when the attack occurred. It was horrifying and sad at the same time and Kyle felt pity for the boy, but then his eyes latched on to the white thing hanging from the light and his heart skipped a beat.

It was Melissa. She had a noose around her neck which appeared to be made from a computer cable. One end was wrapped around the ceiling fan from which she dangled and the other end was tight around her neck. Although it was obvious she was dead, her back was to him and he could only see the left rear portion of her face.

He tripped over something—shoes—and fell to the floor, smacking his face hard enough to stun him. Dazed, he flipped over onto his back and stared up at Melissa as he waited for the world to refocus.

He growled from the pain, took a deep breath and exhaled slowly. He growled again, only the growl seemed to come from somewhere else in the room. It wasn't him, it was Melissa! As he stared at her, her body spun around like a mobile until she faced him. She wasn't dead at all. Well, technically she was.

"Oh, son of a bitch!" Kyle cried. "Not you!"

Twisting and turning, she reached toward him with blackened fingers that looked more like talons. Her toes dug for purchase but found none. She must have tied herself up and then leapt off the bed in an attempt to hang herself. But why had she not snapped her neck and died instantly? Why hadn't the ceiling fan ripped out of the ceiling? She was rather petite. Perhaps she didn't weigh enough to break the mounting bracket that held the fan in place.

She is *just a skinny little thing*, he said to himself. *Damn hot though.*

Upon closer examination, he noted that her housecoat was coated in dark purple and bluish stains which radiated downward from her face. Her eyes, sunken and dilated but as wide open as they could go, were so scary that he nearly peed his pants.

Melissa began to move more intensely, her feet and hands going a hundred miles an hour as she tried to latch onto something so she could get down and attack him. She had that same hungry look on her face that he had seen on other zombies, like his sister.

Scrambling to his feet, he tried to get to the door without touching her. It was a smallish room and it was difficult, especially since the more she fought against her noose, the more she swung back and forth, like a side of beef on a meat hook.

He had a fleeting thought that perhaps she hadn't hung herself at all, that maybe the boy had set a trap when he saw his mother coming at him in such a horrible state. But how had she managed to kill him first and then hang herself?

As he slid carefully past her, he knew that if she got a hand on him she would rip his throat out like she had done her kids. He prayed that the cable didn't give out before he got out of the room. The fan wobbled shakily to and fro. He didn't have long.

The worst part of the entire scene had to be the fact that the poor boy knew that his mother was the one who killed him. It wouldn't matter to a boy that she was just a mindless zombie when she did it. When he went to his heavenly reward the last memory of his Mother that he carried with him would be the image of her ripping and tearing at him with bared teeth and claws. *How horrible.*

He managed to sneak past her frantically swinging limbs and get to the hallway. Carefully, he locked the door from within, just like it had been before, and went into the kitchen.

Melissa was a beautiful woman and the more he thought of her as a putrefying monster the angrier he became. What had she done to deserve such a horrible destiny? Wasn't it enough that she lost her husband and then her own life? To be the instrument by which her children were murdered was more than horrific, it was Satanic. Although it was not abnormal for a parent of a lower species to eat its young, humans didn't.

Life had become so grotesque that it crushed whatever belief in God Kyle might still have had. No God, even an angry one, would allow such a horrible thing to happen.

He had to end the madness before it could spread any further. If he was lucky, the Next Event would end right there, right then.

Rooting through the kitchen drawers, he stumbled upon a good sized meat cleaver that he thought might work but as he pondered over whether it was heavy duty enough, there came a crash from the direction of the bedrooms, followed by dragging noises.

She must have gotten free. It wouldn't take her more than a minute or two to get to him. Ready or not, the meat cleaver would have to do.

He had just enough time to add an ice pick to his arsenal, shifting the meat cleaver to his right hand and switching the ice pick to his left, before she came around the corner. She scanned the room blindly from right to left. Apparently her comprehension skills were not as strong as they might have been if she was alive. It was just enough of a delay for him to get into just the right position to swing the cleaver at her. In his panic, though, he misjudged the distance between them. The cleaver nicked her upper arm but failed to dig into her flesh.

The housecoat ruffled from the slicing action of the cleaver. She peered down at the deep brown ooze that welled up from the wound. *Must not have felt that.*

Momentarily, while she processed the attack, she froze. She was scarier in the bright light of the kitchen than she had been in the bedroom. Her face was purplish black. Tiny black veins stood out on her cheeks and forehead. He could make out small blood clots, probably not hers, dotting her chin, and there was a chunk of intestine hanging from the corner of her mouth.

She was dragging the ceiling fan on the ground behind her. The cable was still tightly wrapped around her neck but she didn't seem to notice it. She leaned forward at such an impossible angle that Kyle realized if he could cut the cable, she would crash to the floor. If she hadn't been undead, he guessed, her neck would have snapped from the pressure on it.

She stepped toward him and raised her arms. The fingers on both hands clenched and unclenched as she edged closer. She had the same plan for him that she had for her kids—dinner.

Thankfully, the ceiling fan was caught on the edge of the doorway and kept her from advancing any further. Once he realized that, it was like teasing an angry dog at the end of its chain. She couldn't come nearer without first moving the heavy fan. Since she didn't realize it was there, she just kept straining against the cable. Things were suddenly in his favor.

He did not back away as that would only pin him against the counters and cut off his exit. Instead, he took careful aim at one of her outstretched arms and swung the cleaver as fast as he could. He expected to chop her arm off cleanly like in the movies, but that's not what happened. The blade cut through the polyester sleeve of her housecoat, burying itself in her ulna. It knocked them both off balance. He staggered but managed to keep himself upright, holding onto the cleaver for dear life.

God help me if she gets hold of it.

When he yanked back on the cleaver, it did not immediately come loose. He had to tug a few more times on it before it finally ripped free. When it finally did, Melissa's forearm dangled limply. He took another swing, burying the steel blade in the bone again.

Then he hoisted the meat cleaver up over his head and brought it down on her arm as powerfully as he could. This time he managed to cleanly lop off the hand. She held up the stump to her face, stunned. Brown drops of coagulating blood oozed up out of the flesh and dripped down her housecoat. It was like her veins were filled with thick oil, which surprised him since he thought that once they died, zombies' hearts stopped beating and their blood stopped flowing. Apparently he was wrong.

Melissa regained her balance and clawed at him with her good hand and her stump. He laughed. It *was* just the tiniest bit comical.

In the instant he allowed himself to be distracted by laughing at her, she managed to grab a hold of his sleeve, latching onto it tightly and reeling herself in.

He pulled away from her but she tightened her grasp on his shirt. He panicked a bit as she reached for his throat.

This must have been how it went with her children. But he was not asleep like her poor children had been. He could see it coming and fight back and he was a lot bigger than her children were. He raised the ice pick, flipped it around in his left hand so that he could get better leverage, and jammed it right through her temple. Then he wiggled it in a circular motion, scrambling her brains as best he could.

That's what you're supposed to do, right? Detach the brain and the body goes too?

Melissa examined her stump as if she had never seen that appendage before. She turned to her right hand as if to compare them. Finally realizing the difference between the two limbs, she understood that she still had one good weapon. She grabbed the hand that was still gripping the ice pick and tried to pry it away from him, but that only made things worse. Every time she wiggled the pick, she was helping to scramble her own brain. Her body responded with random jerks and twitches. She danced like a macabre skeleton.

Realizing what was happening, Kyle wiggled the pick as much as he could for a few seconds, groaning sickly at how ghoulish it was, then backed away and swung the meat cleaver at her other hand. It took two hacks before he was able to break the bones and render that hand as useless as the other arm, but he finally managed it. At that point he knew he had her.

Melissa lurched toward him with both stumps reaching out to him, her face angry and frustrated. She couldn't hurt him without getting very close to him and he couldn't bring himself to lop off her head, so he swiped the meat cleaver across her thighs in hopes of cutting her muscles and crippling her. The initial swing didn't stop her, but on his backswing he nearly cut her in half.

He pulled the ice pick out of the side of her head and jammed it into her chest, hoping that maybe like a vampire a stake through the heart would finish her off. It didn't. She growled crazily at him and stuck him with her stumps. She didn't understand why she couldn't grip him.

Some sort of pus seeped from the wounds in addition to the thick blood. It made him gag. He swung the meat cleaver again, this time in a crisscross motion across her abdomen. Slowly at first her housecoat separated, revealing discolored flesh beneath. The intersection of the cuts abruptly opened wide and her guts fell out. Her stomach sagged out, hanging from her belly like a colostomy bag. Her intestines tumbled to the floor like an incredibly long sausage and other organs he couldn't identify followed suit.

Must have cut the thing that held it all in.

Unaware of her new impediment, she lurched toward him again. She leaned toward him, straining against the cable and inadvertently stepping on her own entrails. The ceiling fan clunked against the wall each time she moved, keeping her from getting any closer. It wouldn't be long before it worked itself loose from the wall and sent her flying into him, but it didn't seem as pressing or scary now that she was basically a torn apart skeleton. Each time she leaned forward, he swiped the meat cleaver at her, cutting her a little more.

At one point, he accidentally sliced open her stomach, spilling its contents on the floor. He hadn't considered that she might have a full belly, but when he saw tiny little fingers and chunks of bloody red meat flop to the floor, all he could do was stare horrified and try to keep from vomiting. There wasn't time to process what he was seeing, though, as the cable tethering her to the ceiling fan finally broke loose. She fell into him. Reflexively, he swiped at her face. The blade sliced through her cheeks and her jaws, sending a pair of teeth to the ground. He swiped at her again and on his backswing he nearly knocked her lower jaw off her face.

"Why am I even playing with you?" he suddenly shouted at the disintegrating monster. She wasn't Melissa anymore; she was a carnivorous creature looking to make a meal out of him. One way or another she was going to accomplish her goal, even if that meant she would have to gum him to death. And he was acting like he had with his family. He needed to suck it up and treat her like the zombie she was.

Delivering a hard punch to her chest, he backed her up a few steps and sized up the situation. Melissa the MILF was gone, Melissa the Zombie was here. She, or *it* as she should be referring to her, had killed the children and apparently attacked at least one infant somewhere in the neighborhood. She—*it*— had to go.

He put his shoulder down and ran through *it* like a running back through a defensive line, knocking it to the floor. Its skull bounced off the tile with a dull thud, not the thud of a live person. What did that mean for the brain within? Was it already rotted away?

He whirled around and brought the cleaver down on its neck, cleanly severing the head from the body. It hit the floor, bounced and rolled across the floor. It came to rest against the back door. Of course, it faced him.

"And now I'm done here," he said as he stood over the nasty thing. Its eyes opened and closed. What was left of its tongue undulated. It refused to die. It didn't know how to die.

The body had slumped into a praying position and froze there, a statue with no head. It was disgusting—a mockery of a supplicant praying to God. It unsettled Kyle.

There were dots of clotted blood all over the floor, the table, and even on the counters. The head, still unaware that it was discombobulated, stared at him with the same hungry look from a puddle of slime. He closed his eyes for a moment to blot it all out, but the images of the disemboweled children in the other rooms danced across the backs of his eyelids and all together, it made him dizzy. He felt his breakfast coming back up, but this time he did not bother to hold it back. He barfed all over the floor. Some of it splattered on Melissa's head.

Once he was finished, he staggered from the home, still retching a bit. As he reached his car he became aware that he was covered in zombie blood and guts. *Shit! Don't want to catch it.* He ripped his coat and shirt off and flung them on the ground.

No one around, he noted. *Do it quick!* He stripped his pants off and climbed into his car. The image of those tiny little fingers on the floor came back to him. Where had they come from? There hadn't been any babies in the house.

Had Melissa staggered to a neighbor's home and eaten their infant child? Recalling that no one had answered their door in the neighborhood before he broke into Melissa's home, it seemed like a likely explanation. There was no damage to any of the other homes that he could see, so they must have let her in. Since he doubted that they would have let a zombie in their homes, it was a logical jump to say that she must have made the final leap into zombiehood in someone else's home.

Jesus. Am I obligated to find the house she was in?

Like most coaches and former coaches, he kept a spare change of clothes in the trunk. Normally they were reserved for rainy days, but if this wasn't a rainy day, he didn't know what was. Luckily, he still had a pair of lined windbreaker pants and a thick sweatshirt in the vehicle. It wasn't ideal for late winter or early spring, but he didn't plan on spending a great deal of time outside.

I should just leave and call the cops. Let them handle it. They get paid to handle stuff like this.

But he couldn't do that. He felt responsible somehow. Armed with a tire iron and a screwdriver, the only tools in his car that could double as weapons, he went next door. He banged on the door once but there was no answer, just as he expected. So he went around to the back door and punched a hole in the glass like he had at Melissa's house and let himself in.

Another scene of horror smacked him in the face. The entire family had been killed at the kitchen table. Their bodies slumped forward onto the table in various states of half eaten decay.

She really did a number on them.

He went down the hall checking all the bedrooms but there was no nursery.

He went to the next house and the scene was similar—two dead old folks sitting on the couch in their living room in front of their TV. *Damn, she had to have done it fast!*

House after house, the scene repeated itself. Every single one of them within a block of Melissa's home contained dead people, yet not a single one of them had a crib or nursery or any signs of an infant baby. But he knew that the fingers had been from a tiny child. They were just so small.

Bewildered, he stood in the middle of the street and looked all around. How could she have killed an entire neighborhood without someone stopping her? Was it possible that she had lingered in some sort of twilight zone between life and zombie long enough to attack everyone in the neighborhood? That's not how the first round of the plague went. Most people turned almost immediately and it became obvious very quickly that they were no longer alive.

Melissa had, though, been sick for better than two weeks before she became a full fledged zombie. Was it possible she snuck out at night, like some sort of werewolf, after her kids were asleep and preyed on her neighbors? That would help to explain Paige's comment about the foul smell her mother had developed.

Out of the corner of his eye he caught motion. It was a man down the street, swaying from side to side as he staggered towards him. It was too far away for him to distinguish who it was, but it was obvious that he was a zombie. Then another shape emerged from the row of houses on the south side of the street. It too walked strangely, too much like a zombie to be anything else. Joining the man in the middle of the street, the pair dragged themselves toward him.

Stunned, he watched as the number grew from two to six in just a few minutes.

Shit! Round two?

Disappointed but calm, he got back in his car and headed for home. Once there he shut his door and began to pile furniture against it.

"Deja vu," he declared as he thought of how quickly life had come full circle.

CHAPTER 22

After two days of heavy duty television monitoring, his fears of another outbreak were proven true. Initially, there had been no reports of outbreaks anywhere but Monticello, but Kyle knew it was only a matter of time. Many people who lived in Monticello worked and shopped in Lafayette, so it wouldn't be long before a sick Monticelloan would accidentally spread the plague.

Unfortunately, Kyle didn't have a large stockpile of food. In fact, he had no food in his apartment, so he was forced to venture out. *I've got to do a better job on stocking up*, he scolded himself.

He went to the local grocery store but it was closed. The windows were all broken out and the lights within were off. He could guess what happened.

The other stores were closed as well. Restaurants too. The whole town was shut up tightly.

It's like they're hiding from vampires or something.

Back in his apartment, which he called The Grotto, he pondered over what to do. If outbreaks were going to become the new norm, he might as well move to the North Pole. Or maybe he was better off moving to Mexico. Either way, living in Indiana was less and less appealing.

If I've got to deal with it, I might as well live somewhere warm and sunny. And if that means that I'm always on guard, so be it.

He imagined a life in Cancun. Tiny, frail grandmothers with pistols blasting errant zombies who happened to wander down the wrong aisle at the grocery store.

Kyle guessed that by the end of the week the outbreak would be a full fledged epidemic—something on the order of the last Event.

"Hmm, full circle," he commented. "How about that?" This time, knowing what the immediate future held, it was an easy decision to make.

"Mexico it is."

The sooner he got started, the better. Perhaps he could beat the monsters there.

He would need a plan. He brought out a tablet of paper where he jotted down story ideas and began to map out a timeline and make a list of things he needed.

At least I kept the box truck!

He spent the rest of the afternoon boxing up his precious books, his own writings, and other items he would need on the long trip. By the time he was finished, it was getting dark.

Too late to start out tonight. I'll wait till morning, I guess.

His stomach growled loudly. "Shut up, there's no food." There was a six pack of beer in the fridge. That would have to do for dinner.

He awoke bloated from the beer but ready for the trip. On the way out of town, he gassed up at the only station that left their pumps on all night. There were no souls anywhere in sight. The whole town was on lockdown still, or had already turned.

His stomach growled again. Through the great plate glass window he could see all sorts of snacks. No one's left to care, I suppose.

There was a large metal grated trashcan next to the gas pump. It wasn't full and he was easily able to lift it. Through the window it went, blowing out the glass with such a racket that he was afraid it would bring all the zombies within earshot. He had to snatch and run.

He went behind the counter, found the plastic bags, and filled a few of them up with anything that looked like it would last more than a day or two. There was a metallic pop from the direction of the truck.

"Shit," he cursed. Was he already too late? Had a horde of undead already found him?

He hustled back to the truck, trying the passenger's door. It was locked. *No shit*, he scolded himself. *I never unlocked it.*

Nervously and weaponless, since he'd left his gun on the seat of the truck, he tiptoed around the front of the cab. He peeked around the corner. No one.

Oh, the gas is done. That's what that was. He felt like an idiot, but then, who cared? No one else was around to see his stupidity.

On the way to Lafayette, he mentally mapped out what he thought would be a quick trip. Meijer was right by the Interstate. He'd hit that place again, like he had during the first Event. There was less chance of running across piles of undead there. Then he'd hit the Barnes and Noble out by the Mall for atlases, maps, and pick up some reading material too. Then it was Highway 52 south out of town and he was Mexico bound.

Comfortable with the plan, he turned on the radio for some music. But of course, there was none. Instead an announcer calmly read a report of a zombie that had turned up in one of the Lafayette factories and attacked his coworkers. The surviving coworkers were taken to one of the hospitals and were "being closely monitored by authorities." Kyle was afraid that was only the beginning.

As he wandered up to the entrance of the Meijer store, he noted that just like the Wal-Mart near his parents' home, there were armed guards at the doors. Two security officers, armed with shotguns and with pistols on their hips, flanked the doors as they scouted the parking lot for signs of danger. It alleviated his fear a bit but not completely.

Inside, he filled his cart with the necessary staples to survive. Most of his goods were canned or dried, but since he had a cooler with him this time, he also bought a few refrigerated items for use over the next few days.

After he had all the food his cart could hold, he went through the alcohol aisle and grabbed two cases of beer and an arm full of vodka bottles. The beer was for the trip to Mexico. The vodka could be used as an offensive weapon or to disinfect any wounds he might come by. In the event he became infected with the plague, he could also get drunk in a hurry and then shoot himself. There was no way he would allow himself to become a zombie. Suicide was the only way out for him.

Next, he made his way towards Barnes and Noble. The skies to the west were darkening. The radio announcer was in the middle of explaining that Purdue University in West Lafayette had cancelled classes because a zombie wandered into one of the lecture halls in the middle of class and ate a few people, including the old white haired professor who stood at his podium yelling at the undead monster to leave.

One student was quoted as saying, "Professor Eggbert just kept yelling at it to go away. He kept screaming that it had no right to interrupt his class and that he would have it removed from campus if it did not leave right away. Then it bit his nose off and started munching his face and he started screaming. Then there was a sick gargle and I saw blood spray from his neck and that's when I ran."

Not completely amazed at the sheer stupidity of the professor, Kyle could do nothing but shake his head and think to himself how out of touch with reality many academics really were. As a teacher and a philosopher, it seemed ironic that as smart as some people were, they did not know how to survive a real crisis.

"And so it begins," Kyle mused as the announcer went on to talk about other outbreaks in the area. At that moment, raindrops hit the windshield. In a few minutes, it was raining so hard that he couldn't see. His wipers didn't move fast enough to beat back the rain, so he was forced to pull over. Not that he needed to. There were no other cars on the road.

"Well, eat me like a doughnut," he remarked upon realizing that he was the only one driving.

But, as something dark moved in his periphery, it became obvious that he wasn't the only one out. He rolled down his window far enough to see that a dead man and woman had locked him in their sights and were hurrying towards him.

"Time to go, bitches," he yelled at them as he dropped the truck into gear and rolled away.

The zombies turned and strolled towards him, shrinking in his rearview as the van quickly left them behind.

Had the sudden, quick warmup been responsible for the resurgence of the zombies? Was the disease heat dependent? Had it set quietly throughout the winter, waiting?

Another zombie came running out of a used car dealer. It made a beeline for the van. Kyle wouldn't have guessed that he was dead except for one small thing: the man did not slow down as he approached. Rather, he ran full speed into the side of the cab. It had about the same impact as a deer would have had. The truck recoiled, shaking slightly as it absorbed the energy.

Shit, here comes another… no, a couple more. Mechanics. They came out of the garage bay attached to the dealer's office. They too smashed into the side of the van.

Sons of bitches move a lot faster now. Maybe it's because they're fresh.

"Time to quit screwing around," he told himself. Rain or no rain, zombies or no zombies, heat or no heat, he needed to get gone. Luckily, he was able to reach the book store. He fully expected to find the mall surrounded by hordes of the undead, a la "Dawn of the Dead," but to his surprise there was not a single person, living or otherwise, anywhere in sight of the expansive building.

Slowly, he turned into the driveway that ringed the mall and led to the outlying Barnes and Noble. He kept the truck in a low gear just in case a bunch of hungry bastards came out of nowhere and he had to get moving quickly, but that didn't happen. He even gunned the engine once or twice just to see if he could draw out a few lurkers, but none appeared.

Not convinced that he was completely alone, he first circled around the bookstore, checking the back door as well as the exposed side of the building. Thankfully, there were no bogeymen anywhere around.

Finally convinced that he just might be alright, he pulled the truck up into the handicapped slots in front of the building and idled the engine. He waited a minute, giving any unseen monsters one last chance to show themselves, then spun the truck around, drove it up onto the sidewalk, and parked across the front entrance, close enough that the only way a zombie could get in was to crawl either under the truck or through the cab. Then he climbed over to the passenger door and got out.

He left the truck running and checked the doors. They were locked but they were mostly glass, so he kicked out one of the lower panels and climbed through. Then he grabbed a book from the clearance rack in the antechamber and pushed the bar on the outside door. It opened easily. Kyle stuck the book in the jamb. When he let the door close, the door gave the appearance that it was shut even though it wasn't.

Inside, the cavernous showroom was dark and tomblike. The air smelled of books. He loved that smell. There was plenty of light at the front of the store where it streamed through the giant windows but very little light reached the back of the store, where concrete walls protected the building's contents. In the low light he could just barely make out the Harry Potter posters hanging on the back wall. They were spooky and evil in this lighting.

Stealthily, he tiptoed toward the information desk at the center of the store, checking each row for potential danger as he passed them by. Thankfully, the front half of the store was empty.

This operation was strictly grab and go. *In and out, no browsing.* He wanted travel guides and maps to get him to Mexico and a repair guide for the truck. Beyond that, if he could find a couple of survival guides it would be great, but if he couldn't he would find a way to manage. Thinking better of it, he decided that a survival guide was a necessity and not an option.

How ironic would it have been to live through two murderous zombie outbreaks but get killed by a poisonous mushroom? Life was just strange enough for things like that to happen.

The books he wanted were all at the back right of the store, huddled together under a huge banner that read "Men's Nonfiction." He made his way there as quietly as possible, peeking down each aisle before moving past them. He suddenly felt the urge to urinate. The bathrooms were right behind the men's section, he knew, so it wouldn't really be out of the way. The problem was that there was no escape from back there, at least none that he was aware of, if zombies should find him. He would die barricaded in a men's room.

He had to prop the door open to get any sort of light back there. The room was filthy, as all public toilets were, so he decided instead to use the women's room. It was palatial and decorated like a hotel lobby. Why women needed such a nice environment for their toiletry concerns he would never understand, but it *was* nice to poop in style.

Why is it that women always complain that their restrooms are nastier than men's?

He finished his business and went back to the travel section. He may not have been the world's most well-traveled person but he had traveled enough to know that you just couldn't beat the Lonely Planet travel guides, so he grabbed one that covered Mexico and others that covered Texas and Louisiana. Then he made his way into the automotive section and found the appropriate repair guide for the truck before sauntering off to find a book that would tell him what types of plants he could or couldn't eat.

Once he had all the books he thought he'd need, and a few he grabbed just for fun—*thought you weren't going to browse*—he stopped by the checkout counter and grabbed a bag for his little pile of books. Just as he slipped them into the bag, he heard a thump on the glass to his left. Startled, he glanced over to find a zombie staring back at him through the window.

The thing was hideous. Its hair was so matted down and so dirty that it looked more like the chewed up lining of a dog's bed. Its eyes were sunken so deeply in their sockets that they were barely visible and its clothes were in tatters. As he stared at it, he could make out the ancient faded uniform of a department store worker.

The stupid zombie just stood there leaning against the glass, staring at him. It looked like it hadn't eaten in ages. There was hardly any skin left on it. Even so, the nasty thing was somehow familiar. It somehow reminded him of April.

Although history had borne out that no matter how weak or rotted a zombie might look, it was still strong enough to take a large, live man down. He'd barely escaped becoming dinner a few times. Still, this one was so bad off that he was sure it posed no threat. He walked to within an arm's length of the window and took a good look at the creature. There were holes in its smock and polyester pants wide enough for him to see that where there should have been flesh there was none. The thing was literally a skeleton. He wondered for a moment what the poor woman might have looked like when she was alive. The name on her nametag read Wendy, which was more than a tad depressing. That's what April's name tag said.

"Wouldn't it be funny if you were actually her?" he mused. Of course it wouldn't have been funny, just par for the course. There was no way April could have survived an entire Indiana summer, fall, and winter as a zombie. Nor was it likely that she would have somehow managed to show up at the exact place and time as he had months later.

But, the more he stared at the creature the more he began to wonder if it was in fact his April. He argued with himself that there was no way she could have survived the posses that cleaned the city of zombies, nor could she have survived so long. But then again, maybe she had wandered into the woods and farmlands around the city and survived on rodents and such. Who could say? Maybe she had lain frozen out in the wilds, just waitig to be reanimated by the warmth of an early spring. Why wasn't it possible? Who would have guessed that zombies really existed? Not he.

He tried to imagine April's beautiful body superimposed on the bones before him but it was almost impossible. Was it conceivable that the dingy, greasy rug on this thing's head was once the same beautiful locks that graced April's head? He leaned closer to the glass, even though he knew it wasn't a smart move. Glass might confuse them for a minute, but if a zombie wanted to get you, a window wasn't going to do anything more than slow it down.

The eyes... this zombie had the same irises as April, although they were sunken deeply and not as bright. They were the same. She had a ring of dark dots in her left iris that he thought at first were some sort of colored contact lens. This critter before him had the same ring. It had to be her! He thought back to the day she'd run out of her apartment, trying to picture what outfit she was wearing. Minus the work smock she wore now, the tatters covering the rest of her carcass could have been the same outfit as she wore that day.

"What happened to you?" he whispered at her, knowing that she couldn't answer back even if she wanted. There was a hole in the cartilaginous covering of her windpipe and he guessed there were no lungs left to push air through the voice box anyway.

But her jaw began to work ever so slightly, moving up and down. Her lips were gone but the tongue was still there, shrunken and shriveled like a raisin. It reminded him a little of a cow's tongue in a butcher's shop. It did not move or work independently as it should have, it just lay there dead.

"God damn!" he mumbled incredulously to himself. He leaned his head against the window, touching his forehead to hers. There was no heat from the glass as there should have been if she were alive. Even though that helped to solidify the idea that she was really nothing but a ghost, it was still so surreal that he refused to believe it was actually happening.

For a few moments longer he stood there, staring into her dead eyes dreaming about what could have been. Marriage, babies, a family, grandkids, a happy life and a simple death surrounded by those he loved. Those were all things he never knew he wanted until it was much too late. In fact, most of the time, when people cited those items as milestones, it turned his stomach. He had no desire for the mundane life that most people cherished. Well, until now. He had only ever wanted to live and write and drink and fuck. That was it. That was all he needed. But now it was too late for any of that.

He was so focused on the possibilities of what could have been that he did not see another zombie lumber up to the window. Only when it growled and pawed at the glass did he become aware of it. By then another was at the window, too. In a few minutes the window was clogged with dead bodies reaching towards him.

"Where the hell did you bastards come from?" he demanded. He stepped backwards from the glass, keeping his eyes trained on April. But as he backed away, the gang of zombies slid along the window, mimicking his movement. April was knocked to the ground and trampled as they pushed around the corner of the building. It was like a crowd of tourists in line to observe a famous relic, everyone pushing the person ahead so that no one gets more than a second or two at the head of the line. The only difference was that he was the relic and as they all shoved towards him to get a 'peek' the chances of them getting to him increased. It wouldn't take long for them to either find the hole in the front door and crawl through it or to put such pressure on the plate glass windows that they gave way. Either way, he was sure that things were not going to end well.

After April disappeared from view, he backed deeper into the store. He waited, too long, for her to spring up from the sidewalk. When it became obvious that she wasn't going to get back up, it was too late. The monsters were already at the front door and one of them had discovered the hole in the glass. It was climbing through even as another zombie was trying to pry the door open. At that moment he saw the wedge in the door.

"Oh crap," he muttered. "That was a dumb idea." Of course, he had not anticipated they would be so smart, since the ones last summer had been so stupid.

The inner set of doors head no lock on them and since the outer doors were about to be breached, he had to do something quickly. He tried to shove a table in front of the inner set of doors but the table was loaded with Bargain Books and was too heavy to move. The crawling zombie was through the outer door. The one behind it was now able to pry it open with no trouble. In a few seconds, the antechamber was clogged with zombies.

"Christ," Kyle cursed. There was nothing to stop them now. He should have run. He should have done something. Now it was too late.

The zombies piled up against the inner set of doors but could not get in. Kyle realized the doors opened out and they had pinned them shut by the crush of the crowd. *Oh thank God for small miracles*, he prayed.

The doors rattled with the pressure of the zombies pushing on them. They were steel but the largest portion of them was still glass, so if the pressure on them grew too great, they could still get in.

He spun around, looking for weapons. Bookstores weren't known for being great armories. He caught sight of the exit sign hanging over the bathroom hallway at the back of the store. He ran to the back and tried the door, but it was chained shut, like most of the fire doors were in these parts. It was illegal to chain them, but it stopped thieves from stealing stores blind.

He had no way to break the thick chain. What to do?

From the front of the store came the sound of breaking glass, followed by the thud of someone hitting the floor. The horde was inside the building.

What have I done to deserve this? Seriously. What did I do?

He could hear them shuffling around, searching for him, bumping into things. He only had a few moments before they found him.

The bathrooms! They had drop ceilings. Maybe if he could get above the tiles, he could hide long enough for them to lose interest and go away.

He ran into the women's room, pushing the plush couch in the 'waiting room' against the door in an attempt to slow them down.

His hope was that there was enough stuff above the ceiling tiles to support his weight. It was easy enough to get up there but what good would it be if he fell right into their wide open maws?

Into the first stall he went, stepping onto the toilet and hoisting himself onto the top of the stall wall. He shoved one of the tiles over and stood up, using the aluminum frame of the drop ceiling to balance himself.

It was very dark above the tiles, but thankfully there was a roof vent that let in just enough light for him to make out the general floor plan of the attic space. It took a moment for his eyes to adjust to the darkness. Down below, a zombie pounded on the bathroom door, startling him. He nearly fell off the wall.

There was a catwalk attached to the wide ventilation shafts that snaked throughout the entire structure. At the far end of the catwalk was a door that must have led to the roof.

An escape! He breathed a sigh of relief. He might just make it out alive after all. There was just one problem. The catwalk wasn't on the near side of the vent shaft. He was going to have to haul himself up onto the rectangular duct that hung low over the ceiling tiles and skitter along it like a rat until he reached the catwalk.

Hope it holds my weight.

Down below, the couch groaned as it moved haltingly across the tile floor. They were getting through.

"Up I go!" he grunted as he hoisted a foot up and hooked it on the thin aluminum frame. He quickly pulled his other leg up and reached for a cable from which the ductwork hung. The metal frame hadn't been built for such weight and it started to bend right away. The small gauge cable that attached it to the roof strained. Luckily though, it held long enough for him to swing his body onto the sturdier air duct.

He crawled along the shaft, ducking steel rafters and dodging support wires. The sheet metal of the ductwork banged and buckled under him as he went. It was very thin stuff, only a millimeter or two thick he guessed. Lucky for him, the builder had situated the ducts within the zigzag frame of the rafters themselves as a cheaper method of support, so that he didn't have to worry about the entire assembly falling through the ceiling, sending him crashing into the mass of hungry zombies below.

While he was busy working his way to the catwalk, the hungry bastards on the main floor had managed to shove the door open and were now inside the restroom. Kyle was no longer over the bathroom though, so even if they somehow managed to get into the ceiling, he'd still have a lead on them.

When the zombies piled into the restroom, most of them were befuddled by the disappearance of the man they knew to be in there. They could still smell him, but as they swarmed the stall and filled the room, he could not be found. So they milled around like cattle, sniffing the air and waiting for something to happen.

There was only one zombie who wasn't fooled by the bathroom ruse. In life his name was Charles Mobley, though his friends called him Booger, and he was as white trash as they came but he was a hell of a human bloodhound. It was a trait he'd carried over to the zombie realm. With each bang of the metal, Booger would rush to the spot underneath the noise and wait for something to happen. He could sniff a meal from a mile away and it was dinner time right now. It would have been comical to watch if it had been a movie, but this wasn't the movies.

Kyle would never have known about Booger if he hadn't accidentally kicked one of the ceiling tiles out. The thing crashed to the floor below and Booger snapped it up, biting into it immediately as if were the best pizza he'd ever tasted.

Scared at first by the knowledge that one of those nasty things was down there waiting for him, drooling after him, Kyle watched the zombie munch the tile insanely. But when Booger finally figured out that the tile wasn't flesh, it looked up at him with as much surprise and anger as he could muster on his decaying face. He growled at Kyle in rage and leapt into the air, grabbing at him but clutching nothing but air. That was so funny to watch that Kyle burst into laughter.

Booger never got his meal. Kyle managed to reach the catwalk and quickly and quietly made his way to the roof access door. It opened easily and he stepped through into warm sunlight.

"Ah," he sighed happily, breathing in the unseasonably warm and damp air. "Beautiful day!" He knew he would survive now. No zombie, not even Booger, would be able to figure out how to get up to the roof. He was safe. He would just have to wait them out.

As he walked to the front of the store, he heard a loud noise behind him. He turned to see the door had slammed itself shut, pushed by a slight breeze.

No matter, I'm not going anywhere for a while anyway.

He had a commanding view from the roof as it was a good thirty feet above ground. He could see everything surrounding the building—the parking lot, the highways that bounded the mall property, and even beyond some of the buildings across the roadways. Unfortunately, he could also see that there was a stream of zombies issuing from the nearest exit of the mall like a stream of ants at a picnic, all single file, blindly following the rotted corpse ahead of them.

There were growls from below. He walked up to the edge of the building and looked down.

"Damn!" he whispered, trying not to draw attention to himself. The mob outside the store had grown much larger. There had to be a hundred or more of the foul smelling fiends down there, with their ranks swelling quickly as more of them arrived every second from the continuously moving line. He watched as they pushed on the glass, finally broke it, and then shoved each other mercilessly through the opening.

The bookstore would soon be overrun by the bastards. He would not be able to escape back the way he'd come. That was problematic but not unsolvable.

"Crap!" he cursed under his breath. He realized he'd left his books lying on the counter in the front of the store. He needed those books. He had no real way of figuring out how to get to Mexico without them. He sat down to think.

A few hours passed. The clouds that had brought the warm front were now just a puff of marshmallows lining the eastern horizon. The air was getting cooler as the sun sank in the west. Perhaps with the cooler night air the zombies would slow down, like lizards or snakes, and he could attempt an escape.

He could only hope that would be the case, since he hadn't worn a jacket and it was still too cold to be outside at night without some sort of coat.

He spent another hour thinking about things. He wondered why he had been so 'lucky' to survive two Events when almost no one else had. It was almost as if he was impervious to whatever bug caused the problem. It was like he was a carrier.

Am I? Am I a carrier? Could that be it?

It felt as if there was a deeper truth there, somewhere just beneath the surface, waiting for the right moment to pop out and tie all the pieces together. Of what puzzle the pieces belonged to, he had no idea. Or did he?

Then came the sound of hope, if ever so faintly. It was the hum of an approaching motor. It grew louder until he could clearly tell it was the sound of a large diesel motor. But there was something behind it, more motors!

He walked over to the front of the building and looked out toward the highway. It seemed as if the motors were coming from everywhere, both east and west of him. He watched anxiously for something to come into view.

Eventually, a single olive drab tank appeared from behind a stand of trees to the southwest of the mall. Then another appeared and behind that was a series of army trucks. It was a convoy!

Kyle started screaming and yelling. He jumped up and down and whooped and hollered. But the convoy ignored him and advanced steadily north along the highway. They couldn't hear him.

"Shit," he said. "They're going to miss me." But how could they miss the mob below?

He took off his shirt and started waving it wildly. It had to catch someone's attention, it just had to!

The convoy kept rolling north. Kyle started to panic. He grabbed a couple of stones that held the rubber roofing down to the building and whipped them pitifully in the direction of the tanks. Abruptly the convoy stopped, as if his tiny useless missiles had offended them.

The turret of the lead tank began to turn toward the building and Kyle started cheering. "Yeah!" he yelled, jumping up and down and waving his shirt. He was saved.

A cruel thought suddenly raced through his mind. They were National Guard sent to destroy zombies. What if they didn't see him up on the roof? If they fired on the building he might be killed along with the hungry beasts below.

"Oh God!" he cried. "But I'm alive! I'm alive and innocent!" Frantically, he waved his arms and shirt like a madman, screaming for them not to fire. It was not zombie behavior. They had to know that. If they had seen the mob below, they must see him waving a red shirt just thirty feet above them. They couldn't fire at a live person, surely!

There was a burst of light from the muzzle of the lead tank and everything exploded into a blinding white light with a thunderous clap.

In that moment, his life played out before him. It was all there, everything from birth to this moment... and so was the sudden, insidious knowledge that he was responsible for all of it.